# The Sharecropper's Daughter

## A Novel by Julie Miliner

Copyright 2011 ISBN 978-0-578-07781-9

Cover art by Porche Photography

Cover model Miss Regan Riley

Many thanks to Margarett and Bobby Wilson who graciously permitted access to the grounds of The Urban Garden, located in College Park, Georgia. The antebellum house and former servant's quarters served as the perfect backdrop for 1930's South Carolina as depicted in The Sharecropper's Daughter.

Dedicated to my mother, Helen Frances

The Sharecropper's Daughter is a work of fiction.

Any resemblance to real persons is purely coincidental.

## Prosperity, South Carolina

De sky o'er Prosperity iz de truest of blue
Bright lak a marigold

Shiny as dew
De air iz sweet wit honey

Trees swayin in de breeze
De fields iz filled with Jessamine as far as de eye kin see

But der are secrets in dis valley dat is hidden o of sight
Dey sneak round like shadows tween de mornin and de night

Can't see dem if you looking, won't see dem if you do
Dey strut round lak honest folk, de truest of de blue

Watch out for when de sky turn sallow
Jus befo de morning sun

De gooses start to cacklin, screaming loud befo dey run
Den its silence across de valley
So loud you think you deaf
Listen now (whisper)...
Dis why de niggers leaving
Dis why de niggers left

Dey string dem up past midnight, dey let dem swing lak fruit

Dey takes dem at dey bidding, whenever it is dey suit
No matter where dem was going or what dem chidren must suffer true
By morning der dem be swingin, in de air dats de truest of blue

**JM**

## Prelude

It was in the way she looked at me. Touching her belly just slightly with her free hand she walked as far as she could along the branch without taking her eyes off of mine. If I hadn't turned and walked away I believe she would have stopped at the bend just to make her point, to tell me silently that I was the source of her pain.

She wanted me to repent in the Lord in the way Negroes and Pentecostals are raised up to do but I wouldn't pretend to look upon her condition as a moral failure. My grandfather would surely roll in his grave. Not because his pure Scottish blood coursed through the veins of this child but because I had failed to righteously stay the path for which he set for his sons in this new world.

It was a narrow path to follow my Pa and his people. They were all Lords of their own land, akin to building bridges and policies to keep it that way. It was easier to meander about as they said my Ma's folk tended to do.

I was the failure the black sheep of the brood. I had no wife and no land except for the bit left me to tend by my Uncle Sion. No food but what I could dig from the dirt or trap in the woods. Odd bird they called me.  No odder than Thomas, I could say.

"Why she looking at you," Thomas asked. "She's going to put the hoodoo on you." He teased, chuckling in his quiet way.

He spit a plug of chaw to the ground with a practiced squirt from the side of his mouth, leaving a fine line of brown spittle along his jaw line.  The smell of it made me want to vomit but instead I quickened my step ahead of him.  He was my first cousin, my Aunt Maggie's baby boy, but we'd been raised like brothers after she took to the odd behavior of eating ash from the stove and leaving her children in the yard to wander about in every direction.  I ignored his call and slipped into the woods just beyond the chicken coup.

His dog yapped after me but after no encouragement he became bored with the chase and scampered back to his lazy spot under the porch.

I ducked around the silver pines and down into the valley where the air was cool.  The floor was cushioned with moss and wet leaves and the itty-bitty medicines the people in the marsh hunted to use for their ailments.

I ran through the shallow water, crossing the creek where it trickled around the blue and black rocks that peeked above the surfaces here and there. I ran toward the Woolley Farm and when I got close I rested for some time before I saw her in the distance. She was making her way to the cabin that she shared with her old nanny. It sat just on the border, in the shadow of the once grand plantation that now lingered land-rich but dirt poor in its wake.

I whistled lightly and smiled at her slight hesitation. She tilted her chin in the air, a practiced gesture meant to let me know that our meeting would be on her terms or no. I whistled again and she stopped.

She turned to face me with her hand on her hip.

"Don't you be coming around here Master Zachrey," she sang in her way. "I don't want to be bothered with you. I got work to do, hear?" She asked, her voice rising slightly at the end.

I stood up and walked toward her. I took the basket she'd been balancing on her head and rested it on my shoulder, holding it there easily with my left hand.  I winked at her.  She rolled her eyes, narrowing them lazily toward the ground and then pursed her lips before meeting my gaze. The light dancing through the leaves of the tall trees magnified the liquid pools of her eyes, clear as a baby's they were. The smell of the sassafras leaves she was chewing on made me want to toss the basket and take her hand.  I wanted to run with her as far and as fast as our legs could carry us, away from this place with its laws and summations.

"What is you doing?" she asked indignantly, knowing well that she could speak to no other white man, white person for that matter, in such a tone. I reminded her of it once and wanted to cut my tongue out for saying it.

"What is we first," she asked after a week of silence, her feelings still hurt enough to bring a strangled tear to her eye.

"Is we a white man and a colored gal or is we better than friends what knowed one another since your granddaddy and my granddaddy?"

I could have whipped her or advised her old nanny or one of her uncle's to beat her for being sassy but it melted my heart when she spoke to me in any fashion.

I couldn't help it.  Maybe Thomas was right.  Maybe she had put a spell on me?  Maybe she slipped some of her urine in my water and now I could see no other but for her.

"Come on silly gal.  I'll carry your mess for you."

"Suit yourself." She walked on ahead of me, her hips swaying slightly more than they had been back at the branch.  I smiled and shook my head, following along behind her like a punchy drunk jackrabbit.

I was older than she was but in these parts had she been a white girl our ages would have been matched just right. We probably would have already married and would already have one youngun or two. We would be living on old Uncle Sion's place, except Thomas would sleep in the barn rather than in the house like he did with me.

"What is it you was fretting over?" I asked.

"Fretting over nothing cept this belly of mine," she snapped.  She turned around to face me.

"You don't know how it is. Everybody want to know what they already know. The bigger I gets the more they suck they teeth and count the days before I drop this... this."

I grabbed her hand. "This baby, Sissy. It's going to be a baby."

I pulled her to me and when her arms went around my waist I could feel her body shaking.

"Shush, now." I said. "It won't be the end of the world. I promise you it won't be."

"When Rebekah over in Hollow Creek had her baby," she reminded me. "They killed it and sent her down county road all because Jasp Bailey be the daddy."

I laid the basket down and wrapped my arms around her. I kissed her lightly on her forehead. She had the kerchief I bought her tied around her head. I pulled it off and breathed in the sweet smell of the lemon oil she liked to rub in her hair.

"John and Cassie live together with their babies. Nobody bothers them," I tried to reassure her.

She retorted. "She's nearly white herself. Folks got to be reminded that them kids are colored at all."

"Yeah," I answered slowly. "But they're colored just the same. Nobody's been out there to kill nobody."

"I suppose it all depends on who you is and who you ain't. You and Jasp Bailey more alike than you and John Morarity."

She didn't have to spell it out that Jasp Bailey's daddy was the sheriff. He was related in more ways than one to the founders of the county. John Morarity was a newcomer who had no family name to taint. He let it be known that nobody had a say on what happened on his property and he didn't tolerate folks talking to or about his children. He kept them close and when they came to town they stuck together like a passel of raccoons all wide-eyed and silent.

She pulled away. "What I'm gone do," she asked before grabbing her basket up off of the ground.

I took it out of her hands and followed her along the path. When we got within a few yards of the edge she turned and took it back.

We parted without a word.

I headed back the way I'd come. When I got to the porch my brother Wilbur was there, sitting on my chair, leaning with the two front legs tilted in the air. He glared at me with his usual look of disgust. Thomas slouched in the doorway and when I checked with him for a hint he looked away, telling me without saying that he'd told Wilbur where I had run off to.

"Can't get enough of that gal, can you?" Wilbur let the chair drop down to all four legs with a bang.

He got up and leaned against the railing. He was my older brother by ten years. The babies between us died soon after our Ma birthed them, leaving a gap too wide for either of us to reach across. He was short and stout like the Brody's and I was tall and lanky, which was more akin to our Pa's people. The physical difference made him work that much harder at being a Shealy.

"You know folk's is talking?" He started softly and slowly like we were friends.

"It don't help having you running all over and around here after that gal. It wouldn't normally matter, Zachary," he reasoned. "But a little birdie tells me this ain't no fly by night type a thing. Little fella tells me you got problems getting your plowing and your picking done for running down to the Whooley place. Little tickle in my tummy says there will be trouble if that baby comes out looking like a Mongoloid with curly blond hair."

I narrowed my eyes at Thomas even though I knew he wasn't so much to blame. Either of us was any match against Wilbur. Thomas slipped into the house and a few seconds later I heard him drop to the ground out of the back window. He was undoubtedly headed down to the pond to hide on one of the boats until he was certain Wilbur was gone.

"Don't you get it, Zachary? You can't run round with a colored gal. Folks won't tolerate it." He shifted the stripped twig of hemlock from one side of his mouth to the other. "If what they're saying is true..."

He was hinting at his son Willie's birthday party the previous Saturday night. Willie turned eighteen and joined the army the very next day. I only stayed at the party long enough to show my face.

"I suppose that gal is more important than your nephew getting killed over yonder."

"We ain't at war, Wilbur."

"But we're dancing in the woods with colored's like we ain't got a care in the world," he retorted.

I looked away to hide my anger. Sissy told me she'd heard somebody that night. I ignored her warning and bade her to dance with me near the clearing at Cedar Pond.

I wanted to tell him it was true, that I'd rather be with Sissy than with anybody else but I knew it would mean a fight. He could beat me like a man beats a child and had done so many times.

I kept my mouth shut and let him say what he would. I knew his wife Barbara Ann put her supper on the table at three o'clock and didn't stand by, not even for Wilbur. It was nearly half past two. I counted the minutes until he would leave.

I found a seat on the bottom step careful to keep an eye on him. If I got a head start I could outrun him any day of the week but he was sneaky enough to catch me if I didn't pay close attention.

"What you got to say," he asked. "Just say." He beckoned with a sneer. We were friends no more. "You ain't a boy Zachary. You're a man now... been a man."

He waved his arm around the farm. "Uncle Sion left you a nice enough piece of property."

"He didn't leave it to me."

"He left it and you're on it. What's the difference?" He blurted.

He took a moment to placate his natural urge to scream and softened his approach to a whine. "Amy will make a good wife for you. She waited for you to come back on Saturday but you had other plans, I suppose."

He'd been trying to make me commit to his best friend's sister since I was barely sixteen.

"She's pretty enough," he curled his tongue around the toothpick in his mouth. "She can cook alright. What more can you ask for Zachary? What more do you want?"

I shook my head.

For all his efforts a moment before Wilbur lost all composure and flew into a rage. "You ain't no prize yourself you dirty four-flushing son of a bitch! Daddy sent me up here to beat some sense into you. I told him you was a lost cause!" He pointed his fat finger at me. "You want a bunch of pick-a-ninnies pulling on your britches that's your business but don't make no mistake thinking you'll raise them here."

He lowered his head, "or anywhere around here."

I readied myself to stand up to run. "What happened to *he left it and I'm on it?*" I mocked him.

He shot his finger up like a piston. "I will kick your ass, Zachary Shealy! I will kick your ass if it's the last thing I do. I can guarantee you that."

He hopped off the porch in a flash but I was halfway across the yard heading toward the pier with enough distance between us to yell back at him.

"Get home to your supper or eat mash with Rowdy in the yard."

I ran to the end of the pier and looked back before diving in. His face was crimson with anger. The thought of him eating supper with his colored farmhand Rowdy was almost enough to make him dive in behind me.

I swam halfway across the pond in ten or so easy strokes and then floated on my back, laughing at him having a tantrum there at the edge of the pier.

He jumped around and cursed for a few more minutes before finally leaving in a huff. Thomas peeked above the rim of the boat he was hiding in and rowed out to where I was. I climbed in and he handed me a hook and line.

We fished for our dinner and docked the boat on the opposite side of the lake. Thomas got the fire started and I cleaned the fish. We gorged ourselves until we were too full to move.

The sun ambled down into the purple valley across and behind Little Mountain. The house grew dark and lonesome like a forlorn and forgotten motherless child.

"I'll go across and get a bedroll," Thomas offered sheepishly.

There was no need for him to feel ashamed. I urged him on, "That's a good idea Tomboy. Keep a lookout for Will and don't forget your harmonica."

He smiled and left down the bank and into the boat. I took my pants and shirt off, still damp from my swim and positioned them close to the fire to dry. I rested my head on my arm and thought about Sissy with the light brown eyes.

I whispered it into the air, "Sissy with the light brown eyes."

After a bit, Thomas rowed back across with blankets and a jar of peaches from the pantry. We passed the jar between us, grinning at how good the peaches tasted.

"Thank the good Lord for Rachel Sue's canning." Thomas remarked, licking the line of syrup running down his arm.

"Uncle Sion finally got it right," I agreed.

"Second time's the charm," Thomas reached for the jar.

"Rachel Sue was his third wife," I corrected him. "His first one died when Kathryn was born. His second one... I don't remember her name, died with the grippe in 18. He married Rachel Sue after that."

"Three's the charm then," Thomas digressed. "She sure kept a full pantry."

I nodded in agreement before walking down to the water to wash the sugar water off of my hands. Thomas followed me down, tipping the jar in the air over his opened mouth trying to get the last drop before rinsing it out.

I yawned expressively. It was nearly nine o'clock and I knew Sissy would be waiting for me.

Thomas watched me as I made a show of laying out my blanket and rolling my pants up to cushion behind my head. He opened his can of tobacco and dug out a plug. He shaped it just right to fit into his mouth and then moved it around until it was in place.

"I didn't mean to tell Wilbur about Sissy."

"Wilbur is a pain in the ass," I told him.

He laughed so hard that the tobacco fell out of his mouth. He picked it up off of his blanket and stuffed it back in. "He ain't never been right," he grinned.

"I'm going to see her," I told him somberly.

His smile faded but his gaze met mine. He nodded his head.

"Alright," he responded. "I'll keep the fire a going."

I put my clothes back on and rowed the boat across the river. I hid it in the brush behind the barn just in case Wilbur decided to walk back up the hill to finish what he'd started earlier. I climbed up to the hayloft. It was dark but I could see her resting against the wall.

I sat down beside her.  I took her hand in mine. We sat that way for almost an hour, gazing out of the opening to watch the moon in the distance.

I pointed, "Sugar water moon."

She nodded, "A little more yellow and it'll be a lemon drop."

I brought her hand up to my lips and kissed it lightly. We eased lower into the bed of hay and fell asleep to the faint sound of Thomas's harmonica.

Before daybreak I awoke to find her sitting against the wall. I smiled at her and she smiled back. "Good morning," she said.

"It'll be a couple of hours before we know."

She looked through the opening in the hayloft and agreed. "In another hour it will be a good morning," she seemed to decide.

And it was, for later that day the baby was born. She was early by nearly two weeks but healthy I was told.

## Chapter One

*Prosperity, Newberry County, South Carolina, 1932*

I was born to a black sharecropper's daughter who was not yet sixteen. As soon as Doc Green saw my white skin  he moved his hand to my face to block the flow of life.

"What's wrong, Doctor," Sissy, my mother, recalled asking.

She was still groggy after a half-day of labor, and confused she says by her adolescent understanding of childbirth. The doctor hushed her with no more than a pivot, his back her only answer.

He flipped my lifeless body into an empty shoebox.  He secured the lid and said just as easily as a snake slithers through grass, "Didn't make it, this one."

Hours later after he'd gone, Sissy woke to a slight rustle from beneath her bed.  The doctor had taken the shoebox and slid it there for what reason no one could tell.  Sissy began to cry straight away.  She was sure the devil had come to get her for the dirty deeds she and Mr. Zachary played.

He lived on the adjoining land to tend what was left him. Trying to make do with what little crop it would yield. Neither of them had much but Zachary was white and Sissy was black and that meant he held the better hand somehow.  She'd tried to steer clear of him but he couldn't let her be.

Her grandmother warned, "You better take the long way around there, gal.  If he get you you'll be got and ain't nothing nobody can do to help you."

The first time Sissy says she thought she would faint having his smiling face so close. She seemed to tremble at the thought of it when she told the story.  She recalled his mouth moving but her ears hearing nothing.  His hands grabbed tight to her arm

1

and into the rows of corn they went. His body pressed her into the cool shade of the corn stalks. She recalled that the ground was still damp from an early morning rain. The smell of his skin choked the air around her as she screamed into the silent autumn morning. If anyone heard, like her old nanny told her, no one came to her rescue. When her scream faded the autumn morning was silent and peaceful once more.

When he rolled over and gave her a smile, his eyes were soft. His chest heaved as he blew the air from his lungs with a whoop. He held out a dollar bill, crumpled and wet from being in his hand.

"Thank you, Sissy," he said it as if his moving mouth awhile back had struck the deal and he was keeping his end of the bargain.

Sissy took the money, scrambled to her feet and ran. He was she says in retrospect not much older than she was. Upon counting the years since she was much smaller playing children's games with his sisters, she surmised that he could have been no older than nineteen or twenty.

She never said she loved him but rather with a twirl of her finger, she sang. "I had him wrapped around my finger I did."

Even so, when she spoke of him she closed her eyes. I suppose to conjure the thought of him but to me, it left the impression that what went on was more than a passing fancy.

"I was as wild as anyone would be without no mama and no daddy. Ludie got the best of both of them." She referred to the four extra years her sister had with their parents purely by the chance of being born first.

"When my Nannie would send me off to tote her basket I could wander all over Prosperity town." She waved her arm around to show how far and wide Newberry County was back then.

Ludie would nod her head in agreement. "Nothing as far as the eye could see but farms what growed tobacco and cotton, corn and potatoes. Yes, sir, there was no better place than Prosperity town."

"I was but seven when mama passed," Sissy often lamented.

"Daddy was gone not too long later with that whore from Richland County," Ludie would recall with a huff.

Sissy always agreed but she had admitted more than once that she couldn't remember that far back. She only remembered being cold and hungry while their daddy was off forgetting that they were mere children and not yet old enough to fend for themselves.

Their grandmother stopped by every morning on her way to the Woolley's to pick up her washing and mending. If she was carrying anything, she'd start hollering for one of them to come out and tote it the rest of the way.

"You, there," she'd sing until Ludie or Sissy would open the door.

She never called them by name. Just to the one who answered would be the one she'd take along with her. It wasn't that she couldn't recall their names. It was more that she despised the fact that their father had named them after his people instead of choosing names from the bible, which was more proper.

She hated Jacob from the start, even though no one could deny that once told he was to be a father he slowed his roaming to a halt. He made a deal with the Woolley's for the small lot closest to the north creek. For a half share of the crops he and their mother Laura tackled the lot into a humming pasture of beans, collard greens and sweet potatoes.

Before long the second baby was born and they had a nice little family - said they were married but really they never were.

They couldn't be because Jake was already married. Tale had it that he had a wife and children too but that was someplace else and some other time. He never spoke on it and as time went by most everybody forgot he'd ever been anywhere but there.

When their mama's belly started growing again, this time with a boy, the old women knew from the onset that this baby would take her home. They forewarned throughout the nine months at the sight of her curried skin and stubborn appetite. They prescribed all types of rues and concoctions but knew all along nothing would stave off the reaper come for his due.

Their clear-eyed premonition came true one cold winter morning. The girls awoke to the smell of the ashy burnt logs from the night before. There was no food cooking and no lights lit. Jake was sitting in a chair outside of the room where their mama and never-born baby brother were laid. He stared ahead into the emptiness.

A few months later their father, with the urging of their grandmother, followed Cavalry's congregation to the river with his daughters. They were overdue to be baptized but it was for the best that they would be saved now rather than later or not at all.

Jake bought a white-laced dress from Mrs. Abbeville. She was a colored seamstress who made a good business sewing delicate dresses and blouses. Her customers were usually the white ladies in and around the town though from time to time a colored lady would darken her door.

When Jacob arrived at her little shop near the side entrance of the apothecary she studied him with an air of peculiarity. When he pointed his thick and calloused finger at the dress that he wanted she held back from parting with it as if in its making it was meant for no other than a white child. Money however is the great separator and motivator in such matters even for the
most pretentious.

When he asked that she replace the pink ribbon for pale green, Mrs. Abbeville cut him the length of satin with a quick snip. She told him she'd sell it for fifty cents but charge an extra dollar to lace it through. She added with a huff that he should be quick so as not to bother a usual customer whom she surmised could be coming along at any moment.

He took his time and counted his money slowly, laying the coins on the table rather than in her outstretched hand.

Later that evening he sat in the chair by the fire and with hands more used to chipping rock and cutting wood he carefully replaced the pink ribbon with the green. When he finished, he placed the dress at the foot of the bed where his girls slept.

Ludie was the oldest. She was a strong girl with a bit of her mama and a bit of him. She gave him no worries and did as she was told. Sissy was the youngest and the apple of her mama's eye. She was a bit on the spoiled side and partial to the peculiar color green as what is found in a mayapple leaf. He knew Laura would have wanted the lace to be just so.

When Sissy found the dress at the end of her bed she was overjoyed. She was still not quite aware of why her mother had gone away and in some sense felt that she would return that very day.

She sat still for her grandmother to press her hair and after a bath in the tub by the fireplace she put the dress on. She studied herself in the little mirror that Ludie held up for her to see. She ran her hand over the shiny ringlets in her hair and then across the front of her new dress. Surely her mother would be meeting them at the river and coming home today. Singing along with the others she skipped along the road and the short path through the woods to the river.

Pastor Thomas stepped into the water along with Deacons Burdette and Jameson. They pressed long poles along the bottom to find a safe and solid place before pushing the poles into the muddy floor to stand as a boundary for the baptism.

Sisters Flora and Shirley chose from the parishioners standing along the bank one by one. They helped them through the water to where Pastor Thomas waited.

It wasn't until Ludie was chosen that Sissy realized that there was a good possibility that she would be next. She had no intention of getting her dress wet and now thought twice about refusing to remove it when her grandmother asked her to do so.

"Your mama's got you spoiled but suit yourself." Her grandmother closed her eyes to the idea of making bargains with youngsters too short to reach good sense.

Earlier, Sissy had stood by and watched the others change from their nice clothes and fold them neatly to carry along with them. Her new dress was the only one that would get soiled by the dirty water.

Her stomach seemed to roll onto itself and just as she was about to run away the sisters took hold of her and pulled her into the cold, brown river.

She pulled and kicked but they were long standing sisters of Calvary. They had not lost their hold on a sinner's walk to salvation in the many years they had served. This itty-bitty thing had no chance of sullying their record. From there the deacons took hold of her arms. By now the dress was ruined. The pale green ribbon was lying limp with dirty water. Just the top of the dress remained white. Pastor Thomas clutched the dress at the neck and covered her face with his other hand.

"Close your mouth little gal." He said and then bellowed loud enough for the whole world to hear. "I baptize this little sister in obedience to God's command in the name of the Father, in the name of the Son and in the name of the Holy Ghost."

He pushed her screaming into the water. When he pulled her up a second later she coughed and sputtered like a fish. The water shed from her face and body leaving her saved on the one hand but with a feeling of betrayal that would not be easily absolved on the other.

She was carried out to the bank where her father wrapped her in a blanket.

Everyone clapped delightedly and as the last person was baptized behind her they sang *Take me to the Water* in long and jubilant moans and crescendos.

Sissy pulled away from Jacob and refused to take part in any of it. When he left some months later she never once asked after him. When he brought food from time to time through the winter, she pretended she wasn't hungry and couldn't have been bothered by his visit. Her grandmother mimicked Sissy's sentiments. Her eyes would narrow at the mention of his name and when he came to visit she quietly found other places to be until he was gone.

Black Jake she called him. He was strong and good looking she would reluctantly acknowledge but blacker than an old burnt log, she would spit. The girls looked just like him, especially the young one.

Years went by. Ludie was coming up on nineteen in the year thirty-two. She was recently married and already with a baby nearly three years old but was still not so much on her own. She and Sissy had moved to live with their grandmother the year prior.

Nanny liked to remind them. "I was on my own far before my year fifteen. I had a baby or two by then." She would mutter names of children they'd never heard of.

"One of them left for the north," she'd say. "And one of them could be sitting right next to me and how would I know?"

Her stories were mostly to herself and ever changing as if she must have had thirty children, all with sad endings. She was often sad beyond repair, bitter still that slavery time darkened her early days to a permanent shadow.

Just now she sat by the door staring out at her garden, trying to get over having Doc Green in her house. She was trying to remember what rue she needed to clear the smell of him away. Sissy was in the bedroom, still sleeping after having given birth to a little white baby. Nanny shook her head. She knew trouble was brewing.

## Chapter Two

Sissy lay there for more than an hour. She could hear her old nanny muttering to herself, going back and forth over one of her concoctions, fretting over a missing ingredient. She heard the tapping of her grandmother's hand as she recited what she could remember like a nick-knack song, trying to trick her memory into letting go of what was missing.

Sissy was relieved to hear Doc Green's name in her ramblings. It was best to stay on old Nanny's good side, lest you wanted to tussle with one of her spells.

Sissy peeked around the door before reaching under the bed for the shoebox. She placed it in her lap and pushed the lid away. Her breath caught in her throat. She stared at the baby inside the box. It looked like it had been born from another family, a white family more likely. She ran her finger across my pink and white hairline. Her heart fluttered at the thought. She pulled the lid back into place.

The only protection for a Negro in Prosperity, or anywhere in the South in those days was to have the good sense to look busy and be invisible all at the same time. Sissy knew it would be impossible to be invisible toting this baby around town.

Everybody knew who and what ought to be in Prosperity. The mayor and elder men saw to it that everything and everybody stayed just so.

Sissy's grandmother stepped into the room. It had been three hours since Doc Green had pushed the shoebox under the bed and declared the baby to have been born dead. Before leaving out the front door he had turned to tell Nanny, emphatically so, that she ought to keep a closer eye on her house and hold. He'd shifted his eyes toward the bedroom and took a pause long enough to make it clear as to what part of her household he was referring to.

Sissy pulled the lid off and handed the shoebox over. I was born. My great grandmother took me from the box. She bathed me, wrapped me in a blanket and waited, fighting, as she recalled, the urge to drown me in the creek herself.

After the sun had passed behind Little Mountain she pushed on Sissy's shoulder.

"Get up, gal," she ordered. "It won't be long before they come out here checking on you. Doc Green won't last ten minutes if they get him in a corner. You done had this little white gal," she shook her head. "You'll be lucky they don't burn this house down... my house down and all of us along with it."

Sissy and Ludie, carrying her own baby daughter Adele, followed Nanny far up into the woods. They were headed to one of the old slave cabins way up on the long lost Avery Plantation.

"Good luck don't follow no child what's first trip is down wise," Old Nanny reckoned as we negotiated the steep and hidden trail.

She swung through the thickest brush with her blade, chopping it heftily in front of us. She held her hand up to get us to stop while she listened with her ear tilted toward the slightest crack or burr. She could see things other folks couldn't and could understand a whisper from a hundred feet away.

"The big house burned down twenty year ago," she explained. "Folks done forget about it."

She cut through a final patch of wisteria and there in the middle of the woods was a row of tiny houses. They were stacked one beside the other for as far as could be seen in the dense light. They were covered in crawling vines and yellow

Jessamine left over from bygone days. Some of the doors were missing. Others had been left open. A few still held on to tattered pieces of burlap that had been tacked across the openings. The material, soft after years of wear, swung gently in the evening breeze.

They walked along the front of them until Nanny found one that she liked. She lit the candles from her satchel and started a fire on the stove with bits of leaves and switches that she'd been picking up along the way.

The fire filled the little room with a glow that felt warm and safe. Her granddaughters watched as she found a small pot, filled it with water and pulled a crooked piece of burdock root from her pocket. She cut the skin away with her knife and laid the pieces of white root in the boiling water. The smell of earth drifted like a spirit into the room.

She spoke to it softly, telling it to tend to its business.

"Shush that baby," she whispered. "Shush that baby."

She cut another piece and laced it to a string to make a necklace. She handed it to Sissy. "Put it around her neck," she ordered.

Sissy took it. She glanced at her sister for confirmation unsure of what it would do. Ludie looked away, refusing to help her understand that boiling burdock root would keep the baby from crying or that by hanging a piece around the neck would erase any signs of colic.

Soon after, Nanny hefted her sack and blade across her back to return to her little house. The sky was dark and the woods were darker but she made her way along the invisible path nary a worry about losing her way.

The next morning she lied to Wilbur. "I ain't seent her," she said.

She was sitting on the steps in front of her little house. A bowl of pole beans rested in her lap. She snapped them in half one-by-one with a swift turn of her wrist.

"I ain't seent her." She repeated in response to his narrowing eyes as if he could somehow read her mind.

The baby chicks ran across his feet. He kicked them aside, sending one or two into a roll across the dusty yard.

He lifted his ear into the air. "Is that a little birdie telling me that there's a baby whining about?" He asked in a singsong manner.

Nanny kept snapping the beans, not missing a hitch in her rhythm.

"I don't know what little birdie you talking about Mas Wilbur." She said his name in pieces, leaving a pause between the wil and the bur.

He turned his head to the side, looking at her sideways like when a donkey checks to see if whoever is close behind is near enough to kick.

"Little itch in my ear tells me your Sissy gal done had a bitty baby about the color of water." He chucked his head straight, "Which ain't an easy thing for a black gal as black as your Sissy gal to do."

"My Sissy ain't had no baby." She said it with a slight smile, as if it was a joke Wilbur was telling, stringing her along like white folks tended to do with the poor coloreds. "Maybe you're talking about that gal down in Frog Level? Maybe it be the one over on the other side over yonder by Cedar Pond... or the one off in Gilbert Hollow?"

There were plenty for him to choose from. She gave him but a sampling but knew to keep her voice low and songlike so it would seem as if she was being helpful to the man. It was a fine line to converse with white folks, she knew. She had learned much during her seventy- seven years, the least of which was how to handle crackers like Wilbur.

She looked up at him then. She set the bowl aside. Wilbur put his hands on his hips. He knew well that he couldn't do nothing with this old woman, stubborn worse than a Billy goat.

He pointed his finger. "What they're doing is against the law. You know it and I know it."

When she didn't respond, he continued. "She'd better be gone away from here by now, your Sissy. If she got any sense in that happy high toting head of hers, she better take a notion to follow them others what's finding what theys finding up and over yonder." He gave her a long look until he became satisfied that his message had sunk in. He turned on his heel, kicking chicks here and there, and left the yard. He got nearly halfway across the side garden before turning back. "I better not see no yellow headed pick-a-ninny running around here neither old nanny. I just better not."

He stomped away in a huff, too simple to recognize how many yellow headed colored children there were running around these parts already. Nanny picked the bowl up, saying low enough for him not to hear, "Damn crazy fool might ought to stop listening to little birdies."

She carried the bowl into her middle room and came back out with the broom and a handful of salt. She sprinkled the salt where Wilbur had been standing and then along the path he took home. She swept the broom back and forth humming one of her lullabies. "That ought to keep him out from around here," she spat in the dirt.

She looked up to study her memory for the haunt her own grandmother once put on the old master. The one that made his bowels run over till he was empty. He died in a cramp of

13

twisted and dried bones like a stump in the ground. Was not a drop of water left in him but for the loosy-toosy covering the floor like a layer of sugar-water molasses that smelled like shit and death.

The big house was burned to the ground and the whole mess of them got sold down south to be dispersed this-a-way and that. That's how she ended up on the Shealy plantation. That's why she couldn't remember the taint her old grandee used. Pity she thought, shaking her head for that and everything else she could no longer recall.

On the way back across her yard she grabbed one of the older chickens strutting around in the garden. She pulled it by its legs and quickly flipped it over to snatch its neck with a quick jerk of her arm. She marked an ex in the dirt with the handle of the broom and sat the chicken on it. She went inside to heat the lard.

She waited until dark before returning to the old slave cabin in the woods with the cooked beans and fried chicken. She didn't bother studying the field for Wilbur; she knew he wouldn't come back around until after a rain had washed the salt away from the path.

"You all got about two days," she said without saying that she wouldn't be traipsing through the woods no more. They stared at her in the bit of light from the candle. "I'll leave it to you," she gestured with her hand toward Ludie, who shook her head with a frown.

"Look, now," Ludie reminded them. "I got to get back to mine." Her husband wasn't too much for nonsense even though she lived in one house and he still lived at home with his folks. She still cooked his dinner and washed his clothes but he stayed by his daddy's house near Batesburg. She knew by now that he would be fit to be tied. "Herman is going to kill me if I don't get back. I told him I'd be back before night fall." Nanny chuckled, "I suppose he can't say too much."

Ludie set her mouth into a frown aimed at Sissy. "I suppose we'll just hide up here in this cold and starve to death." "It's some nice figs nearest to the thicket." Nanny pointed off in the direction of the old plantation. In years gone by there had been more than a hundred fig trees lined up in neat rows for the folks to harvest. The ones that survived grew wild now, leaving most of the fruit to fall to the ground to rot in the heat or be snatched up by animals and wild birds. This late in the season there would be slim pickings.

"I'll bring your daddy on Thursday if I can get word to him," she spoke to Ludie. "Thursday," Ludie protested. "By then I might as well stay here."

"Meet me down there near the big poplar," Nanny told them before gathering herself up to return to her cabin, "...just after dark, hear?" Ludie took her blanket and climbed onto the pallet beside little Adele. She turned over to face the wall. Sissy followed Nanny to the yard and then returned to fasten the log across the door to secure it. She sat back down at the table.

"I'm sorry for your troubles," she said to Ludie.

When she didn't get an answer, she rested her head on her arms. The next morning, the room was still dark but it was so small it was clear to Ludie that we were alone.

"Sissy," Ludie hissed.

Sissy was gone. Ludie looked down at me in the covers beside her. "Your eyes were so big," she told me later. "...just sitting there looking like wasn't nothing wrong with this world. Two days old and already an orphan was what."

Sissy left me just after Ludie had fallen asleep, sneaking through the woods in the dark to Zachary's place. He was hiding from Wilbur just like she was. When she didn't find him in their usual place she scrunched down low at the wood line to study the other side of the lake. She saw the tiny glimmer of firelight. Even from there she could smell his pipe.

She eased into the cold, dark water and waded silently across knowing well that it would take three times as long to go around through the woods. Thomas's dog met her on the other side, wagging its tale for a scratch behind his ear. She heard Thomas. "Who goes there," he whispered loudly.

"It's Sissy," Zachary recognized her.

He met her with a blanket, wrapping her in it and helped her back to where he and Thomas had been camping since she left.

Thomas gathered his things. "I hope she didn't let nobody see her," he complained.

"She didn't, damn fool." Zachary warned him.

Thomas hung his head. He was already ashamed of saying what he was thinking out loud. "I'll watch out for Wilbur."

"Thank you, Thomas." Zachary responded softly.

Sissy sat silently next to the fire while Zachary rubbed her arms with the blanket. He found a shirt and slacks in his sack, "Put these on before you get yourself sick."

She did as she was told, knowing that she'd probably die anyway. She remembered hearing what her grandmother said about bathing after having had a baby.

"Don't bathe for thirty days lest you gone die," was a popular enough superstition.

It had women all over and around these parts doing chores in foul and stained dresses for weeks or months after giving birth. Some of the white folks believed it just the same.

"Your brother's been down to my Nanny's house. He been telling her that he's going to find me. He say he knows I done had a white baby and he ain't taking no excuses if he get his hands on me."

"Shush now." He told her. "He ain't doing no such a thing."

She sat up and looked at him with her eyes furrowed and her mouth set like a snake about to strike. She wanted to beat some sense into him but when he leaned away and laughed, she started to cry. Every tear ever made fell out in a flood.

"Look here," he said, trying to wipe them away. "We're trying to get you dry and here you go getting yourself all wet again." He pulled her into his arms and let her cry.

"I'm sorry Sissy. I know you're scared but I promise you, Wilbur won't harm a hair on your head and neither on the baby's head."

"I want to get out of here," she choked through her tears. "I want to get away from here."

"Where do you want to go?"

"I don't care," she said. "Wherever the bus will take me. I don't care."

"Thomas," Zachary called for his cousin. "Go across there and bring the truck back over and around."

Thomas got up and whistled for his dog. A few seconds later, they could hear the oars and the slight lapping of the water against the side of the boat as Thomas made his way across the lake.

If Wilbur happened to be on the other side Zachary's plan was to stand fast and shoot him when he crossed. He kissed her on her forehead and they settled into the covers to wait. A few hours before daybreak, Thomas returned through the woods from Old Red Oak Road. He added wood to the fire and set the frying pan to heat without saying a word. He cooked fresh eggs he'd carried over from the coop and then he passed a plate to Sissy.

"Go on," Thomas cajoled Sissy when she hesitated. "He don't eat eggs. Them's for you."

Zachary winked at Sissy and got up to gather her clothes. When she was finished he took the plate down to the water to wash it off. He studied the other side of the lake over the morning steam floating over the surface. He was sure Wilbur was there, no doubt looking for something to cross with. The cook fire and the smell of food would make it easy enough for a five year old to find them now.

He took Sissy by the hand to lead her through the woods to his truck. They drove all the way to the bus station in Columbia.

She bought a one-way ticket to wherever the first bus leaving was going, which happened to be New York City. She would have preferred Chicago since her cousin Jeremiah had left for there the summer before last. No one had heard from him since but he'd told her before he left that she should get out of the south. He'd said he would help her if she came to Chicago. She was in no position to barter just now. She paid the fare and ran back across the street and climbed into Zachary's truck. He hugged her one last time and then pulled his hat down on her head, patting it on the top for good measure.

He gave her every bit of money he had, twenty-seven dollars, which seemed like a fortune to her. "It's all I got," he told her.

"When you get to where you're going, send me a letter with your address and I'll send you more."

She nodded her head but he knew she wouldn't do it. She could barely write her own name and was far too proud to ask anyone to do it for her.  He stayed in the truck and watched as she boarded the bus.  She was still wearing his shirt and pants. He waited until the bus was far down the road, imagining that it might stop, open its doors and she'd hop off and run back to where he was. It was a folly of a thought and he knew he was the bigger fool for even imagining it.

## Chapter Three

Childhood from my adult perspective was swift, like the naked branches of a late winter forest. In my memory of it, there was no color, just pales of gray with dull and lonesome silence. Tears never fell from my eyes. They spilled on the inside, drowning my soul with sorrow and my heart with heavy despair.

After Sissy left, I was left with my grandfather Jacob. He lived with Sylvia, a woman who had two children of her own but had not an ounce of motherly love... especially for a half-white baby whose own mama was headed north.

"Get out of that window before you catch a draft," she barked. She was sucking the marrow out of a chicken bone with such a practiced motion that the bone was falling apart in her hands. She dropped what was left of it onto her plate. She pointed her greasy finger in my direction, and like a trained monkey her son reached over and pulled me away from the window. Sylvia narrowed her eyes. "Don't you start no crying, you hear?"

"Put her in the cellar, mama," her daughter, who mimicked her mother in every way, suggested. "You want to go in the dirt cellar, gal?" Sylvia played along. I shook my head.

Her son shoved me further away from the table. "Talk, gal," Sylvia hollered. "Don't nobody understand you."

"No, ma'am," I answered.

"She hungry, mama." Her daughter advised with a nasty sideways grin.

"No, she's not." Sylvia countered with a dry chuckle. "She don't like to eat. Do you gal? She'd rather stand at the window and wait for her granddaddy. Don't you gal?"

She stared at me as if she might decide to pop me in the pot and cook me for tomorrow's dinner. My eyes widened at the thought. She took the look as one of defiance and reached around and pulled me to her.

"You want to try me, little gal? You think just because you got them light eyes that somebody wants you? Let me tell you something little gal, your own mama don't want you. You better find you someplace before I send you down there to play with the rats and the cock-a-roaches."

She let me loose and I ran to the other room. As afraid as I was of the dark, it was the only other room in the house. Any place was better than where they were. I fell over a pair of shoes that had been left in the middle of the floor. I scrambled the rest of the way to the window, hoping that Sylvia couldn't hear the loud drumming in my chest.

I stood at the window and watched as the sun melted down on the far side of the sky. I knew my grandfather would be home before long. I trained my eyes on the bend in the road and like magic there he came. It was akin to a vision and at first I didn't believe it was true. I stood there until I heard the latch on the front door lift. I walked across the room to just inside the door and waited.

"Hey, there," he walked in and greeted everyone in his quiet way. I heard him rinse his hands and face at the basin before fixing a plate. "Where's the baby?" he asked.

"Ain't no babies in this house," Sylvia retorted indignantly.

"Where's the youngest one living here, then?" He replied. "She eat anything this evening?"

"She won't eat. She's finicky that one. That's why tain't nothing to her but skin and bones and all that hair on her head."

"Frank Lee," He called for me quietly.

I suppose Sylvia pointed or jerked her head toward the room. He stood in the doorway for a second before seeing me there beside the wall. He picked me up and carried me to the table.

"There you go," Sylvia muttered. "Treating her like she can't walk, can't talk, and can't eat on her own. There's nothing worse than a child what's spoiled."

My grandfather ignored her. He sat at the table to feed me from his plate, talking to me softly, telling me about his day. Sylvia and her children glared at me from their separate vantage points around the table.

When he finished, he carried me out to the front porch. He lit his pipe and rocked me slowly while watching for what he called a sugar moon, one what carries more light than the sun. He pointed to it off in the distance. It was true; it lit the road and field across the way so brightly I could see the jackrabbits hopping to and fro.

He smoked his pipe and rocked me slowing in the rocking chair. I fell asleep in his arms, oblivious and unaware of his letters to Sissy asking her to come for me. He knew by now that he couldn't continue leaving me with Sylvia. So far, his first and second letters to Sissy had gone unanswered. I suppose she couldn't have been bothered. After all, she now held a favored position with a white family on Long Island, caring for their all-white children. She had a new name since Sissy was too poor, the white mother had decided. Her new name was to be Susie. The white children didn't even bother adding Miss to the front, and often shortened the back to a whine. Sissy just grinned and raised those white children while I, her only child, began moving from one relative to the next and then on to strangers as my welcomes wore thin.

Each time, my grandfather was there to send me off with luck, he would say. "Throw me luck," he would cajole until I would say it for myself.

Many of them I don't remember but for a blur of hushes and scorn, except one who became my buffer for a short while. Her name was Annie Bell Ephron. I, and the other children, called her Miss Bell.

She was a woman like many others who took in children one by one as their mothers moved north for work. The children were treated well, meaning they were largely ignored when not picking, cleaning, or carrying something or the other for Miss Bell. As long as their mama's sent regular payment for their care, Miss Bell was happy, and if she was happy the children were happy.

She reminded us every day as she plopped grits, or meal, or dry bread with jam at the setting of those children whose payments arrived. She often let the others go hungry until even she could no longer stand the sight.

I somehow became her favorite for the years I lived there. She still scrubbed my body at bath time till I feared the skin would rub off, still whipped me with a switch if I moved too slowly in fetching, and she still passed me over if three dollars didn't arrive from up north when it was due. But from time to time, she gave me a smile, or when it rained, she'd carry me way up on her shoulders to keep my feet from getting wet. It was an odd gesture of tenderness I know, but endearing at the time nonetheless.

She was a tall woman with large hands and sturdy shoulders. When she carried me up high it felt like I was riding on a throne... if only for a moment. When gifts arrived for the other children, she'd put the ribbons in my hair telling the actual recipient that their nappy heads wouldn't hold no bow. When shiny patent leather shoes arrived from Philadelphia she laughed at the frowning face of the hapless receiver, telling her that her mother must have been crazy to think their big ole feet would fit the shoes. The children would cut their eyes at me, and store their anger for later when Miss Bell dozed off on the porch after supper.

I begged God to release me, to show me the slither of an opening to allow me to escape but when he did, three days before my fifth birthday, it was to a place that seemed much worse. I was shaken from my sleep by rough hands to my chest. A dark shadow hovered in the early morning haze. I was slung from the bed before it became clear that my mother, after nearly five years, was come to fetch me. I certainly knew I had a benefactor but the true definition of mother escaped me. I knew one thing. This woman frightened me. Miss Bell could be cruel but she and the other children were all that I knew. My mother yanked and pulled, searching for the white children's outgrown clothes she'd sent, screaming from Miss Bell to me, to tell her, show her, where my belongings were. I tried, but could not utter a word.

"...she, mute?" My mother asked. Her mouth was twisted, and her hands were ready to let me loose at the thought of a dysfunction.

"Naw, she ain't mute," her cousin, Precious, who lived a few doors down from Miss Bell declared. "I done heared her talk befo. I told you Annie Bell done made the child too scared to speak to her own kin. I sees her every day."

Precious cut her eyes at Miss Bell, "...won't even let me talk to my own kin." Precious twisted her lips into a sneer and jerked her head in Miss Bell's direction.

By then Sissy had made up her mind. She didn't need no clothes, no shoes, no nothing. "That's alright then. I'll get her some new clothes in New York City!"

I looked up at her. New York, I thought? I hoped whatever New York was it would be nicer than this woman who had such a clutch on my nightdress that I was nearly walking on my tiptoes.

She dragged me out of the front door and down the stairs of the little house. Miss Bell stood on the porch with the rest of the children clinging close, all eyes, watching the spectacle of the three of us climbing into the big shiny car that was sitting on the dirt of the front yard.

"Look at her," Sissy smirked. "Crying like a big old baby fixin' to lose that three dollars ain't ya?"

I turned in the back seat and looked out of the back window. Miss Bell's arms were outstretched towards the car. Tears streamed down her face.  Her mouth tracing the words my poor baby, over and over.

"Sit your ass down in that seat." Sissy grabbed my leg from the front where she was sitting. I jerked around and held tight to my bladder, which was on the verge of spilling over. Her cousin Precious, who had climbed into the back seat too, looked down at me.

"I told you, she spoiled," she said it with an emphatic nod of her head.

"Go on, drive," Sissy instructed Buddy, the driver.  I was soon to discover Buddy was her current boyfriend and I was to call him Daddy. I never did and it didn't matter because he, like others to follow, never lasted for long. Precious got out a few doors away. I stared at her through the side window as the car moved away. Dirt lifted from the road in a cloud of dust as the taillights caught her still yapping away about me and my ways.

Sissy kneeled in her seat to hang out of the window. She yelled for Precious to come on up to New York City and get away from "backwards assed Newberry County."

She laughed, thinking that it was so funny that black folks remained in the South. I took her laughter for a shift in her disposition and smiled when she looked at me.

Her mouth twisted, "What are you laughing at? Lay your ass down and go to sleep."

I moved to curl my feet beneath me, to do as I was told but she pointed her finger at me and barked, "Don't you put your feet on that seat!"

I leaned my upper body to the seat, leaving my legs dangling over the floorboard. I stayed this way, full bladder and all, until the sun climbed high over the lonely and narrow highway that led to Richland County.

When morning came, Sissy instructed Buddy to pull over. "I got to pee," she said.

He skidded to a stop without hesitation. I sat up, trying to prepare my mouth to speak.

"What's wrong with you?" She yanked her seat forward. "Get out the car before you wet that seat."

I scrambled out of the car prepared to follow but my bladder didn't wait. Pee spilled down my legs into a puddle at my feet. Sissy, who had already started towards the trees looked back. "Come on, here, damn it." Then she saw the urine still spilling to the dirt.

"Look at you!" She pointed her red lacquered fingertips at my feet.

The polish caught the early morning light like the sparkles at the bottom of the creek near Miss Bell's house.

"What is you, a two year old baby?"

She turned and left me standing there. I was afraid to look at Buddy. He'd gotten out of the car to see what Sissy was so perturbed about. "Heh," he grunted before walking down to the trees behind Sissy. They disappeared into the thicket and I heard my ma squealing and branches cracking. I stood there in my puddle of urine and waited.

My stomach growled. I longed for the sticky oatmeal that Miss Bell had undoubtedly served to the other children that morning. Never mind that Roger, the oldest boy there, liked to thump my head with his hard knuckles if my elbow touched his, or if he thought I was ugly that day. I'd been gone from Miss Bell's for only a few hours but it seemed like an eternity. After awhile Sissy and Buddy came out of the trees. Buddy zipping his pants up, and she adjusting her dress. She was smirking and twisting her hips and still teasing Buddy, when she looked up and saw me.

"You got something to put under Miss Pissy Girl," she asked.

He went around the car to search and she, as quick as a flash, grabbed the back of my nightdress. She lifted it to swat my rear end for every word. "Next time you tell me if you got to go. Hear?"

My heart nearly stopped as I tried to hold my balance and catch her hand at the same time. She switched her grip from the back of my nightdress to the front. She grabbed it up in a bunch and pulled my face to hers.

"You hear me," she asked again.

I nodded yes. She grabbed me tighter. "What you say?"

"Yes, ma'am." My mouth moved.

"Alright, then." She shoved me away. "Hand me that here," she reached for the rag Buddy had pulled out of his trunk and placed it on the back seat.

"Now, you sit there and don't you move. Buddy don't want his car smelling like piss, do you Buddy?"

By then Buddy was back in the driver's seat.

"Sure don't," he said and put the car into gear.

We drove for another while before she began to point out turns to Buddy until finally she began to scream out of the car window at people she knew.   She directed him to pull to a stop in front of a rickety little house that was leaning dangerously to the left. The old man sitting on the porch was dressed like he was going to church. His black skin contrasted sharply with the crisp white of his dress shirt leaving the image in my mind's eye to forever appear one-dimensional. He barely looked up from his chore of carefully trimming the skin from a large green apple.

"Hey, Daddy," Sissy yelled. "Look who I brought you."

She stepped out of the car and pulled the seat back with one hand.

"Come on, here."

She jerked her hand towards the outside of the car. I slid off the seat and onto the dirt yard. The stairs were built up with pieces of rocks and wood that led up to the lopsided slate-colored house.

Children from the house next door stopped throwing sticks at each other long enough to scratch their dusty legs and gape at the visitors to my grandfather's house. Sissy gave my shoulder a push and nodded toward the house before twisting up the steps like a movie star.

"I bet you didn't think you'd see me no mo," she leaned down to Papa Jake and gave him a quick hug.

"Ludie say to tell you she love you and she's doing fine. She's working and I'm working... you know, that's what made me take so long to answer your letter."

"Um huh," he replied and brought a piece of apple to his mouth.

"I would have come before now but the Marshall's, that's what their name is that I work for; they couldn't do without me until just now. I finally told the Miss look here, I got to go! I got to go take care of my business. Anyway," she waved her hand towards Buddy. "This is Buddy. Buddy, this my daddy."

Buddy ambled up the stairs, barely making the landing and having to take a giant step to regain his balance. "Pleased to meet you, sir," he greeted Jacob with a big grin.

"Come on, here," Sissy gestured to Buddy. "Who home," she screamed into the house. The screened door slammed behind Buddy as they disappeared inside.

The children from next door moved closer. One, with little braids sticking in every direction on her head, stuck her tongue out. I looked in the opposite direction and hoped the lot of them would find someone else to bother.

After awhile, I brought my attention back to my grandfather. He slid another piece of apple into his mouth. He smiled at me ever so softly. I hadn't seen him in more than a year. I wanted to run to him but my shyness had me planted in the dirt like a beetroot.

The children started chanting "Goosie, goosie, goosie gander," and moved closer.

A boy wearing no more than a pair of dirty underwear, his bellybutton the size of a plum sticking out ahead of him, threw a small stone in my direction.

"You all get on out from over here." Jacob said. I could barely hear him but the children scattered away. He slowly brought another piece of apple to his mouth.

"You gone stand in the yard all day?" He asked me. His voice sounded like a song.

I climbed the stairs until I stood at the top. He gestured for my hand. I held it out and he took it and guided me closer to him. He carefully cut a piece of apple and held it up. I opened my mouth and he popped it inside. When I bit down, the juice filled my mouth and started my taste buds to dancing like I hadn't eaten in a week.

"You like that, don't ya?"

Papa Jake smiled. His cheeks were high and shiny black. His eyes were soft brown almonds and his teeth were scattered but you could tell by the wrinkles around his eyes that he didn't allow that to keep him from a good laugh.

"What's my name?" He asked.  He raised his chin just so and popped another piece of apple into my mouth. I hunched my shoulders forward. His eyebrows rose.

"I'm your Papa Jake," he reminded me.

I nodded in agreement. I knew he was my Papa Jake but my mind was on my stomach, which was growling just now.

"What's my name?" He asked again, cocking his head to the side and raising his eyebrows.

"Papa Jake," I replied around a mouthful of apple.  He chuckled.

"And you... your name is Frances Lee."

I nodded yes except that wasn't my name. They called me Frank Lee at Miss Bell's. I had to remind myself to answer Papa Jake when he called me by the other name.  He was nodding his head satisfied that we were on common terms when his nose wrinkled at the whiff of high dry piss floating in the air around me. He held me away from his Sunday suit. My heart began to hammer at the thought of another sour relative.

"Looks like you need a change of clothes." He stood up to lead me by the shoulder into the house. The inside was dark and the hallway was narrow. I could hear Sissy away in the back someplace. She was talking louder than anyone else, baiting the crowd with a story that led them just shy of a juicy climax just out of their reach up north in New York City!

Papa Jake and I veered away from the noise at the back of the house. We ended up in a musty smelling room with so much furniture in it we had to walk sideways to get around it. The bed was so high that whoever slept there had to step up on a two-step stepstool to get to the top. Papa Jake hefted me to the top step and pulled a cardboard box from under the bed. I watched him fumble around in the box until he found the dress he was searching for. He held it up for me to see.

"How you like this one?" He asked. The dress was white cotton with little puffy sleeves that had pale green ribbon laced around the bottom of each puff. My breath caught in my throat. The dress was the prettiest I'd ever seen. None of the dresses the mamas had sent to the girls at Miss Bell's could match the one Papa Jake held up in front of me. He clucked his tongue with a shift at the corner of his mouth and winked.

"I reckon you like that a mite better than that nightdress."

He took my hand and led me to a basin of water sitting on a dresser in the corner of the room. He pulled a rag from a shelf and handed it to me.

"You wash up. There's the soap," he pointed. "When you get done, come on back to the kitchen."

He winked again and left the room. I dipped the rag and quickly washed my body with the cool water. I skipped the soap trying my best to get into the new dress and back into the presence of my new friend. Once dressed, I gingerly walked along the hallway toward the voices coming from the kitchen.

With every step, my heart thudded against my chest more urgently.

As I rounded the corner into the kitchen I found everyone there, leaning forward in their seats, listening to a story Sissy was telling. You'd have thought they believed she was the savior come back to pull them from the clutches of Lucifer.

"...and I walked right up to that white gal," Sissy was saying. "I told her, I pays my money and I tends to see the movie in whatever seat I choose!"

"You talked to a white lady like that?" They whispered.

"What white lady? Just cause they white don't make them no lady. Ain't that right, Buddy?" She urged Buddy to get in on the celebrity.

Just then someone spied me standing in the shadow of the kitchen door. "Who brought that little white gal in here?" Everyone turned and looked.

Sissy slid off the counter where she'd been sitting. "That ain't no white gal. That's my baby, Frances Lee! I pulled her out from Annie Bell's last night. That heifer was taking my money and wasn't feeding my baby. Look, she ain't nothing but skin and bones."

Sissy stuck her hand out and began counting down each thing Miss Bell hadn't been doing.

"She wasn't giving her the clothes I was sending. I was sending some good stuff too... new shoes, dresses, sweaters, everything! That heifer was giving my baby's things to her own kin. I had to come get my baby. I been working hard sending five, six dollars every month... and this heifer was taking it and putting it in her pocket. I had to come get my baby."

All eyes were still on me. Each one trying to determine from the features in my face, in the texture of my hair, where the white blood started and the black blood stopped.

"She got some pretty hair," one said.

"Sure do," others chimed in. "I seen white folks darker than she is..." and "Look at them cat eyes."

"She's shame faced," Sissy informed them, as if in saying it, she would be relieved of any responsibility if I turned out to be slightly retarded. She grabbed my arm and pulling me into the center of the room. "We're going to have to get her out of that, ain't we?"

Papa Jake was leaning on the counter near the back door, slowly stirring a steaming cup of tea. Buddy had fallen asleep. He sat with his mouth wide open, oblivious to the seven other people in the room.

"Where you get that dress?" My ma asked holding me away from her so she could see. "That dress belongs to me."

She turned to Papa Jake as if he'd given away an heirloom. "Who gave that dress to you?"

"I gives it to her," Papa Jake volunteered. "She washed herself up and put it on like I told her."

"Harrumph. It's good somebody's looking out for you. That Annie Bell took every stitch of clothes I sent."

"You hungry," the lady over at the stove asked me.

She was Jasperella; Jasper for short and Jake's newest wife.

Whatever she was cooking smelled so good it was making my stomach cramp. She reached over and stuffed a piece of greasy sausage into my mouth.

"What do you say?" My ma jerked my body back practically before Jasper could pull her hand away.

"Thank you, ma'am," I stumbled around the sausage and saliva filling my mouth.

"Don't talk with your mouth full neither," Sissy warned me.

I stumbled a "Yes, ma'am," out anyway. Too afraid she'd smack the food out of my mouth if I didn't acknowledge her warning, even if it meant disobeying it.

"Somebody go get me a comb. Let me comb this child's hair,"

Sissy instructed the youngest person in the room besides me, my cousin Adele, to get up from her perch on top of a pile of newspapers to fetch a comb. Sissy moved to a chair away from the kitchen table and wedged me in between her legs.

By now the piece of sausage was gone. I stared at Jasper, hoping she'd understand my silent request. She didn't seem to. Adele came back with a comb, a brush, and some thick black hair grease that smelled like tar. Sissy pulled and yanked on my hair, swatting me with the comb if my head wasn't positioned just how she needed it to be, while she told more stories about up north in New York City. Everyone in the room, except Buddy and Papa Jake sat at the edge of their seats as if her stories were golden and were spilling from a 24-karat spigot.

When she finished, the four tight braids had my head feeling like it was in a vise. I was afraid to say a word. She nodded at her handiwork and then handed the comb, grease and brush to me. She told me to put them away. Adele got up and jerked her head for me to follow her down the hallway to yet another room at the back end of the house.

You could tell the rooms were poorly planned additions because the floors shifted up or down an inch or two whenever we crossed a threshold. The hallway dipped so low to the left that it felt like the fun house at the county fair.

The room had a big bed smack in the middle of it like the last one. There was a little more room to move around but all along the border there were large rusted nails hammered into the walls; each one holding what seemed like a foot width's worth of clothes. Adele and I had to duck here and there so as not to run into them. There were clothes hanging on the back of every door and bags and boxes with more stuff was situated on the floor. These people must be rich, I thought.

Adele jumped to the bed and then pulled me up with her. It was high like the first, with layers upon layers of tattered quilts and blankets from bygone days.

"What's your name?" Adele asked me.

"They calls me Frank Lee." I offered, hoping she hadn't heard my other name, which I had already forgotten.

Adele accepted it. "That's your mama out there?" She pointed with her thumb.

I could tell from her twisted lip that Adele wasn't impressed with Sissy. I twisted my lip to match hers.

"Yeah," I nodded my head.

"What she say about New York true?" Adele whispered.

I hunched my shoulders. "Don't know. Ain't never been. She's taking me with her. Guess I'll find out. Don't want to go." I offered.

"Shoot. Anyplace is better than here. I wish I could go with you. My mama lives up there."

Her mother was Ludie, Sissy's older sister. She'd been in New York since Adele was about four and from there the girl had been shifted around nearly as often as I had.

Adele picked my hand up and started digging the dirt from under my fingernails. "That ain't my mama in there," she explained. "She Jasperella, Papa Jake's wife. I stay down at Aunt Juney's." She jerked her head toward the window. "She's mean."

I stared at my cousin hoping she wouldn't suggest we go down to her house. I'd met enough mean people for a lifetime. She continued to explain the intricate and delicate relationship between our relatives. "Aunt Juney won't come down here because Papa Jake told her not to bring her you know what down here no more. They're sister and brother but Aunt Juney don't like Jasperella and Jasperella don't like Aunt Juney. I comes down here because Aunt Juney don't know how to cook."

"What she eat then?" I asked, letting Adele switch to my other hand as if I was sitting at her manicurist's booth on Fifth Avenue someplace.

She shrugged her shoulders and curled her lip again.

"Don't seem like nothing but her coke cola's, one after the other."

Adele mimicked our Aunt Juney swilling down coke cola after coke cola. She looked up to make sure I was paying attention, before lowering her voice just so. "I sneaked a sip. They taste nasty to me."

"Me, too..." I lowered my eyes with indifference even though I had no clue what a coke cola was. We sat there on the bed for hours. She told me everything about our family that I'd missed out on by living with Miss Bell.

When Jasper called us in to supper my ma was gone off someplace to visit some of the folks around the way. Buddy was still there, asleep and snoring loudly on the floor of the back porch.

Papa Jake made a show of pulling the chairs away from the table for each of us as we sat down to eat. Jasper giggled and quickly covered her nearly toothless mouth with her hand. She had to be nearly forty years old but she acted like a schoolgirl around Papa Jake. Between the food and Papa Jake telling riddles and silly stories, it wasn't long before I wished I could stay right here with him and Jasper and Adele. I pretended that my life had just begun, there and then.

After dinner, Adele and I helped Jasper wash the dishes. Papa Jake went to the front porch with his pipe and tobacco. The smell of it made me feel safe but the feeling wasn't to last.

Sissy showed up from wherever she had disappeared to, Buddy woke up and my musings quickly evaporated away. When it was time to go, I stood beside Papa Jake on the porch hoping he'd tell Sissy to just go on away without me. He gave me a little smile but otherwise didn't try to keep me from her.

"Take care of that girl," was all that he said.

Sissy laughed. "What else I'm gone do?" She replied, jerking the back seat forward for me to climb inside. We made it down the road for a bit and then Sissy pulled a sheet of paper from her pocket. She began navigating Buddy to a little yellow house.

"It's over by the water plant," she directed him.

Buddy did as he was told; turning, backtracking, and finally stopping in front of the house they were looking for.

"Get out and go on over by that tree," she instructed him.

"What I got to get outta my own car for," he protested.

Sissy turned in her seat and gave him a look that convinced him not to argue. He swung the car door out with his foot, stepped out and stomped over to a tree on the other side of the road. Sissy got out on her side and taking a quick look back she pointed a finger for me to stay put.

I watched as she walked up the front walk. A man stood on the steps in the shadows of the front porch. His hands were deep in his pockets. A cigarette dangled from the left corner of his mouth. When he spoke, the red tip on the end bobbed up and down.

After a few minutes she turned and pointed toward the car. He took a step or two down the stairs to get a better look. I could see then that he was a white man. My eyes widened as he moved closer to the car. He handed Sissy something from his pocket. It quickly disappeared into her blouse.

The sun had ambled its way behind the little yellow house and as he walked toward the car his features darkened to a blur. He stopped a few steps from the car window and tossed his cigarette to the ground. He blew the smoke from his lungs. It escaped into the air around him like steam from the swamp.

He stepped one foot closer and his face came into focus. His blue eyes stared into mine. He neither smiled nor frowned. He touched the window briefly and for the second time that day my features were sized up against each other. After a moment he seemed satisfied. He put his hands back into his pockets and walked away.

Sissy watched him until he had disappeared around the backside of the house and then she waved at Buddy to come on. He scrambled back to his car.

"What he give you?"  He wanted to know.

Sissy swiveled her head in his direction and lifted her nose in the air.  "You don't counts my money," she said, her voice smooth as velvet, "and I won't count yours."

  By the next evening we were in New York just in time to celebrate my fifth birthday.  I wouldn't return to South Carolina for seven years.

## Chapter Four

Sissy studied the girl lying asleep on the couch where Buddy had carried her. After all of these years of being away she had let her imagination change the reality of who her baby really was. With skin so light Frank Lee was almost as white as the Gilbert children on Long Island. The only difference was the slightest and most delicate glow that lingered around the child like a shadow.

Sissy traced her finger over the girl's lips. They were full and almost as perfect as the one's on the stone-chiseled cherub that danced above the door at the Herald Square Hotel on 31st Street. In fact Sissy thought, they were more perfect.

Sissy sat on the floor beside the couch. She watched Frank Lee's breathing and thought back to the first time she saw her daughter. Even then, hours after her birth she knew the girl could ruin so much. She counted the seconds between inhale and exhale while she watched the fine and tiny hairs along the child's hairline rise and fall. The pulse beat its rhythm in time with the child's heartbeat. Sissy could hear it. She could see it thumping there through the dress, the very same dress that she had stubbornly worn to the river twenty years before. The pale green lace was faded but it was still the garment's finest attribute. She shook her head at the idea of her father holding on to it for so long.

She placed her hand over Frank Lee's heartbeat. She let it knock against her palm. She should have been happy but her mind raced over matters she hadn't anticipated before. What would the white people think if they ever saw her? They would want answers to questions they already knew the answers to. Like one day when Mrs. Gilbert asked her if she was late, even after seeing her walk into the kitchen at six- forty-five. Or when Mr. Gilbert sometimes gave her half pay and then asked if he'd paid her enough, as if he dared her to contradict him.

The challenges of it all were enough for Sissy to make silent promises to the sleeping child. Promises she knew she wouldn't and couldn't keep. She knew her limitations but her heart was melting and the urge to embrace this child was a strong one. She knelt closer to the girl to smell her, to marvel at the sweet marble apple scent in her hair and to regret the dry tear that still traced a line from the corner of her baby's eye into the curling hair at her ear.

Sissy wet her finger and gently wiped the evidence of the girl's tears away. Frank Lee stirred and shimmied closer to the edge of the couch. Sissy froze and waited until Frank Lee settled before inching her back and away from falling.

Ludie walked into the room. "Look at that baby," she whispered in the way one speaks to little children. Sissy tucked the light blanket around Frank Lee before turning to her sister.

"She's so light," Sissy remarked softly, as if she was regretting her decision.   Ludie sat on the arm of the couch. "I told you she looked like a white girl.  Precious told you. If you put a hot comb in her hair and leave her downtown at the department store sure enough nobody would know the difference."

"She don't need a hot comb."

"I said a light hot comb... anyway," she digressed. "I meant a light one."

Ludie looked closer. "She got blond hair in there."

She lifted one of Frank Lee's plaits to study the different colored strands from sandy to darker brunette. "I don't remember Mr. Zachary having that color hair. I suppose some of its yours and some of its his."

Ignoring the reference to the girl's father Sissy mused, "maybe I ought to put some shoe polish in it."

"You could put a little Murray's oil in it. You could take her down to Ruthie's and let her put a dye on it but hell, you can't hide that white skin no matter what color her hair is. The darker you make her hair the lighter she gone look."

"Everybody's going to talk."

"Everybody's going to talk no matter what. You had to have known that when you decided to go get her."

Sissy ventured, "We got Indian in us..."

"Well, sure... I suppose we do..."

"On Mama's side, I think we got Indian in us."

"Well, sure...she could have gotten straight hair from the Indian in us. She could have got her light skin that way too. Sure..."

Ludie glanced toward Sissy, who met her gaze before smiling. Ludie laughed at the idea of conjuring up Indian blood in a child who was clearly mixed with white.

"It ain't nobody's business no how," she reasoned. "She sure is a pretty thing. Precious says she's smart too."

They both glanced back at the girl who was now curled around the blanket, clutching it like a rag doll. Sissy nodded her head in agreement.

## Chapter Five

New York City was nothing like Sissy had described. It may
have been the land of opportunity for some but to me it was
noisy, dirty and confusing. We lived in a five-story walk-up on a
Hundred-Thirtieth Street in Harlem. There were twelve other
families in the building and a small nightclub called the
Mandalay Bar in the basement. Music from the bar, mixed with
sirens and cars from the street made me wish for the quiet
sounds of Newberry County.

My bedroom from the day I got there to the day I left nearly
fifteen years later was the hallway between Sissy's bedroom
and the tiny living room. The kitchen was too small for two
people to stand in at the same time and the bathroom, which
everyone on the third floor shared, was outside of our
apartment clear down at the other end of the hallway.

"Take the toilet paper when you go," Sissy instructed me. "And
don't forget to bring it back when you're done. Them folks from
chaka-laka and jinga-linga," she pointed down the hallway,
raising her voice so they could hear, "they don't know how to
buy nothing but curry and cheese."

She fanned the air in front of her face, "Close the door so my
stomach won't start acting up."

She pushed me back inside and sat on the couch. She fanned
herself with a newspaper. "I don't know why I listened to Ludie
about taking this place. Its smells like a zoo and that bar
downstairs sounds like one."

I perched myself on the edge of the chair and watched as she
flipped through one of the magazines that she'd brought home
from the place where she worked. She stopped to gaze at the
pictures, pointing to one of a lady with gold, curly hair and

bright red lipstick. "I bet she doesn't smell nobody cooking goat cheese at four o'clock in the morning."

Besides the smell of their food Sissy *was* able to tolerate the West Indians who lived in the building. It was another thing when it came to the white people who lived there. There were two of them, and if either of them tried to speak to her, she ignored them. She called them low class and forbade me from speaking to them as well.

"Stay away from Mr. Benson. You'll know which one he is. Don't go near him no matter what he say to you, hear?"

"Yes, ma'am," I answered.

"He lives down on the first floor near the back," she pointed. "He looks greasy and smells greasy," she leaned forward and lowered her voice. "I want to call him white but I think he's something else... maybe Italian or something like that."

She sat back and tossed her hand toward the bottom floor. "One is at the back of the building and the other at the front. Both of them must be simple minded else wise they'd be living uptown somewhere and not over here."

The colored people in the building gave the rare white residents hell for, as Sissy liked to say, "If Negroes don't have nothing else in the world they have Harlem. If one of them is too sorry to find quarters with their own kind, shame on them. Mister Adam Clayton Powell ought to figure out how to make it so."

Adam Clayton Powell was the new pastor at the Abyssinian Baptist Church on 138th Street after having followed his father into the pulpit. Sissy was especially fascinated with him. She started planning what she would wear to church practically before he finished his sermon from the week before. She quoted him often and for a good little while found a reason to say his name at least once every day. I didn't know who he was but would have guessed they were the closest of friends.

When we went to church however, we sat so far back in the pews, if we got in at all, that all I ever saw of him was a glimpse. His voice boomed over the crowd like a giant God and every time he hit a compelling point, the women around us fanned themselves and chirped "my lord and savior" as if he may have been the second coming of Christ.

Abyssinian was the most popular church in Harlem. You had to get there early or you would end up outside listening to the sermon from the huge speakers that were set up for latecomers. When we didn't get there before the large red doors closed Sissy would take my hand and turn on her heel. We'd return home. No church that day.

Ludie laughed at Sissy. "You ought to know better," she warned.

"That man has a line of women long enough to circle around that church two, three times."

"What are you talking about," Sissy argued back. "Some of them women are old enough to be his mama."

"What about his wife then?"

"What about her?" Sissy smiled slyly. "I don't know why you're worried. He's not my type anyhow."

Ludie laughed. "Alright, not my type."

If Sissy liked a certain type, I couldn't tell. Her beaus came in all shapes and sizes, light skinned to dark skinned to medium brown. When one of them dropped by she would push me outside into the hallway. The first time I stuck close to the door. When she got sick of me knocking and whining she came out and led me to the stairwell. It stank so badly that I was compelled to venture down the stairs and out to the courtyard.

"Who's that white gal?" The folks hanging around would ask out loud as if my ears were there for looks and not for hearing.

"I think she belongs to that gal up in Miss Martha's old rooms."

I could feel the blood rush to my face. They stared and talked about me as if I was a monkey at the zoo.

"What is she doing with a white baby?"

I couldn't tell who said it because I never took my eyes off the ground.

"If she don't be careful she's going to have a little black baby to go with that white one."

"She must be shame faced," they surmised about me. "What's your name," they teased me. "We won't bite."

When I refused to answer they eventually lost interest. I sat like a statue on the stoop, scooting from one side to the other when people wanted to pass until Sissy's visitors finally walked past me on their way out. I scampered back up to our rooms and slipped inside, hoping she wouldn't chase me away.

Her favorite boyfriend was a man they called Pearl. He was my favorite too. He worked upstate someplace and only came by once in a while. He always smelled nice and nearly always brought me a piece of root beer candy. He called me Junior for some reason.

"Come on, Junior," he'd say and then put his large heavy hand on my head to ruffle my hair.

"I believe I have something for you in one of these pockets of mine."

He'd pat his breast pockets and then his pants pockets until finally revealing the candy hidden in his other hand.

"Why they call you Pearl," I asked him.

"Well," he said, sitting back to cross one long leg over the other, h e held his hand three feet or so above the floor. "They been calling me Pearl since I was about this high. You got you some pearly white teeth, they used to tell me."

He ran his tongue across his teeth and winked at me. "These not the same teeth," he knocked on them with his knuckle. "But, they're pretty close to the ones I had back then."

I tilted my head to the side in wonder. Sissy called in from her bedroom, "stop worrying Pearl, Frank Lee."

"She's not bothering nobody," Pearl told her. "You not bothering nobody, is you?"

I shook my head but knew enough to keep my mouth shut.

"Come on, now," he goaded Sissy. "We don't want to miss the revue. If you miss the revue," he advised me, "you may as well skip the whole movie and go straight for the ice cream."

He checked his watch and shook his head before getting up to walk across the little room. He tapped on her door. "It's nice enough to walk if you shake a leg."

"Shake a leg? You think I'm fin to walk for thirty blocks? You must be out of your mind, Pearlie," she laughed at the idea as she opened the door.

Pearl whistled when he saw her. "Well..." he nodded his head. "It was worth the wait."

We walked out to Seventh Avenue and waited for Pearl to hail a cab. We rode down to the Lafayette Theater to watch a movie like a regular family. I was in love with Pearl. The only problem was that he never stayed for very long.

"Come on, Pearl," I'd hear Sissy say late into the night. "Dance with me. You have time. Dance with me. Just one more song."

"Alright, woman," he'd give in and I would hear them dancing in the living room just a few feet away from where I was pretending to be asleep.

"When are you going to move back uptown, Pearl?"

He stopped, "You said you wanted to dance."

"Can't we dance and talk at the same time?"

"Come on now, don't start with that. We've been here before and there's no need to go back. You know we can't live together."

"We did fine."

"Oh," the dancing paused again. "I guess you don't remember chucking my clothes out the window?" he laughed lightly.

They started dancing again.

"Frank Lee needs a daddy," I heard Sissy whisper.

Pearl took a long pause, "She's a sweet bitty thing, Sissy."

"She's sweet?" she asked.

"Well she is but I... you know, I can't do it." He looked at his watch.

"You can't or you won't?"

"I don't want to fight with you." He held her close, finally placing his hands on her shoulders. "I'm too old and I'm gone most of the time."

"I know you got that train to catch," Sissy relented. "Go on, then. Go where you got to go. Do what you got to do."

He tried to kiss her on the cheek but she pulled away. My heart beat rapidly against my chest as I tried to hold my breath and keep from crying. I wanted to run to the door and hold on to him, to keep him from leaving but I knew this was grown folks business and way out of my league. I listened as the door closed. She waited for a moment then walked across the room to stand at the window to watch him exit the building. She stood there quietly before lifting the needle off of the LP and switching the record player off. She went to bed and in the morning her door was closed. It stayed that way all day.

I played in the living room and ate crackers with peanut butter and jam. Midmorning or so, Ludie called from downstairs in the courtyard.

"Sissy," she called. "Sissy."

I poked my head out of the window. "I'm coming up," she said, "Open up the door."

I smiled and ran to unlock the door. It was Ludie's day off and we'd be going shopping!

Sissy had what they called a day situation. During the week, she left every morning before I got up and went out to Long Island to Jennifer, Jessica and Thomas Junior. I had never met them but I knew everything about them, including how they smelled because I wore their clothes when they couldn't or wouldn't wear them any longer.

Ludie on the other hand was a live-in maid. She stayed on Long Island most of the time. She kept her rooms upstairs in the same building as ours even though she only came home once or twice a month.

"I been there before," she'd say. "Giving up my room and then when the white folks don't want you no more you don't have nowhere to go. They tell you in the morning they don't need you no more and you got to be gone from there before lunchtime. You could have been there twenty years and it wouldn't matter none. Get your stuff and go." She smacked her hand on the table.

"I've been there before, sure enough." She nodded her head in my direction. "I'll keep my rooms so if they tell me to go... I have some place to go to."

She was nothing like Sissy. She would hold my hand and let me go with her all over to pick up food to cook that evening; meat from the butcher, vegetables from the Chinese market, spices from the Jamaican man up on Broadway. She'd talk and tell me stories and when she'd ask me what I thought, I'd shrug with a smile.

She'd poke me and say, "I'll tell you what you think. You think it don't make no sense for stew meat to cost over forty cents a pound. That's what you think." Then she'd laugh with her head thrown back at the thought of a five year old having such a thought.

I'd skip alongside her and wave to everybody she waved to. When I walked with Sissy she never spoke to anyone and no one ever spoke to us. If I forgot who I was with and spoke to the butcher or bakery lady, Sissy would jerk me back and tell me to keep family business in the family.

A Hundred-Thirtieth Street was a different place when Ludie was there. By the time we got home from the store, word would have traveled that she was in town, and out of nowhere

Parris, her sometimes boyfriend, would be waiting in the courtyard.

Other folks would have stopped by and left messages with Mr. Johnson on the second floor that they'd be back later too. She cooked enough for twenty people whenever she came home. Her friends and some of our cousins who lived in the city would drop by with bottles of liquor or wrapped meat they'd taken from their employer's Frigidaire's.

Everybody had a high time and I'd get to stay up and be a part of folks who smiled at me and pinched my cheek. Sissy would come in with one of her boyfriends, or find one already at the party, and not pay much attention to me at all. When newcomers found out that I was her daughter they'd be surprised that I wasn't Ludie's since she'd be the one smoothing down my hair or slicing a piece of pie for me to eat. At the end of the night when the few who didn't care if they showed up late at their jobs the next day were spread out asleep on the floor or at the kitchen table, Ludie would sit by me on the couch and tell me about her daughter Adele.

"I miss my girl," she'd say. Her words slurring over her last shot of Johnny Walker Red. "My Adda-lee..." she called her. "I wasn't but fifteen. I had no idea what was going on. By the time I put two and two together I was right up on my date... had her on my mama's birthday. My grandmother never said a word, just carried me to the bedroom and told me to shush up all that fussing. When I thought I was about to burst sure enough, my Nannie handed her to me. Ha!

Herman and me, we got married but his daddy wouldn't let him come live down there where we was and said I couldn't go live with them neither. How in the world was we supposed to be married with his daddy telling us what he wouldn't allow?"

She confided in me as sincerely as if she was talking to a grown person.

"Herman didn't have no money... couldn't make no money cause he worked for his daddy and his daddy wasn't about to give him no money. Shoot. What else was I supposed to do? I couldn't bring a baby up here, no how. Your mama was already up here talking about how rich it was. I had to leave and wasn't nobody up here to look after her while I worked." Her eyes welled up. "I do miss my girl, I do."

I let her hold my hand until she fell asleep.

# Chapter Six

On the first day of school Sissy greeted me with one of Jennifer or Jessica's good dresses, one that I hadn't been allowed to wear until now.  Their clothes were always too big or too small. The red and black plaid jumper she laid across my bed was so big it would last from that day clear to the third grade.

I ran my hand across my newly cut hair and wanted to cry. The day before, Sissy had taken me to the barber and told him to cut the stuff off, which he did under loud protest.

"Is you crazy?" he asked. His hands were on his hips and his head was cocked to the side.

"I told you what that lady said," Sissy shot back.

She didn't care that everybody in the shop had stopped what they were doing so they could hear the story again.  She pulled me around to stand in front of her and held her hand out. "Look here. See how skinny she is? She's five years old and no bigger than a mouse."

She held one of my braids above my head. "It's her hair. Miss Reba... you all know Miss Reba, don't cha?"

She looked around the small barbershop. She waited for them to nod their heads that they knew Reba the voodoo lady from a Hundred Twenty-Fifth Street.

"She say it's her hair and I'm not going to argue with her about it. She say it's draining the child's energy and if I don't cut it off and gives it to her, this child won't grow no bigger."

The barber pulled the towel that was draped over his shoulder. He whipped it across the seat to remove the hair that was left from his previous customer. He shook his head.

"I don't know about Miss Reba. One time she told this fella that if he wanted his wife to love him like she used to he had to offer up one of two things."

He held up two fat fingers. "A fat, juicy steak," he said loudly. "Or..." he paused dramatically, "A cup of blood."

Sissy covered my ears. The barber went on with his story, which was reaching a high enough pitch for me to hear what he was saying even with her hands on either side of my head.

"Of course the fella thought the juicy steak was the right answer so he went to the butcher and bought the biggest steak they had. He carried it over to Miss Reba. When she saw it, she told this fella that he could go home and his wife would love him like she used to. The man went home and found his wife had run off with the mailman. He ran back to Miss Reba and found her eating the very last bit of the steak. He cried, Miss Reba, what happened? My wife left me! You was wrong! I want my money back! Miss Reba pushed herself back from the table..."

"Did she have her pistol?" One of the other customers asked.

The barber nodded his head. "Yes, she did. She pushed back from the table and said, listen here. You wanted your wife to love you like she used to. You got what you paid for. She didn't love you then and she don't love you now."

The fella asked, "but why did I have to choose between a steak and a cup of blood?" Miss Reba looked him up and down and then she told him, "If you brought the cup of blood instead of the meat the result would have been the same. The only difference would be that I would still be hungry."

Sissy dropped her hands away from my ears. "That story isn't true and you know it."

"How you know it's not true? Anyway," he pointed at me. "What is it she said? She's skinny because of what?"

"Don't worry about all that." Sissy lifted her chin in the air. "Is you a barber or ain't you?"

He shook his hand at her. "No, no, now." He twirled his finger around in the air. "The sign going around about out there say this here is a barber shop but that don't mean I'm a cut this little gals hair just because some gun toting voodoo woman say so."

He crossed his heart with his finger and said up to the ceiling, "Excuse my language."

Sissy opened her purse and pulled out a dollar bill. "Listen here," she said. "If you don't cut it, I'll take her over to Cecil."

The barber took the money. "I didn't say I wasn't going to cut it. I'm just trying to understand, is all. He pointed the straight edge razor in my direction. "Feed her ham hocks for the next three weeks, she'll grow one inch and stretch wider by two."

He laughed so hard tears fell down his dimpled cheeks. Sissy dismissed him with her hand, "Go on, now," she told him. "I don't have all day."

He loosened my braids and ran his hands through my hair. "I bet you could sell this downtown some place. They'll make a wig out of it." He leaned around to check with me. "What you say about that? You want to make some money?"

"I done told you I got to take it to Miss Reba. Go on with your slow self," said Sissy.

He shook his head. "Sorry, baby." He said to me before turning to Sissy. "Look at that sad face. Are you sure you want me to cut it all off? How about half? She don't look all that small to me."

He checked around the shop for a consensus from the other customers.

Sissy put her hand out. "Look, if you can't do it." She wiggled her hands for the money back.

He picked the scissors up and snipped across the back. He held the handful of hair for Sissy to see. Everyone in the shop gasped. They shook their heads as he clipped the rest. When he was finished, all that was left was a half inch or so. I looked like a chicken wearing the red and black plaid jumper. It barely stayed on my shoulders as I walked behind Sissy for the three blocks to PS157.

She walked in ahead of me, overdressed in high heels and a skintight A-line skirt with a matching jacket and purse. I wondered if she would go to work with it on. If she did, I wondered whether Jennifer, Jessica, and Thomas Junior would even recognize her out of her usual starched white dress and the flat black shoes.

The office was pointed out to us. Sissy brushed past the other mothers and children who were standing along the corridor in a nice polite line.

"Excuse me but I got to catch the number 14 down to 42nd Street in an hour. All I need to do is tell you what her name is and where she lives."

The secretary looked up at Sissy. Her pink rose lips pursed together in hopes they wouldn't reveal the disgust she felt at having to work above East 86th Street.

"How old is she?"

"She's six." I was five.

"What's her name?"

"Frances Lee Shealy." Sissy answered.

I thought my name was Frank Lee period.

"What's your name?" The secretary asked Sissy as her perfect penmanship laced my name across the registration form.

"Why you got to know my name? I ain't starting to school am I? You all be wanting to know things ya'll don't need to know!"

Sissy grabbed my hand. The secretary looked up from the form. Her pale green eyes were blank puddles. Just behind them she hid the fact that she wanted to spit at the thought of a nigh-high colored girl holding up her line. She used her calm and patient voice.

"We need to know your name just in case she gets sick. How would we find you if we don't know your name?"

"Oh... well, in that case, my name is Sissy. S-I-S-S-Y." She pronounced each letter with practiced precision.

"And your last name?"

Sissy stared at the woman until the answer apparently became inconsequential.

"What's the father's name?"

Sissy's face turned ashy. She checked behind us to see if we had an audience, which indeed we did.

"His name is Zachary... but, he don't live nowhere around here. He lives back home in Prosperity, South Carolina where we come from."

I looked up at Sissy. I was amazed that she knew so much.

"Zachary?" The secretary asked.

"I told you he don't live nowhere around here. Why you got to know his name for?"

The woman pursed her lips even tighter and through clenched teeth, she ordered Sissy to sign the form.

Sissy jerked her hand from mine. She turned on her heel and left me standing there in the office.

"If you don't sign, she can't go to her classroom." The secretary sang, her voice rising with each word.

After the sound of Sissy's heels clicking down the polished hallway faded and we heard the outside door slam, it became apparent that she wouldn't be returning no matter what the consequences were for me.

The secretary pointed to a line of chairs and told me to sit. I perched on the edge of the first seat, certain that they wouldn't let me stay for long. I remained there through bells and rings, children moving from one place to the other, teachers walking in, teachers walking out, all of them glancing at me and then taking a double take to size my features against their own. At the end of the day, when the final bell rang, the secretary pointed to the door. I walked home on my first day of school having never started school at all. The next morning I didn't stop at the office. I followed the other kids to a classroom where there were kids who were my size. The teacher had so many new students she never wondered about me. Within a few days my name was added to her roster.

I found my first friend. Her name was Collette. She was quiet like me and smelled like garlic toast. We held hands and stayed out of the way of the other kids. She told me she was Italian but I didn't know what that meant, so I told her I was Italian too. Her mother sent two pieces of everything in Collette's lunch pail - one for her and one for me, the other Italian girl. I went home with her after school one afternoon and found out right away why she smelled like garlic, the whole house did. Her mother eyed me from across the kitchen while Collette and I ate homemade cookies. The next day Collette told me we couldn't be friends anymore because I wasn't Italian. I didn't understand. Neither did she but for the rest of the year I sat on one side of the classroom and she sat on the other. No one else played with us and we didn't play with each other.

## Chapter Seven

 The fall that I matriculated to Junior High School, Ludie
received a telegram from back home. Her daughter Adele was
acting up. It was decided that it would be a good time to visit
the folks down home.  It was perfect timing because Ludie had
just been let go from her live-in job. A few days before, the
husband had wanted her to tell him where his wife
disappeared to everyday at eleven- fifteen.  Ludie knew where
the wife went but she also knew she'd found another woman's
lipstick on his collar more than a time or two, so she refused to
tell either story unless she could tell them both.

The three of us, along with Sissy's new friend, Mr. Clovis, who
was actually the husband of a woman who lived up on a
Hundred-Fifty-Eighth Street, left the block before dawn. We
drove south with a basket of chicken and a dozen hard-boiled
eggs.  Ludie and I were in the backseat clapping our hands to
the juke joint rhythm and blues playing on the radio.

"Alright," Ludie shouted as she swayed back and forth.  "That's
what I like."

"Is Adele going to live with us? Is she going to go to school?" I
asked over the music.

"Don't you get yourself all up in grown folk's business," Sissy
warned me.

"I don't know, Sugar." Ludie answered me. "I suppose she's old
enough to do what she got to do either way. How old are them
kids you go to school with?"

I thought about it. "Oh, there's some that are twelve and some
are fourteen, I suppose."

She took a moment to figure up Adele's age. Counting on her
fingers, she took a pause to get it right.

"She ought to be, let's see... I want to say nearly sixteen by now. They probably won't let her go to school. You think?" She asked me, genuinely concerned about the possibility.

"How much school do she need?" Sissy interjected.

I could tell Ludie wasn't happy about Sissy's comment but it made me wonder. "Can I stop going to school?" I asked.

Sissy laughed.

"What's funny?" Ludie asked.

"This child," Sissy answered. "That's what's funny."

She turned in her seat to face us. "It's the law that say you got to go, not me. You can read and write can't you? What more can they teach you? Somebody has to pay for food and clothes. Somebody has to pay for a roof over your head."

She turned back towards the front. "I was working by the time I was eleven. You can work and let me take a break."

Ludie smirked. "I don't believe you was working that young."

"What you say," Sissy shouted. "I was washing for Miss Forrester down home when I was eleven years old. I remember it if you don't. That lady nearly bit my finger off."

She held it out to show a tiny scar that was still slightly visible after twenty years.

"Talking about I run off with one of her night dresses."

"What," Ludie asked skeptically.

"Oh, yes." Sissy nodded her head. "I didn't do no such a thing! If I did, what was I gone do with it? It would have been as big as a bed spread! You know that thing was probably took off the line by some drifter living up in the woods. Shoot. She might have taken it herself just to keep from giving me what she owed me. Whoever it was they took my first payday with them when they did. I'll never forget how mad I was... but I worked, yes I did. You can work too," she nodded at me.

"Things were different back then, Sissy," Ludie reminded us. "Everybody had to put forth some effort back then."

"What else was there to do?" Sissy agreed. "You might as well work to get a little bit of money in your pocket."

The music on the radio went out of range. Ludie leaned forward and flipped the switch off.

"We was happy," Ludie shifted into a better position. She closed her eyes and repeated herself. "We was happy to work. Of course, we didn't have nothing else to do."

"No TV, no roller skates, no soda pop," Sissy chimed in. "No time to carry on. No time to act a fool. No school."

"If I was you," Ludie advised me. "I would stay in school as long as they let me. Once you're grown there's no turning back. Ain't that right, Clovis?"

He looked at me through the rearview mirror. "Um hum." He said, with a wink

## Othello (Theo) Minor

He was born at the tail end of a childish dream. Chasing the devil at his very first breath, taunting him with clever disguises but in the end the boy proved a poor match to the strength of the serpent.

## Chapter Eight

*Asheville, South Carolina 1931*

His mother sat dumfounded at the back kitchen door. The big hotel where she worked loomed behind her like a huge and grey-stoned giant. The sweet, mouth-watering sensation that first loves always leave behind was overwhelmed by the heavy realization that he was gone.

She chastised herself for telling it. A few more weeks with him would have been better than feeling her heart tearing to bits just now. It didn't matter, between the wagging mouths of the day maids and her growing belly it was only a matter of time before he would have known.

It seemed sensible to tell him on the off-chance that he would take her in his arms, sweep her off her feet, and carry her and their baby to higher ground but such was not the case. He did what they all said he would do. He left. At twenty-eight years old she should have known better but contrary to everyone's understanding, this was her first foray into a love affair. Her heart ached with as much pain as that of any sixteen-year old girl's.

"Dora Dear, what you doing out here? You don't have to be to work till Thursday." Mariah teased.

She knew. Everybody knew including the white folk why Dora Dear was sitting on the woodpile looking pitiful. The hotel, the grandest in Asheville, was no less a gossip shop than a low country juke joint. The whites may not have tarried with the coloreds but they were listening just the same.

Dora tried to ignore her. She wished she'd go away. She knew what everyone was whispering and what Mariah was standing there gloating over. Mariah sauntered over, her narrow frame switching from side to side in a slow amble.

"Where Jesse at?" she asked, knowing full well that he was gone nearly four hours by now.

Dora kept her eyes trained on the ground. Angry as she was to have let such a thing happen, she didn't want Mariah to see. She had kept her knees closed her whole life without as much as a good glance at the boys hanging around.

When it came time to find a husband, most of the men her age were already taken. Those that were not were either mean, or lazy or slow-witted enough to need a mama more than they did a wife.

She met Jesse just like everyone else. He turned up one early morning at the edge of the tree line that surrounded the hotel grounds. Mr. Thornton, the kitchen boss, was always looking for honest Negroes and Jesse looked honest enough. Thornton was the kind of white man who only saw black folk in one-dimensional shades. They were honest, clean, or hardworking... never more than one or the other. When a colored worker proved to have more dimensions than Thornton could initially fathom, he would call them unfortunate. He'd shake his head as if they'd surely be passengers on the chain gang by morning.

Dora was in charge of the rooms on the second floor. She changed the linen, washed the sills and made sure there wasn't a spot of dust anywhere on the furniture, floor or ceiling. Miss Lane had often praised her workmanship. Once Jesse started in the kitchen however, Dora Dear's two year record collapsed like a bumped cake in the oven drops to the bottom of the pan.

Eliza, her baby sister, who got her the job in the first place, saw Dora running up the side dirt path to the hotel many a morning with her skirts and bloomers lighting in the wind. By the time Dora got to the second landing through the pantries and back stairs, she was already musty and the sun had barely come up for the day.

"What's keeping you past six Miss Dora Dear?" Eliza mimicked Miss Lane. "Is it your rheumatoid arthritis or did your auntie die again?"

Eliza stuck her nose in the air as Miss Lane often would. "I've housekeeping to run, don't you know?"   Dora fanned past her sister and hurried to the closet to get clean linen and buckets.

Eliza followed behind her in a near frenzy.

"Is you crazy?" She poked Dora on the shoulder.

Dora Dear turned to her sister and grabbed both of her hands. She pulled her close and whispered, "I'm not crazy. I'm in love!"

Dora rushed away. She was barely able to contain her glee at the thought of Jesse Boy Miner.  Eliza rushed after her sister. She was careful to check the far end of the massive hallway to be sure Miss Lane was not sailing toward them in her full and flowing petticoat and aprons.

"What you mean, in love? You're too old to be acting this way. Jesse Miner's not nothing but a hustler and a shifter. Youze crazy to believe what he say!"

Dora wouldn't have been able to hear her sister's warning even if she tried.  Jesse's spell had her heart floating on warm butter and any words of reason dissolved away like sugar in water.

"You don't know how it is, Eliza. Jesse is different. You ought to try to see.  He's not a hustler." She laughed at the thought. "He sure ain't shiftless, neither."

Even now four months later full belly and all, Dora Dear smiled at the thought of Jesse's manner.  Just silly enough to be trusted and just handsome enough to be proud, he had ideas she'd never heard of before. He knew of places she'd never imagined; California, Boston, the Gulf of Mexico.

He called her titillating.

"Tita-what?" Dora Dear blushed.

He was lying on her bed, the lamplight just catching the ripple of muscles across his mahogany brown belly. She was hopping on one foot, wrestling with her long stockings and trying not to giggle off balance.

"You're titillating," he repeated. "It's a word that means lovely and enchanting."

Dora Dear giggled. "Then why don't you just say that then?"

Jesse rolled off the bed and grabbed Dora around the waist. He rested soft kisses along her back and shoulders. She nestled into his embrace, too delighted to remember to wish for the moment to last forever.

She shook away the memory and got up from the woodpile. She walked away from Mariah's teasing and headed back to the rooms she shared with Eliza. That morning she'd told her, "I won't be here when you get back."

Eliza was doing her hair in the little spotted mirror that leaned against the washboard. She hesitated for only a second.

"Jesse and me..." Dora continued. "We're going to Boston... umm, Boston, Massachusetts. Up north."

She watched Eliza's back afraid of the pause. When Eliza turned around, Dora nearly lost her nerve.

"I know we said we would stay together when we left down home, Liza," Dora rushed. "I want you to come with us but

Jesse... he say we probably need to do this by ourselves, you know?"

Dora unconsciously rubbed her hand across her belly. When Eliza's eyes followed the movement, Dora quickly dropped her hand to her side. She stared at Eliza solemnly.

"How far gone are you?" Eliza asked. When she didn't get an immediate answer, she asked again. "How far?"

"Three months."   Eliza shook her head without saying out loud that three months was too late to fix.

"He's different," Dora defended Jesse.

Eliza set her comb aside and walked across the room to Dora. She put her arms around her. "I know he is, Dora.  I'll be here if you need me."

Dora clutched the gathering of her sister's skirts. She dreaded the separation. They'd been together all their lives and had identical dreams of attending the nursing school in Nashville. By spring they would have had enough money for one and within a year the other would have been able to register for classes.  Dora wished her sister could see the good in Jesse but she knew she was already asking for too much.

She opened the door to their neat little room. She climbed into her bed and hoped Eliza would pretend the morning conversation had never happened.

Miss Lane either didn't know or pretended not to know that Dora Dear was pregnant until the day the boy was born. She accepted the story that Dora was sick with the stomach cramps for two days and then she pretended the baby being kept in the kitchen had been there all along.

There was an unwritten understanding that the new babies that miraculously appeared from time to time wouldn't be underfoot for long.  Within a few months, Dora found a woman to care for her boy away from the hotel.

She named him Othello after a story Jesse had told about a great king born before Christ.  She didn't dare tell Eliza the reason.  By then it was best not to mention Jesse's name at all.

"But why Othello," Eliza pressed her. "I never heard of a name like that."

She played with her nephew near the fireplace in their room.

"Won't you pick something from the Bible? At least give the boy a chance."

By the time Othello was nine months old his name had been shortened to Theo.  He wouldn't understand it to be anything otherwise for many years to come.

**Chapter Nine**

His earliest memory was of the sound of the train chugging up and down the backcountry through the heat and cold of one southern state after the other. In those days the cars that were reserved for Negroes also transported the odd goat or pet chicken and as a result the cars were never clean.

The smells, compounded by Theo's vivid imagination of monsters and goblins racing through the rushing forests made the trips unbearable.

He traveled with other children, sometimes cousins or looser relatives who were pushed on board to travel to unsuspecting aunts or uncles as he was. He sat still, his eyes large and silent, hoping for the train to stop, wishing for it to quiet its lurch. He learned to eventually ignore its rumble but he never stopped his search for winged creatures flying alongside the car.

It wasn't that Dora chose to send her boy, her beloved son away but without a husband it was nearly impossible to care for him around the long hours she worked at the hotel. She and Eliza tried different shifts but sending him home to Bertha Ann, one of their young nieces, seemed to be the wisest choice. Dora rode with him the first time. After that, a square of cardboard with his name scribbled across it was simply placed around his neck so that his relatives on the other end could recognize who he was. A lunch of fried chicken or a boiled egg or two was pressed into his hands along with his sack of clothing. He was pushed up the steps to the train with sometimes a teary but more often a hasty goodbye. After his third move he learned to mimic mannerly behavior without actually getting to know his surroundings very well. What was the use? He was furious with his mother, and even at the early age of five years, he blamed her for all of his troubles. When she was able to gather enough money and time off from work, she took the train to spend time with him. The experience only left her with more regret because he tried his best to pretend she wasn't there.

"How are you going to ignore your own mama, boy?" his Uncle Joseph asked before grabbing the boy's shirt to jerk him back to the center of the room. "You ought to be grateful anybody cares about you enough to travel overnight to see your ashy behind."

"No, Joe. Don't pull on him. It's alright." Dora smiled.

She didn't need for the boy to talk. She just wanted to see him, to touch him, if he would let her. He was a fine boy. So strong and dark like his daddy. By now she could remember only the best things about Jesse though she dared not mention them out loud. No one wanted to hear good things about a man who left her while she was pregnant and too pathetic to even marry her before leaving.

Theo stood there, refusing to look at anyone in the room. Neena, Joe's wife stared at her husband from the table. Theo could feel her silent anger over the fact that they had been coerced into taking him in the first place. She didn't like Theo and had made it clear from the start.

"Why you got to let him live here, Joe? He's not strong enough to help. You know he don't do half as much as Little Joe but he eat as much as you do."

Theo could hear her whispering to his uncle late in the night. He kept his belongings close. He knew it wasn't true anyhow. He was stronger than lazy Joe and he barely ate anything, with Neena always serving him last what was left in the pot getting cold.

Theo spied his mother's shoes from the corner of his eye. He despised her standing there with her feet close together like a guest in her own brother's house. He could feel his face getting warm; a sensation he knew would bring tears. He sucked in his breath and with as much strength as he could muster he pulled away from his uncle's grasp. He pushed past his mother and out the door.

He ignored his uncle's screams for him to come back and get what was coming. He glanced back before turning the corner at the fence post. Neena's head bobbed sanctimoniously up and down like a bug-eyed bullfrog. His mother stood where he'd left her, in the doorway alone.

He ran past the other houses in the shanty and the dry goods store on the square. He passed the boys playing on the dusty front yard where the white children went to school and then the fields where most of the Negroes worked during harvest season.

He ran until his lungs burned and his legs felt heavy with rocks. His nose was running and his eyes were blurred by the red hot tears pouring from them but he refused to stop until he reached the river. He crossed to the other side at the low point and climbed the rocks to the ridge. He made his way along the edge until he found the clearing where an enormous gray rock covered the ground. Everyone called it a meteor. The old timers said it fell from the sky and that the mass of it lay below the surface for more than a mile deep. Theo climbed on top and sat down. He rested his hands on the cool surface and waited for it to calm his rushing heartbeat. Eventually he curled up and fell asleep on the hard calming surface.

He dreamt about a safe place, someplace away from everybody he knew. When he awoke, a mist of rain was falling softly through the opening at the top of the trees. Falling, falling from far up in the sky. Each drop sparkled as the afternoon light caught it in its losing battle with gravity.

"Come on here. Come out of the rain." It was his mother's voice.

He lay there contemplating the urge to ignore her but the light was dimming at the top of the trees. He knew he'd be too frightened to be left there alone once it got dark. He gathered himself off the rock, sliding easily to the ground. He leaned away from his mother's outstretched hand and walked past her. He retraced his steps back the way he had come. Dora Dear trailed behind him, happy enough to walk in his footsteps.

"I'm sorry you don't like it here," she ventured. "Your Uncle Joe and Auntie Neena say you don't want to stay. I'm trying to find you someplace. I am..."

Theo heard her but refused to respond. He'd heard it before.

"Do you hear me, Theo? I'm looking for us someplace to be... you and me."

She'd said us. Theo stopped. He turned to Dora. He couldn't remember ever living with her, in the same city even.

"Are you moving to Greenville? Here, by Uncle Joe?" He asked.

He wondered what she would do. It appeared that it was hard for Joe and Neena to raise their children and keep food on the table.

His mother didn't have a husband. He didn't have a father.

"I'm moving north," she replied quietly. "There's better work up there."

Theo waited. He was afraid to get excited or to anticipate that she would take him with her. He held his breath.

"I can't take you with me," she said.

Theo didn't wait. He turned on his heel and ran ahead.

"...yet, Theo." Dora called after him. "I can't take you yet but I'll send for you, baby. I will."

## Chapter Ten

Theo moved from Joe and Neena's to his Cousin Maggie's in Boatwright, Alabama. From there he lived with his grandmother near the border between Brevard, North Carolina and Greenville, South Carolina. She meant well but was far into her eighties and couldn't care for herself much less keep up with a young boy.

Finally, he moved to his Uncle Percy in Tennessee. Nearly ten years had gone by and he was still no closer to living with Dora Dear than he had been before.

Percy stumbled into the room. He tottered toward the center to stand just in front of Theo. His stagger could have been attributed to the slight tilt of the floor, which sloped marginally toward the heavier furniture along the far wall but it was more likely the tiny bottle of rotgut in his shirt pocket. His body swayed as if it was atop a heavy tower blowing in a topsy-turvy wind.

The old man had been propped in the front seat of the junk car that sat near the remains of the burned house across the yard. The fire was four years gone by but the house still sat like a ragged and black reminder of that dreadful night.

If you tilted your nose in the air just right, you could still conjure the smell of the devil's rolling black smoke and the image of the red hot fire licking from the tip of his torch like a serpent's pointed tongue.

By some accounts, the fire was started by Percy's moonshine still that was set too close to the back door. Everyone was screaming and carrying on with Percy's wife Sula running back and forth.

"Mary in the house! Mary in the house!" she kept screaming. "My Mary in the house!"

Her sister Mary along with Mary's baby daughter Petunia perished in the fire. By that next early morning, Percy and Sula, along with the neighbors who ran to help, stood in the fire's glow, too tired to do more than watch it with torn spirits and somber thoughts of their losses.

The old car, like the burned house, still sat in the yard. It was Percy's place to moan his thoughts over whisky or wet rye. It was where he often fell asleep to awaken in the wee hours curled up on the re-laid floorboards at the backside of the car's shell.

"I know you been selling my liquor, you good for nothing jackass!"

His uncle's voice spit past the alcohol still on his tongue.

"Go on now and leave that boy alone, Percy," his Aunt Sula tried.

Slowly, as if he was pulling a pure white dove out of his magician's hat Percy took the bottle out of his pocket with his thumb and forefinger. He twisted the cap off as demurely as a cat cleans his paws and then he emptied what was left in the bottle by throwing his head back as far as he could without stumbling over backwards.

When it was empty of the very last drop he threw the bottle towards his wife, which she easily dodged.

"Alright now, Percy," she raised her voice slightly above her normal monotone. "You hit me with that bottle and won't nobody be fixin' your supper when you ready to eat."

"That boy got his hands in my still." Percy placed his hands on his hips to steady his sway before lowering his glare towards Theo.

"You know that was more than a year ago. He's not been messing with your belongings, have you Theo?"

She pronounced his name as if it ended with an A. She was from Gullah country down off the coast of Georgia and she minced her words like often using bidi for chicken or dayclean for tomorrow.

You had to pay close attention when she spoke or else you could miss her meaning all together.

"Get some rest, honey," she sing-songed to her husband,"Dayclean you be fine."

Percy remained where he was. He crossed his arms and released a belch that stayed in his chest a couple of seconds before letting it loose without a care to whomever it may offend.

"This my house," he reminded them. Making it clear that under no uncertain terms would he let down his watch on this nephew what was put on him without his say.

Sula shook her head in dismay. She went back to her chore of hemming blankets for the undertaker. She was paid sixty-five cents for each one; which she felt was too much to pay for something that would be going in the ground straight away.

"Life is just an arm long," she offered her own brand of advice. "You can reach clean across it and before you know it, your fretting won't be worth the time it took. They'll be wrapping you in one of these coveralls before long."

Theo had been waiting for nearly two years to fight Percy and like every other fifteen year old boy anywhere else in the world, he thought he could win.   It was a folly of a thought since his uncle was nearly a hundred pounds heavier, two feet taller and unbeknownst to Theo had worked for most of his life at the rock quarry, either in custody or as a laborer.  His muscles even after some years were well tuned after hefting a sledgehammer like most men tote sacks of hay.  Theo tightened his lips and hid his fists inside his pockets.

The next morning on his way to school he tested the idea on his cousins, both of whom raised their eyebrows high before falling to the ground laughing.

"Is you crazy? Percy ain't no lightweight. I seen him fight before. If you got any sense in that head of yours, you better stay out of his reach," Tee Pee warned him before holding his fists up to mimic a snapping motion.

"He'll mash you until you snap in two, fool!"  Charlie chimed in. "Catch him in the morning, after he been drunk. He'll be too sick to fight."

"Naw, nigger," Tee Pee pushed Charlie away. "I'm telling you. Don't fool yourself. If uncle gets his hands on you, you're finished! He ain't no lightweight."

Theo tightened his lips in defiance and walked on ahead. His cousins ran up on either side jostling him here and there to get him out of his foul mood.

"Box lunch day on Sunday.  How much you gone pay for Etta to feed you?" Tee Pee reminded him of the churches' biggest fundraiser. One that Pastor Bertrand would be hollering about for weeks to come.

Theo pushed them away but they came back just as quickly. They knew he had money from selling sips from Percy's bottles of rotgut in the schoolyard and behind the church after bible study on Wednesday nights.

"You got enough by now to buy everybody something to eat."
Tee Pee rubbed his hands together and thought of Lucille's
baked plums.

Charlie licked his lips as though he could read his brother's
mind.

"Theo's too cheap," he countered.

"What am I going to give money to Bertrand for? That mess is
for grown folks. His Miss is going to have to find another
somebody to buy her a fancy hat," Theo retorted.

Charlie started mimicking the way Pastor Bertrand walked,
holding his thumbs under his suspenders and waddling back
and forth.

Tee Pee slapped his leg, laughing at his brother. "Calvary sure
don't need another hat," he agreed.

"I'm not studin Etta May," Theo answered. "I'll make my own
lunch."

Charlie ran ahead, "...and sit by yourself and eat it too."

Theo raced after him but Tee Pee came from behind. He
grabbed Theo around the waist to twist him off the dirt path
and into the bushes. Theo quickly scrambled back to the path
but by then his cousins were far ahead of him. He dusted
himself off and walked the rest of the way to school by himself.
He thought about Etta May Simpson, always smiling at him like
they had some sort of a secret. He wouldn't pay two cents for
her box lunch, even if it had fried chicken in it.

The last time the church sold boxes to raise money, a fight
nearly broke out when the pastor's brother Tommy bid five
dollars for Harriet Kilgore's box lunch, which was four dollars
more than her boyfriend could afford.

"You can pay your five dollars," her boyfriend had announced loudly, "but Harriet won't be sitting with you when you eat it."

Tommy snatched his money back from old Miss Mercy, the church secretary which made *her* son, who was sitting clean across the church yard make his way to her side.

He was ready to fight anybody who was "grabbing money out my mama hand!" His chest was puffed out like an old greased rooster. A good shine of sweat was already rising across his forehead.

Pastor Bertrand had to calm everybody down by holding off the three men and reminding them in his booming voice that "God was the joy of salvation and that their lack of fear would lead them to torment in hell."

Then he plucked the five-dollar bill out of Tommy's hand. He looked at it closely between his short fat fingers, turning it this way and that before raising his eyebrows at his brother. "Looks familiar, Tommy."

Tommy let his mouth drop open in a show of innocence but none-the-less didn't argue when Bertrand gracefully returned the money to Miss Mercy and handed the box lunch to the boyfriend.

At the time, Bertrand had brushed his hands together to indicate that the show was over and everybody could get on with what they were doing before it started.

Theo shook his head as he climbed the stairs to the school. He took his place at his table near the window. He ignored Etta May's silly grin. He knew that by now his cousins had tickled her ear with some tale about him and her box lunch. He could hear them snickering at the table they shared behind him. Miss Jones rapped her stick on her desk and held her hands upward, raising them slightly for the children to stand.

Chairs scraped across the wooden floor as the students stood to cover their hearts with their hands. They faced the flag to recite the pledge of allegiance. Afterwards, they bowed their heads and recited the Morning Prayer.

Theo was one of the oldest boys in the class. The only reason he showed up at all was so he could see Etta's sister, Naomi. She was Miss Jones's helper after having reached the top grade the summer before last. She had plans to attend Allen University, the teacher's school in Columbia and had hopes to replace Miss Jones at the end of the next school term after Miss Jones and Eddie Walker got married.

Naomi sat at a small table beside Miss Jones's desk. If Theo wanted to buy anybody's lunch on Sunday, it would be hers.

"Why you waste your time coming up in this school every day of the week," she asked him later in the morning after the other students had left to go home for lunch break.

Theo was pretending to read one of the books that the white school had delivered the day before. They had arrived in a large box filled with primers and boxed puzzles. When Miss Jones found the books on the bottom of the container, she lifted them in the air as if she'd found the last and long lost Holy Grail.

She'd cradled the books to her chest and with the starry eyes of a dreamer; she searched the class for worthy recipients. She had handed one to Theo and was, just now, reading the other while sitting under the shade tree across the play yard. Naomi closed Miss Jones's grade book and placed it on the desk. She walked across the classroom to Theo's table. He could smell the soft scent of the grapefruit she was preparing to eat. The skin had already been pulled away from the fruit and she was carefully removing the tiny pieces of pith from the slices in her hand.

Theo could feel her staring at him but he kept his eyes on the book.

"Where do you get all your sense from Mr. Theo? Is all the boys got good sense in South Carolina? Is that where you come from?"

She offered him a piece of grapefruit but pulled it away when he reached for it. She brought it to her mouth and wrapped her lips around it, taking a slow bite while watching and waiting for his answer.

"I'm from North Carolina. A place called Asheville."

She shook her head as if Asheville could be on the other side of the world.

"Never been," she held another piece of grapefruit toward him.

When he reached for it she pulled away again and then brought the piece to his mouth.  She held it there for him to take a bite. She popped the other half into her mouth and smiled at him.

"What's it like?" she asked, holding her hand out for him to take another slice of the fruit.

"No place is much different from the next." He picked a grapefruit slice out of her hand.

"Is the folks nice?"

"They're about the same."

Naomi checked on Miss Jones before sitting on Theo's table. She took the book out of his hands and laid it down beside her. She picked his hand up to study it, turning it over to check his palm.

She traced her finger along his lifeline before comparing it to hers for a moment.

"See here," she traced her finger over the crease in the center of his palm, "This here is your life line. Some folks got a long life coming and some folks don't."

The line in her palm was clearly longer than his. She brought his hand to her lips and kissed it lightly.

"Folks with short lines got to live their life like they mean it. They can't waste time because they don't got much of it."

He pulled his hand away and got up to stand beside her. He pressed his lips to hers. They were still sweet from the grapefruit. He held them there until he could feel his heart grow warm, a sensation he decided was what love must feel like.

She didn't pull away and when he stepped back, she smiled at him coyly. It was the first time he had ever kissed a girl and the first time a woman, young though she was, had ever been kind enough to encourage it.

"How did you get to Maryville if you from Asheville?" Naomi asked.

Theo shrugged his shoulders. "I come by train."

"I know how you come. I mean why did you co me? Where's your mama? Where's your daddy?"

"Don't know my daddy and my mama's working up north. I live with my uncle and my auntie."

"I suppose that's better than getting sent to the home for the colored in Henderson."

He shrugged his shoulders again. "Suppose so," he answered and then asked. "Why you not married yet?"

"Why *you* not married yet?" she retorted.

"Because I'm fifteen," Theo smiled.

She leaned back and crossed her legs. She glanced quickly out of the window to be sure Miss Jones was staying put. A few of the students were coming over the hill but the teacher was still there, her nose in the book as if she'd be there for the rest of the afternoon.

"Well, I'm seventeen but I don't intend to marry anybody from around here, that's for sure."

Theo asked, "What's wrong with the fellows from around here?

She shook her head. "They're not for me." She stared at him long enough to make him blush.

"I been here two years," he offered as if to test his standing.

Naomi got up from the table and walked a few steps away before turning back.

"That isn't long enough to say you from here. You're not from here until you can say your daddy's daddy's daddy is from here."

After school Theo and his cousins were supposed to gather coal off the road near the mine. The wagons and trucks that came daily to haul it to customers all over the state dropped a good bit of it as they passed across the rocky and muddled road. Theo told them to go ahead.

He waited under the tree, his eyes trained on the front door of the school. When Etta May passed on her way over the hill, he ignored her curious stares. Ten minutes later he watched

Romulus, a boy from their class who was forever being punished for something or the other, leave after having performed his punishment of cleaning the blackboards and sweeping the floor.

Romulus had a deep frown cut across his face. Miss Jones often told him. "I don't folly with folks what don't have good sense!"

For a teacher, she was a quiet sort. She used her hands to bid the students forward, to stop them, to raise them or to choose the one for whom she needed an answer. If her hands were otherwise engaged she fixed her face in various different expressions meant to direct the students in one way or the other. When she spoke it was often to cut you quickly and decisively into line.

"If your mammy didn't teach you," she'd point to the corner, sending whomever the offender was to stand there for the rest of the afternoon.

Romulus walked by, still frowning, narrowing his eyes at Theo as he passed. Normally, Theo could sympathize with him but just now he was preoccupied with waiting.

Miss Jones came out next. Just as the sun was going down behind the line of Cyprus trees growing along the ridge, Naomi stepped out. She closed the door firmly behind her. The burnt orange sky was nearly translucent and a cool evening breeze lifting up from the valley. She pulled her sweater closer and walked across the yard. When she saw Theo, she held her hand out for him to take it as she passed. They walked hand in hand in silence until she finally spoke.

"Everybody wants me to take over when Miss Jones gets married."

He looked at her. "You're a good teacher," he said seriously. Naomi curled her lip and fluttered her eyes as if she would have expected him to say just that.

"Pastor says it's an honest job for a gal like me."

Theo nodded, yes.

She stopped and let his hand drop. "That sounds like I don't have no other choice."

"You want to go to the teaching school, don't you?"

"My daddy is making me go. Pastor is making me go."

"It seems like you like being a teacher."

"It's not fair. I want to go other places... you been to other places," she accused him. "If I teach down at that school, the only way I'll go any place is inside a book. One of these old mash mouths will end up being my husband and I'll have babies and then I'll be stuck right here forever."

"Maryville is alright," he offered. He was sincerely confused by her confession.

"Is it better than where you from?"

He shook his head and laughed. "I'm not from any place," he assured her.

"But is it better than where you been?"

He shrugged his shoulders but when she put her hands on her hips in exasperation, he thought for a moment.

"I lived in a place called Tupelo, Mississippi when I was real little. I remember the folks there worked out in the field picking cotton. Even the little bitty kids had to haul a sack. I stayed in Brevard County in North Carolina with my mama's mama for a while. I had to sleep on the floor," he smiled.

"I stayed in Boatwright, Alabama and in a place called Anderson, South Carolina, except they called it Electric City but I don't know why."

"What was the best place?" Naomi wanted to know.

Theo kissed her on the cheek. "Right here, Naomi. It's the best place so far."

She smiled and took his hand again. They walked for a while down the darkening road toward her daddy's property. When they got to the bend in the road, Naomi stopped.

"I can go the rest of the way," she offered. "My daddy don't like some folks." She twisted her mouth and looked away so as not to say anything disagreeable.

Theo stepped back and waited while she ran up the path. When her dog started barking he heard her tell it to shush and then he heard the bang of the outer door as it hit the latch.

He put his hands in his pocket and waited there near the trees for more than a half hour. He finally turned back toward Percy's house. It was the last place he wanted to go but there wasn't much to do in Maryville, Tennessee after dark, except get caught by the white boys on a bad day.

He walked her home the next night and again the night after that. On Friday Etta May glared at him from her seat across the classroom but Theo didn't care. His cousins teased him all the way home but he barely heard them. When they got to their house, he didn't even turn to tell them goodbye. He walked up the hill and made his way the long way around through the woods to his uncle's place.

He could hear Sula inside reciting one of her Br'er Rabbit tales, which she did all times of day and night. It mattered not that she was alone or if others were around and not necessarily listening. She still told the stories the same, with excitement, pauses and depending upon the character with high tones and low.

"Buhr Rabbit laid there in the road pretending like he was dead, uhm huh. Buhr Rabbit seent the farmer pass him by with a thousand head of lettuce for to sell at the fair. Buhr Rabbit wait for the farmer to pass. Clump, clump, clump said the wheels on the wagon. Clump, clump, clump till the wagon pass Buhr Rabbit laid dead in the road and he jump up and run through the woods on up ahead to lay the road again, pretending like he be dead. The farmer stop this-a-time. He say what going on with all these rabbits laid dead in the road?"

Theo could hear her chuckling at the story that she'd been retelling since she was a child. He crouched down under the window to listen.

"Buhr Rabbit wait for the farmer to pass before he run through the woods up ahead and laid in the road for the one, two, three time. When the farmer come upon him for this three time, he say enough of this! Dead rabbits is dead rabbits. He snatched up Buhr Rabbit and toss him on his thousand head of lettuce. He rub his stomach jes so. Before long, he think he going to stop and cook him up some rabbit! Buhr Rabbit wait for the farmer to be on his way before he throw off one head of lettuce then two and for long it be a thousand head of lettuce laid along the road behind the farmer's wagon."

She chuckled again. Theo could hear her tapping on something to the rhythm of her tale.

"Buhr Rabbit hop off the empty wagon and pile up his breakfast, lunch and dinner for that day, the next and the next after that. Poor farmer done lost his wagon full of lettuce and his rabbit dinner too. Buhr Rabbit... sneaky Buhr Rabbit!"

Sula finished the story with a flourish as if she was reciting it to a cathedral full of wide-eyed children. Theo crawled under the house to his hiding place just under the backside of the porch.

He shimmied his tin out from between the red bricks and then leaned against the backside of the cool pillar. He could feel the damp dirt seep into the backside of his trousers but decided that since it was Friday they would be going into Sula's Saturday wash anyway so no matter.

Inside of the tin his most precious treasures were laid on top. The large cat-eye marble that one of the white boys left in the dirt next to the pharmacy downtown, a tin metal key from the 1940 World's Fair that his mother give him the last time she came to visit and an eagle's feather he found in the woods one day.

He set them aside and carefully counted out five dollars from the coins in the bottom, all money he made from stealing bottles from Percy's stash. The still was deep in the woods behind the house.

Percy's cellar, which Theo had watched him dig more than a year ago, was back off beyond the creek in a hollow in what folks called the Indian mound. They say it was where some colored folks mixed with Indian blood were buried. There were certainly a lot of holes in the ground that were easy to fall into.

"When it gets to raining real hard and the water's running good it pick up them mestee and wash what's left of them up the river, caskets and all," Tee Pee claimed.

Mestee is what they were called. They had dark skin and long oily hair. They were known for spewing crazy predictions midway between colored folk's haunts and Indian witchery. Some folks say they still lived up in the mountains or deep in the woods. They were blamed for all sorts of things up to and including missing chickens and missing women.

Theo had managed to save eighteen dollars towards his plan to move north. He put the five dollars into a brown paper sack and then carefully replaced the tin in its hiding place. When he crawled out from under the house and walked around to the front, he was surprised to find his uncle sitting quietly in the front seat of the old car. Theo walked by as if Percy wasn't there. Percy kept his eyes trained on something in the distance pretending as the boy did that the other didn't exist.

Sula smiled when he walked in, busy as she was decorating her box lunch for Sunday. It was more than a day away but she took elaborate steps in making her box the most attractive. She lined it with a fine and fitted material that she sewed together to sit perfectly on the inside. The outside was always different from one time to the next and this year she had collected itty, bitty pieces of pyrite. The little pieces of rock were laid out on the table along with a bottle of Franklin glue. She was carefully affixing the fool's gold onto the outside of the box one side at a time.

"Hey there you, Theo," she chanted.

She stepped back from her creation so he could see. She put her hands on her hips and closed her eyes. She raised her face to the heavens for the praise she felt was due. "How you like me now?" she asked.

Theo nodded. "That's your best one yet Auntie Sue. Your best one yet."

He tested the pyrite between his fingers. She had been pounding it with the side of a flat-faced rock even though Percy's hammers were sitting on the back porch in a box with his other tools.

"Oh yeah pastor gone tell it!" She grinned, speaking of how Pastor Bertrand would likely do a little dance upon seeing the box.

She waved absentmindedly at the pot on the stove too busy she was to stop what she was doing.

"All two a you got plenty in the pot." She reminded Theo that Percy had yet to come in to eat.

Theo hesitated before picking the lid off of the pot. Sula was the only one of his aunts that allowed such a thing. He would have gotten a smack or two had he touched a pot on Neena's stove. He peered inside at the collard greens with bits of wild turkey meat mixed in.

He wanted to wash up first and at least get out of his damp trousers but his growling stomach convinced his hand to reach for a bowl. He ate his supper whilst sitting on the kitchen stool and watching Sula apply the glue to the final side of the shoe box. She sprinkled the tiny bits of stone onto the surface singing softly as she went about her business.

"Soon and very soon," she sang. "We going to see the King. Soon and very soon we going to see the King. Soon and very soon we going to see the King. Hallelujah. Hallelujah we going to see the King. No more crying there..."

The screened door slammed as Percy stepped into the room. He stood there for a moment and then he turned without a word and went into the front room. They heard him fiddling with the radio.

Sula looked around the box at Theo.

She whispered. "Good luck say shut you mouth and open you eyes."

Theo nodded in agreement. He put his bowl on the counter and went in the opposite way from the front room. He somehow managed to stay out of Percy's way all day Saturday too.

Sunday morning he waited for them in the front yard. He rested his hand on the bag of money hidden in his pocket. He intended to use it to buy Naomi's box lunch. Sula stepped out onto the porch in a flowered dress and a string of chinaberries laced around her neck.

She had pinched a bit of color to her cheeks and wore a lipstick better suited for a darker woman but she was still beautiful enough for Theo to clap his hands together upon seeing her. She blushed past the makeup on her face.

She grinned. "Not looking too bad for a geechee gal what pick up me foot and run forty mile to get where I was going."

She held the decorated box up for him to see.

He nodded. "Pastor's going to like that."

He held his hand out to help her traverse the stairs and then reached for the box to carry it for her.

"No, no, no." She held it away from his reach. "I intend to carry it myself.  Thank you, sir."

Percy came out after her.  He was wearing his Sunday suit and carrying one of the kitchen chairs across his back.  He walked past Sula and Theo and went on up ahead without a word. When they got to the main road they met with the others who were headed toward the church.  Theo caught up with Percy, Tee Pee, Charlie, their Daddy, and older brothers.

Sula walked with her people who had come up from Alcoa.  Her sisters all walking barefooted so as not to get their church shoes dirty from the walk.

They all assured Sula that her box would take the prize.

## Chapter Eleven

Pastor Bertrand gave a shortened sermon not so much so because he knew potato salad and collard greens were slowly seeping through the cardboard boxes that were lined along the wall, but because he knew he'd have many an opportunity to remind his congregation throughout the afternoon of their probable yet redeemable failures in the eyes of the Lord.

He let them loose to the spectacle of box lunch day, one he hoped would generate enough money to pay the final note on the lot he'd bought to build the new church upon. He had big dreams and big plans that he wasn't sure this congregation could give him. Nevertheless he intended to take the long walk whether they were with him or not.

The land was further north and closer to Knoxville. A distance he was certain they would not have approved of. He had been conveying the funds clandestinely for the past two years to Able Sinclair, the frowning and freckled faced redneck who owned it.

"This land been in my daddy's name and my granddaddy's name since the War of the Americas," Sinclair had informed Bertrand on the first day they met.

It was unlikely that the story was true but Bertrand stood by with his hat in his hands patiently waiting for Mr. Sinclair to finish his pitch.

"I'll sell you a piece of it for a fair price." He spat a plug of chaw into the winter lilies that were sprouting on the side of the road, staining their white petals brown with tobacco juice.

They were the first flower of spring but just then they seemed to immediately regret the distinction. Their heads bowed as they wilted to the ground.

Bertrand knew the statement of fair play was what white folks said before any transaction having to do with money. He knew it was devil talk for "I'm going to give you a price and you better grin and bear it for you will get no other."

It was a proposition Bertrand was willing to take. He was aware that Negroes living up that way were making more money than in Maryville yet they still pined for a down home church... without having to travel down home to get to it. His plan was to give them their church in exchange for the extra dollars they'd drop in the coffer.

But for now it was Box Lunch Day and it was these folks and their nickels and dimes that were important. He clapped his hands together to bring everyone's attention to the table closest to the steps. Miss Mercy was taking a seat and setting the cash box before her. The ladies carried their lunches out and laid them in a dignified form around Miss Mercy so that theirs would be within easy reach.

The wives and sisters of King's Chapel AME were a creative bunch. They had taken great effort to adorn their boxes with brightly colored material or flowers. In Miss Hemphill's case, she had pulled a patch of dark green ivy leaves away from the side of her stone barn and glued them around her box in a circular pattern. The others were as elaborate but none of them were a match to Sula's.

Hers was by far the most enchanting. The sun caught its million points of sparkling stone, compelling everyone to ooh and ahh over it. Sula stood as speechless as a blushing fourteen year old bride. Bertrand waited for everyone to gather around for the bidding. He started with the youngest and passed through the children's boxes quickly with the highest bid being a mere eight cents. When Deacon Foley carried Sula's box up the stairs to him, Bertrand pretended that it weighed a ton.

"Good Jesus," he boomed. "How many of you fellows had to carry this box up in here? I bet it took a dozen. Praise the Lord!"

Everyone clapped delightfully while fanning the flies and heat away with their kerchiefs and church fans. Some of the younger men stepped forward to jostle for a spot, all of them knowing well that what was inside would be well worth their money.

"Oh, yes," Bertrand hollered. "As beautiful as it is, I am certain the outside won't match the fine and delectable and delicious collard greens..." he bellowed.

Everyone cheered and the guys up front pushed at one another, all raising their hands ready for the bid but Bertrand was not ready to accept it yet.

"Fried chicken," he raised his voice even higher. "And," he looked at Sula and asked, "Corn on the cob?"

Sula nodded her head up and down like a bay colt fixing to gobble his first apple of the day.

"And chocolate cake," Bertrand raised his eyebrows in wonder.

He knew it would be chocolate because chocolate was Sula's all time favorite. She made it whenever anyone died or whenever a baby was born. She made it for birthdays all year long and she made one every time they had a box lunch day.

Sula's sisters pushed in on either side to hold her hands while the young men bid one over the other to take possession of the prize.

Percy sat under the old oak tree playing dominoes with his brother and two cousins just a few feet beyond the church boundaries. They were forbidden to play on church property so they always brought their own chairs and a square of wood to play on just out of reach of Bertrand's jurisdiction.

"How much you think Sula gone get for her box this year?"

"Don't know, don't care." Percy raised his hand in the air and slapped a domino bone onto the table. He added with a smile, "I fills my belly for free."

Just then the crowd hollered loudly when Charlie B won Sula's box with a bid of one dollar and ten cents.

Percy grimaced. "A dollar and ten cents," he shook his head. "I ought to be selling plates if folks paying that much for what Sula cooking."

Charlie B danced up the steps to accept his prize. He bowed to Sula before following her to her table to enjoy his lunch. When he offered to share the box she shook her hands. "No, baby. Eat your half now and my half later. I got plenty where that come from."

Foley handed a pink, laced box to Bertrand. The pastor looked over from top to bottom before holding it out for everyone to see.

"Now this one is dressed like a princess. I bet I know who it belongs to."

He pointed toward Etta May and Naomi who were sitting together at their table. Theo's heart started thumping like a drum.

"Which one of you fellows got a nickel in your pocket?" Bertrand teased the crowd.

Etta May and Naomi's father sauntered across the lawn. "I got that nickel."

He held the silver coin up for all to see.  Theo wasn't sure if the box was Etta's or Naomi's or both. His hands started sweating and just as he was about to muster up enough courage to speak, Deacon Foley put his hand up to stop their father from coming any further.

He dug deep in his pocket and pulled out a quarter. "I raise that donation to twenty-five cents!"

His voice jumped three octaves as if his bid was a thousand dollars.

"I think I got another quarter in here," Naomi's father grinned good-naturedly.

He pulled the coin out of his pocket.  "That's mighty fine of you." Pastor Bertrand rubbed his hands together, "especially since the sweat from your back sowed the seed what cooked the food."

He laughed and his adoring congregation laughed right along with him.

"I'm in for sixty." Johnny Boy, one of Theo's cousins, raised his hand.

"Show me your money," Bertrand said.  He put a little dance in his step, "Show me your money."

Johnny Boy unfolded the change from a handkerchief.  He ignored his mother and sister's glares from where they were sitting.  He held his hand out to show six dimes.

"I want to do what I can to support the church," he said, shifting his pants up from the side.

He had just been released from doing time for the county. The money he was spending was what he'd earned for more than a month of labor. He could hear his mother grumbling. "Sixty cents is too much to flash around when that's all you got."

Bertrand waved his hand over the crowd. "We got sixty cents and a sit down with two lovely young ladies. Two lovely young misses what made some fine fixings that I know gone put a smile on your face."

Johnny Boy crossed his arms. He turned toward the crowd as if his bid couldn't possibly be beat. Old Ramsey, who was nearly ninety and swore to be damned if he wasn't born in Africa and transported here on a ship called The Molly, raised his finger and mumbled, "Add my nickel for sixty-five."

He moved about as slow as an inch a minute. Everyone knew that if his bid won he'd probably forget to claim it, though Bertrand would not forget to retrieve the sixty-five cents. Johnny Boy's arms dropped in disgust. His mother and sisters, looking like a cackle of blackbirds sitting on a tree limb, gleefully relayed "um hums" back and forth at each other.

Theo was sitting atop a picnic table with Tee Pee and Charlie, both of whom were pushing him this way and that every time someone raised the bid on Etta May and Naomi's box. He finally got up to walk closer to the crowd.

His plan made so much sense the day before except now with Percy not far away he wasn't too sure it was such a good thing to be prancing around with a pocket full of money.

When he glanced toward Naomi, she winked at him and before he knew it he was bidding a dollar. Everyone turned his way and Naomi lifted her hand to cover the smile spreading across her face.

Bertrand said, "Well, all right then."

When Ramsey turned to see who outbid him, he held his hand up to wave away any further part in the competition.

"We got one dollar... going one time... going two time..."
Bertrand held the box out to Theo who handed the money over
to Miss Mercy.

When he turned around, Etta was standing there waiting. She
smiled coyly and took Theo's arm and pulled him through the
crowd to the table where her family was sitting.

"Afternoon, Theo." Naomi greeted him. She moved to the
opposite side of the table as if he was just another one of the
students from the school.

Their daddy was already eating, hovering over his plate as if
someone may snatch it away.

"Who this?" he asked, his mouth full of green beans.

Etta May pulled the top off the shoebox. "This is Theo," she
blushed.

"Who his daddy?" their father wanted to know.

"He's Mr. Percy and Miss Sula's nephew."

She put a plate in front of Theo and placed a sandwich of sliced
ham and tomatoes on it.

Their father pointed his fork at Theo. "Bertrand baptize you?"
He asked.

Theo shook his head, no.

"Is he going to baptize you?" The father raised one eyebrow.

Theo waited for Etta May to spoon a heaping of potato salad
onto his plate before answering. "I already been baptized...
more than once."

"That so," the father asked?

"Yes sir. One time in North Carolina and one time in South Carolina."

"That so," the father asked again.

Theo studied him. He wasn't sure if an answer was expected, the same answer at that.

"Alright then," the father went back to his meal.

He continued to stare at Theo every few minutes or so.

Theo ate his overpriced lunch *with the wrong sister.* He tried to ignore his cousins who were across the yard making fun of him, and his uncle who was wondering aloud about how anybody could make a whole dollar from picking coal up off of the road.

He tried to concentrate on the food but when Naomi walked off to talk to Johnny Boy, it tasted even worse.

Etta May asked him. "How you like the baked beans? You want some more? I cooked them for two hours."

She breathed the words as if she might hyperventilate at any moment.

"They're alright, Etta May," he answered.

"I put molasses and onions..."

"I don't like onions too much."

"They itty-bitty little pieces, if at all," her father butted in.

He held a fork full in front of his face to study it. "I don't even see any," he smiled at his daughter. "I taste them though."

His smile faded as he turned his attention back to Theo.

"Yes, sir," Theo agreed in theory if not with enthusiasm, "They're the best I ever had."

He shoveled the rest into his mouth so as not to have to keep talking. "Do you want more," she picked up the bowl.

Theo shook his head. He stuffed the rest of the sandwich into his mouth as well. He chewed until he could swallow and then gulped the iced tea to wash it all down. Etta May pulled another sandwich out of the box.

"I made you two. Don't you want the other one?"

"It was very good. I'll take it for later." He stuffed it into his pocket. "Thank you, Etta May."

He got up. "I'm pleased to meet you, sir." He extended his hand to the father but let it drop after her father kept eating.

"Your daughter is very pretty, sir." Theo smirked because even though Etta May grinned out of control he was talking about Naomi.

He walked across the yard to Sula's table.

Sula shook her head in dismay when he sat down. "Talk me, Theo. Talk me or no," she said.

"Nothing to say," he replied.

She shook her head.

"A rooster don't cackle when he find a worm but sometime he don't need to. He strut his neck just the same," she recited mournfully.

They both looked to where Percy was sitting and found him turned in his seat facing in their direction. Bertrand didn't allow liquor on church property but there was no doubt some was being consumed over the line where Percy was sitting.

Sula shook her head. "Me, one and God..." She bemoaned.

Folks started leaving after awhile and when Sula helped her sisters pack their baskets, Theo told her he'd be along soon. She looked up at the sky.

"Sugar moon this evening," she reckoned. "It will be as bright as the daytime."

He lay back on the bench and watched the moon rise high above the trees. Johnny Boy played his fiddle for the folks still hanging round. Ginia started singing and the guys starting tapping their toes and sipping the bottles that had been hiding in their trousers all day.

Theo moved closer and before long one of the bottles got passed to him. He took a sip and then another. He started clapping and singing along with the others. Percy be damned he thought. He'd get home when he got home.

Later on he stumbled along the road, jiggling the change in his pocket still agitated over spending a dollar on Etta May's lunch. He was headed to his bed when he was surprised to find that instead of going home he'd subconsciously redirected himself toward Naomi's house instead.

He shushed the dog with Etta's May's ham sandwich and tiptoed around to the back of the house. He could see Naomi through the open window asleep on the bed with Etta May and their three younger sisters. He didn't make any noise but Naomi suddenly opened her eyes.

"Who that?" she whispered.

She got up quietly and stooped down by the window.

"Who that," she asked again.

"It's me. Theo."

"You playing with fire," she smiled.

"I want my dollar back," he whispered.

She lowered her head. "You been drinking?" she asked.

Before he answered she held her finger to her lips and then disappeared into the room. She came around the side of the house and quietly bid him to follow her. They walked down by the river.

"You're too young to be drinking, Theo."

"I didn't drink that much."

She fanned the air around him. "You stink like you spilled more on you than in you."

He laughed too loudly. She immediately took his hands to get him to quiet down. He leaned forward and kissed her. She pulled away and hissed, "If my daddy wakes up he'll shoot you, boy."

Theo held his hands up in surrender and then pulled the four dollars in change out of his pocket. The bag immediately broke and the money spilled to the ground. Surprised, Naomi stepped out of the way.

"What in the world?" she stammered. "Where did you get all this money from?"

She knelt down to retrieve the coins out of the dirt but it was too dark to see most of them.

"Aren't you going to help? Don't you want your money?" She asked him.

He knelt down and felt around for the money but after finding a few coins he stood up and dropped them back down to the ground.

"It's ok," he said. "I have to get home, Sula's going to be waiting on me."

"What about your money?"

"You can have it."

She looked at him queerly. "Etta May likes you..."

"But I don't want to be with Etta May. I want to be with you, Naomi."

"I'm too old for you, Theo. You know that." She stood up.

"You're not that old... I'm not that young."

His head was surely spinning. He blurted, "I'm headed up north. Won't you come with me? Nobody will know how old we are."

She paused for a long time. He smiled halfheartedly, "You'll get to see what's outside of here."

"No, Theo," she said softly. She held the money she had picked up out for him to take. Instead, he wrapped his arms around her and held on to her as if he may never let go. When he finally pulled away he walked up the bank soundlessly and then disappeared into the darkness.

The dog followed him to the road, hoping, Theo supposed, that he'd get another ham sandwich. Theo patted his pockets. "Sorry boy, I got nothing to give you."

When he got to Percy's house the junk car was sitting empty. Theo didn't see his uncle sitting on the dark side of the porch, waiting. Not a word was uttered just the blur of what seemed like a wild, black leopard attacking so fast that all Theo had time to do was shut his eyes.

The smell of his uncle's anger mixed with rotgut, homemade tobacco and a daylong sweat from sitting under the tree playing dominoes was, altogether potent enough to freeze Theo in his tracks. Tee Pee was right; Percy had him in a grip that was slowly cutting off his ability to breathe.

Sula came running out of the front door. She held her nightdress close around her neck to keep the chill away. "Percy! Percy!" she screamed. "You too much on him! Let him be!" she screamed.

When Percy didn't let go, she looked up at the ceiling of the porch and uttered, "God hold me just now so I don't catch the death." She let loose of her nightdress and grabbed Percy.

"You gone mash him till his eyes roll back! If you kill that boy it be the last time you see my face! The last time, I'm warning you!"

Percy adjusted his grip even tighter, ignoring Sula until she grabbed up her nightdress and pushed past him down the stairs.

She looked up to find a sure enough sugar moon to light her way. She nodded her head at it as if it wouldn't have been any different if she drew it in the sky herself.

"I'll be by my Lottie house. Fend for yourself, hear?"

Percy let Theo go and stepped over him. The boy slipped to the floor. Sula kept walking.

"If you done killed him," she raised her hand in the air. "Explain it to the Mister what gone hang you and tell Saint Peter at the gate that I tried to stop you."

Percy went inside, slamming the door behind him.

# Chapter Twelve

The next morning Theo woke to the sound of the church bells ringing. Sula was sitting on the steps beside him, counting them off.

"Seventy-one... seventy-two. Could be Mr. Ramsey, got twenty more to go. Seven-four... Could be Miss Mercy, got three more to go. Seventy-six... seventy-seven...," She waited as the last ring paled into silence.

She shook her head and brought her hand to Theo's face. "Miss Mercy done died. The church bells say so."

She sighed heavily. She looked at Theo for a moment. His neck was bruised and his shirt was torn.

"I left my babies long time past. One of them is bound to be like you."

She looked off into the distance, still rubbing her hand softly over his head.

"Percy's not going to let you stay. Best you be on your way before he get up and out."

She looked back at the front door. "It won't be long."

A lump crawled up into Theo's throat and he could feel the hot tears pushing at the back of his eyes. He knew that if he spoke he'd be crying like a baby. Sula looked away at the sky. "How the sky stand," she asked? "Do it look like a good day for picking up he foot," she asked the trees?

They swayed in the wind; an answer Sula took for a positive one.

She nodded her head emphatically. She helped him to his feet. His sack of belongings was already packed and sitting by the bottom step. He climbed down and disappeared under the porch. When he came out, Sula had walked out toward the road ahead of him. He stuffed the tin box into his sack and ran to catch up.

She reached out to hold his hand and they walked the rest of the way together.

"Every grin teeth don't mean laugh," she offered her best advice.

Theo nodded his head. He hugged her and kissed her on the cheek.

"Go on now," she told him. "I'll see you with Tee Pee and Charlie."

"No, ma'am," Theo told her. She looked shocked, "Where you going? Percy be fine. He not coming to look for you. I won't let him do that."

"I never stay no place too long. I've been in Maryville long enough, Auntie Sue."

She seemed to think about it for a moment. "You going by your mama?"

He nodded.

"Let her know you coming before you get lost up there with all them folks."

She pulled him to her and sang him a simple lullaby. She told him to follow for the seven stars.

"You be fine," she said. "You be fine."

"Yes ma'am."

They parted.  He walked along the road toward town.  At one point regretting that he'd given Etta May's ham sandwich to the dog but nonetheless he felt somehow relieved.  He changed his clothes and washed up by the river. He counted out the seven dollars he would need to board the bus to Boston and then he walked the rest of the way to town.  He paid his fare and waited for the bus to pull up to the depot.

It was early and Maryville was still asleep. He looked toward Naomi's house. He thought about begging her to come with him one last time but he knew some folks talk about leaving but never do.

## Chapter Thirteen

Dora Dear married a man named Jimmy Wilson in 1942, five years after arriving in Boston. At the beginning he reminded her of Jesse Miner until she discovered most of what he said was simple-minded nonsense.

He worked downtown and called himself a doorman at one of the finer buildings but in reality he was a low-level porter, and the building wasn't even all that grand. He wore a little uniform, the same one that he washed out every other evening. He conked his hair and pretended to have Choctaw Indian in his blood.

"I got Choctaw Indian on my mama's side. Her hair was straight just like the white ladies on Newbury Street," he'd say, more often when he was drunk but at least once a week regardless. After four years, she finally convinced him that Theo wouldn't be any trouble if he moved north to live with them.

"I ain't asking you to keep up after any of my kids, am I, Dora? I don't see what's wrong with him staying down south. I stayed down there myself until I was old enough to come up here on my own. Hell, my kids still live in the country! Shit. I told you when we took up together that I didn't have money to be raising other folks' kids."

Dora Dear ignored Jimmy. He was always talking big at the mouth when it came to Theo coming to Boston. She was working just as well as he was. It wasn't like he was taking care of anybody. She paid half of their rent and bought most of the groceries on top of it. She kept right on stirring the stew, ignoring him like she always did. He was a big talker. She wasn't going to let him talk her out of allowing Theo to finally live with her.

When Theo arrived at the station, Jimmy wasn't there. He was off somewhere pouting. It was better this way Dora determined as she greeted her son. "Look how big you are!" she exclaimed.

She could hardly believe that he was taller than she was. "Only fifteen years old." She shook her head at the idea.

She held her arms out and he leaned toward her for an awkward hug that somehow turned into a pat on his back.

He looked around and let out a low whistle. "This is nothing like Maryville."

Dora shook her head no. "You're in the big city now, honey. There's a lot to see and even more to do."

She nodded her head and then laced her arm with his. Theo ran his fingers along the building as they walked, feeling the brick and cobblestone.

"This must be made to last until the end of time." His voice was heavy like that of a full-grown man.

They walked across the street and along the sidewalk where the iron gates surrounded the public gardens at the South End. Dora bought popcorn and lemonade and they walked across the grass to a spot near the water to sit for a while. A musician played his trumpet close by and a man practiced some sort of a dance on the walkway. People were standing around watching him and putting coins in a bucket every now and then.

Theo studied him. "Why are they giving him money?" he asked.

His mother shaded her eyes from the sun and looked to where the man was pretending to walk along an invisible line. He was holding his hands out in front of himself to guide the way. His face was painted white and his lips were rubbed with red lipstick.

She shook her head slowly, "I can't imagine."

Theo laughed when the man simulated running in slow motion. When he bowed low at the waist and elaborately doffed his hat, his audience clapped. Each person then dutifully dropped more coins into the bucket.

Theo looked at his mother in awe. He shook his head. "I think I'm going to like it here," he smiled.

He stood up and tried to do what the mime did, which made Dora grin with pride.

"I think you'll be fine," she said. "Living here has been good for me."

Theo studied the landscape around the park, turning around slowly in a circle.

"It's so big. I bet Maryville could sit right here in the park and have more room besides." Theo waved his arms around.

"I believe you're right. Once you start to school and get some friends it won't seem so big after a while."

She looked up at the sky and figured it was time to get home. She gathered his bag off the grass and held her hand out for him. They strolled back toward the entrance where Theo stopped to stare at a statue of George Washington.

"I read about him," Theo told his mother.

He wanted to touch the statue but there were flowers planted all around it. He studied it in awe. He couldn't imagine how it was made. Naomi would know. He wished she had come.

They walked arm in arm toward Dora's house. On the way, they passed the laundry where she worked. She stood in front of it proudly.

"If it wasn't closed for the day I'd take you inside to meet Mr. Fleming," she explained. "

He's not the owner himself. His brother Tom is."

She lowered her voice. "He used to be the owner until he let it get away."

She tipped an invisible cup toward her mouth. "Of course," she added. "Tom Fleming don't know a lick about the laundering business. I suppose it's not too much to have to know. I'll be three years in March," she told him. "Miss Maggie's been here longer, but after her I'm the next in line."

Theo studied the clean glass along the front of the building, running his hand along the painted name across the middle. He peered inside.

Dora did the same, she pointed out the counter and where the clean clothes were hanging. "We work back there at the back. I got to get here early though. Mr. Fleming promises some of these folks their cleaning back by the end of the day."

"They get them in on their way to work and they like to pick up on their way home." She smiled, proud that her orders were always ready.

"Do you think they'll let me work here too?"

Dora Dear started back up the street. "Oh, no, honey. You'll be in school."

"I want to work," Theo retorted. "I want to make my own way until I go to the army. I quit school. I ain't been in over a year," he lied.

Dora stopped, her heart rushed to thump loudly in her chest. Jesse Boy Minor was long gone but the thought of this boy going without schooling was enough she knew to break his heart.

"But what do you think we been doing all this for? You can't work. That's why I work so *you* can go to school. So *you* can be somebody like your daddy would have wanted."

Theo's body recoiled in the way one shifts away without moving their feet. He thought about reminding her that the only reason he was here at all was because that's just where the bus ticket he bought took him. Instead, though, he took a deep breath and laced his arm with his mother's. He wanted to get along with her. He wanted this, whatever this was - the music in the park, white folks walking on the same sidewalk and not even seeming to notice; the easy money to be made for painting your face white and shadow dancing to silence.

"I'll go to school if that's what you want."

A smile of relief spread across her face. It made him smile. They walked on and after a while she started telling him about how she got to Boston. "I was living in New York with Eliza, but the family I was working for moved up this way." She shook her head. "I didn't want to leave but I had to work and they were nice enough. It turned out that the Missus didn't like it... said it was too cold."

Dora shrugged her shoulders. "What's the difference in thirty degrees in Boston or thirty degrees in New York? I told them to go on back without me. I did some piecework at home for a while until I got on with the laundry."

She leaned over to whisper even though there couldn't have been anyone within earshot who cared. "Mr. Fleming don't like it but I still take in a bit of laundry around in the neighborhood. You know how folks are though. They're cheap and after a while they want somebody to mend their stuff for nothing, or when it's time to deliver, they pretend they're not at home."

She shook her head and laughed lightly. "Every little bit helps though."

She stopped. "Here it is."

She nodded toward the steps leading to her front door. She held him back. "Now listen. I want to let you know that Jimmy may be a little snappy at first. Don't let him give you even a bit of worry. Let me worry about him, hear?"

Theo shrugged his shoulders. He wasn't worried because he could take care of himself.

She had a setup of wooden boxes behind the couch with a narrow bedroll set on top. Dora untied the roll and laid it flat. She sat down and patted the top.

"It's comfortable enough," she raised her eyebrows. "Somebody brought it in for cleaning and never did come back to pick it up."

She patted it again. The wooden boxes underneath faced with their open ends out so he could store his belongings there. Theo walked around the couch and sat down beside her. He nodded his head.

"Thank you. It'll do just fine."

Jimmy came home an hour or so later. He walked directly to the bedroom, never taking a moment to acknowledge the presence of Theo who was sitting in the living room directly in his path.

When Dora Dear heard the front door close she dried her hands on a towel and followed Jimmy to the bedroom. She closed the door softly behind her. Theo sat in the living room and listened to them argue, at first in mumbles and then louder.

He was used to people arguing about him, in fact, it happened everywhere he'd ever lived. Finally, the bedroom grew quiet. Theo got up and leaned at the wall near the window on the far side of his bed. He peered out, careful not to burn his hands on the radiator near the wall. He looked down at the street and then as far to the left and as far to the right as he could see.

If Jimmy wouldn't let him stay, Theo thought, he'd walk right out of there. He'd take a right turn and keep walking. There'd been an old colored man on the bus who said that if you walked south from Bean Town you'd end up in New York smack dab on Broadway.

That's what he'd do if the little man in the little blue suit came out of the bedroom and told him to get out. He'd go straight to New York and he wouldn't look back. He sat down and leaned back on the bed and watched the sun drop behind the rooftops over Boston.

As the sky got darker, he could see his reflection in the window. He stared back at himself. He never wondered where he'd inherited his coffee colored eyes or dark tone; in truth he didn't even know his father's name and was so used to being called a bastard, he didn't care to know.

He sat there through the night never sleeping just waiting, preparing himself for what tomorrow would bring

## Chapter Fourteen

The next morning, Dora went to the kitchen and started breakfast. Jimmy came out of the bedroom in his uniform as if it was just an ordinary day. The creases in his pants were as sharp as they'd been the night before after having spent the night carefully laid between the mattress and box spring on the bed. He was pushing a brush briskly down his jacket as he straddled the arm of the old green chair. When Theo sat up, he simply stared back at the man who was staring at him. Neither said a word. Theo wouldn't have if the house were on fire. He hadn't backed down to his uncles and he wouldn't start backing down to little niggers like this one.

Jimmy though was a talking man. He was the first to start a conversation and was always the last to shut up.

"Your mama say you want to go to school," Jimmy grimaced.

He'd never gone to school himself and he wasn't about to pull the weight for anybody else to go. "That's alright with me as long as you got some work going on, too."

He waited for the boy to respond. When Theo didn't, Jimmy continued. "Your mama say you was all the way up to the seventh grade. I didn't know they let Negroes go to school in Tennessee. Is that so?"

"Yes, sir," Theo grudgingly answered.

"Yes sir what? Do they let Negroes go to school or was ya in the seventh grade? Yes sir to everything or yes sir to one thing or the other thing?"

Jimmy grinned, showing gold-rimmed front teeth. He licked his tongue across the gold. It was a habit for which folks weren't

certain was a tic or a way to remind them that he had
something they didn't.

"Both." Theo's lips tightened.

He sized Jimmy up. They were about the same height but
Theo's build was solid next to Jimmy's thin frame.   Jimmy
licked his lips. He wasn't about to let a boy disrespect him but
he knew how easily a situation could get out of hand.  His
uniform was more than a minor concern.  He fretted over it like
it belonged to him - in fact, had it tailored to fit his short arms
just right.  In actuality it belonged to his employer and if it got
ripped in a scuffle with this hoodlum from Tennessee, Jimmy
would have to pay for its repair.

He stuck his chest out and re-traced his tongue across his teeth.

"There's a butcher down there on the corner around by
Cochran, your mama will show you where to go. They had a
sign in the window looking for a boy."

"They're looking for a day worker." Dora leaned around the
door from the kitchen where she'd been eavesdropping on the
conversation.

Jimmy closed his eyes for a second before cutting them in her
direction. "What do that have to do with it, Dora?"

"Theo's going to school during the day."

"Theo got to eat, too. Don't he?" Jimmy turned to Theo. "You got
to eat don't you, boy?"

Jimmy stood up, not waiting for a response since he knew he
probably wouldn't get one anyway.  "I got to catch that 22
before I be late.  Dora, you got my lunch ready?"

Dora winked at Theo as she handed Jimmy his bag lunch.  They
watched Jimmy prance out of the apartment.

"Don't worry about him, hear?"

"I'm not worried." Theo responded in his deep voice. "Where did he come from anyway?"

"Come on to the table and eat this breakfast I made for you. I'll tell you all about it."

She sat in Jimmy's seat and he sat across the table in hers. "I told you I was doing some piece work." She reminded him. "I went to make a delivery up there to the building where he works."

She rocked her head back and forth to indicate that there was more to the story but to make it short, "We started meeting up and after a while we got this place."

She looked around the small apartment. "I like it alright."

She saw that Theo was finishing his eggs. She got up and brought the pan over to put more on his plate.

"Does he have any kids?" Theo asked.

"He says he does but he don't even know how many."

Theo looked at her skeptically.

She laughed. "They're all back in Alabama. That's where he's from."

"Alabama," Theo nodded. "No wonder."

Dora Dear laughed lightly. "No wonder."

"Come on, here." She gathered his dishes. "You don't want to be late."

Theo washed up and got dressed. They walked toward the school together.

"You're not scared, are you?" she asked.

"I'm not afraid of anything," Theo answered.

He said it in such a matter of fact way that it frightened her a little. She wanted to say he was like his father but it had been so long ago she wasn't sure that her imagination of Jesse Minor was greater than the reality ever was. She relied upon a scripture from the bible instead. "God says do not be afraid for he is your shield."

She took his hand and they walked up the steps to the school. It was so big compared even to the City Hall in Maryville. Theo's eyes went automatically to the ceiling and then around toward the massive hallways that ran for what seemed like miles in every direction.

They were early and the only students in the building were already in the office waiting in chairs along the wall with their parents. They all looked up when Theo and Dora walked in. Dora carefully filled out the forms and signed her name in big shaky letters across the bottom. She breathed in when she finished as if the task was the hardest one she'd have all day. She smiled at Theo and gave him the lunch she'd made for him along with fifteen cents.

"Buy a soda or something," she whispered before leaving him there in the office.

He sat down to wait along with the other new students. Each one was called until he and one other boy was left waiting.

"Where you from?" The boy asked.

Theo thought about it. Where was he from? "North Carolina," he decided.

"No wonder," the boy teased.

Theo laughed because it was ironic that he had said the same thing about Jimmy.

He asked, "No wonder?"

The boy smoothed his hands along either side of his lapel. "It's all in the clothes, my man."

He wagged his finger along Theo's pants and shirt. He shook his head. "Look what you got on, man. You had to be from some Carolina."

Theo looked down at his clothes. This kid was probably right.

"What about you?"

"I was born in Kentucky, man but I been here long enough to call it home."

He held his hand out. Theo shook it. "Everybody calls me Tony."

He pulled a tiny comb out of his pocket and ran it through his close-cropped hair.

"Theodore Minor." The receptionist called. "Theodore Minor," she called again after no one responded.

"Anthony," she pointed. "Who's your friend?"

Theo realized she was calling him. "My name is Theo," he corrected her.

"Come on up then." She waved him up and handed him his assignment card.

"Anthony will show you where to go. Can you do that, Mr. Pierce? Do you think you can stick around long enough to show Mr. Minor where his first class is?"

Tony remained in his seat for a second longer than Theo would have to prove Theo supposed that he was the bad ass of the school. They ended up in most of the same classes. By the end of the first day they were fast friends and true to the receptionist's predictions Tony didn't stay in school for long.

Theo tried but quickly realized that being at the top of his class in Maryville meant very little in Boston. He dropped out in a matter of weeks. Instead of going to school he and Tony along with Raymond and Billy Belton, whom they called Bell, met every morning to hop the trolley to Scollay Square. Sometimes they went to South Station to watch the trains coming and going but after an hour or so the cops usually chased them away.

They shared Dora's bag lunch for breakfast and if they didn't have any money they stole fruit or candy from the markets on Washington Avenue. Tony showed them how to pick the pockets of unsuspecting ladies on their way into R. H. Whites or Gilchrist's department stores and if it was too cold there was always a way to slip into The Howard to watch movies or sleep in the balcony undetected for most of the day.

In the evenings Theo pretended to do homework. Jimmy sat with eyes narrowed, certain the boy was telling lies. When Theo spoke, it didn't matter about what Jimmy would clear his throat loudly and grimace as if he could read the boy's mind. "All I want to know is when are you going to get a job?"

Dora was about to lift a forkful of green beans to her mouth. She let the fork drop to the plate.

"He's in school and he's doing good." She nodded at Theo for confirmation. "Why do you have to make a fuss?" She asked Jimmy.

Jimmy kept his fork pointed at Theo but spoke to Dora. "Don't worry about me making a fuss. I'm a man! I'm the man of this house, damn it."

He turned his head to face Theo and pointed to the bedroom. "By the way, I'm missing fifty cents off my dresser this morning."

Theo's mouth dropped open. "I didn't take any money," he looked at Dora.

She shook her head, no. "I know you didn't take it, baby," she assured him. "I didn't see any money on the dresser," she told Jimmy.

Jimmy turned back to Dora. "So does that mean it wasn't there? Is that what you're trying to say? I'm lying? I didn't have two quarters in the evening and when I got up this morning they was gone?" He tested her.

"I'm just saying, Jimmy. I didn't see any money or quarters or whatever."

She got up and took the change purse out of her pocketbook. She moved the coins around before finding a quarter two dimes and a nickel. She put them on the table next to Jimmy.

"I told you I didn't touch his money," Theo protested.

Dora shook her head and sat back down. Jimmy scooped the money up. "He still needs to find a job," he said.

Dora took a deep breath, deciding Theo supposed, to preserve some semblance of decorum by sitting up and readjusting herself in her seat. She silently picked her fork up and gathered the green beans together on her plate before replying. "He come here to finish his schooling."

She measured her words slowly and clearly, leaving no room for confusion. "When he gets ready, he'll find some work. School will be out for the summer, he'll find a job when he gets out of school."

Theo looked down at his plate. He was afraid to imagine what she might do if she knew he barely ever went. When Jimmy tried to respond, Dora slammed her hand on the table. The movement startled both Jimmy and Theo alike.

"That's all I'm going to say about it Jimmy. This boy is staying in school until summer comes. I'm paying his way. Not you. Now, you got your money. Leave it alone." Her eyes closed to the idea of another word being spoken.

Jimmy shifted his glare from Dora to Theo. For the rest of the meal, instead of looking at his plate he stabbed at the food blindly bringing it to his mouth and chewing loudly before swallowing.

Theo felt bad enough the next morning to actually show up at school. His resolve was fleeting however and he didn't make it through the day. By then though, he couldn't find Tony or Ray or Bell so he walked to the park by himself.

He found the spot on the hill where he and Dora sat his very first day in Boston. The mime was gone. A woman, dressed in black had taken his place. She was singing mournfully and swaying slowly from side to side as if she might be demented. A short time later a police officer eased her away as if it was his usual task to undertake every afternoon.

By four o'clock, Theo decided to surprise his mother at the cleaners. He walked the short distance and waited just outside the opened back door. The steam from the dryers floated languidly through the opening. He could hear Mr. Fleming ranting about some clothing that he didn't think had been cleaned properly and he could hear his mother laughing nervously.

"Oh, yes sir," she answered. "I'll have to wash them over again."

"Well that's not good enough, Brownie," he called her.

Theo peered around the opened door. His mother stood there, her fingers were laced together in front of her like a schoolgirl.

Theo felt the same anger he'd felt when he was a boy still living at his uncle Joe's house. Mr. Fleming held the shirt above Dora's head to show the other workers. He was the Fleming brother who didn't know well enough that the shirt was of a muslin material, the color of which was meant to be off white.

His brother walked over. The tip of a pint bottle was sticking out of the pocket of his day coat. He placed his hand on her shoulder.

"What's happening here Dora," he asked.

His brother butt in, "I don't know about this one, Talbot."

Talbot moaned, "We'll take care of it. Won't we Miss Dora?"

"Yes, sir, right away for you, sir." Dora gushed.

"No, now... not right away." He shook his head. His jowls jiggled freely as he spoke. "Tomorrow will be fine, won't it Tom?"

Tom Fleming tossed the shirt on the floor, making it a certainty that it would need to be laundered again.

"Go on, now, Dora. Go on home until tomorrow." Talbot Fleming slewed his words.

When she walked out of the back door and saw him, her eyes brightened. She placed her hand on his left cheek and kissed the other. When she saw his frown, she shook her head. "Don't let anything he says worry you."

He pulled away and walked on ahead.  She followed him.

"White folk are going to be white folk," she laughed. "The shirt is muslin. Muslin is yellow. It's going to always be yellow. He don't know," she explained. "He don't know a thing about it."

Theo turned around to face her. "Why didn't you tell him that then?"

"What for, so he can tell me to get my things and go? You want them to tell me to find work someplace else?  How will that help anything?"

Theo shrugged his shoulders. "It would just be better."

"It's better already," she ignored his fretting eyes and laced her arm through his. "It's better already," she repeated.

## Chapter Fifteen

"It's like this," Jimmy explained over dinner one night. "You got the Jews over there in Hollywood," he pointed towards Canada with his fork. "You got the Irish-Catholics down here on Wall Street," he pointed to the floor. "That's it!" He pressed his finger repeatedly on the tabletop like it was a one key typewriter.

"There's nothing left for the Colored folk, the niggers as you may say." He wagged his finger in the air, "not a thing but cleaning up the messes they make."

Theo kept his eyes on his food, careful not to let Jimmy see the disdain in his eyes. Every thought that fell from Jimmy's face was a regurgitated notion that he'd picked up in his elevator or at least as much as he could retain to twist into nonsense.

"Colored folks, they don't got a thing going for them," Jimmy shook his head. His fork hung in the air. The piece of roast beef that was had already fallen back to the plate.

He stabbed it up again and turned his fork this way and that, examining the meat carefully. "How much you pay for this roast, Dora Dear?"

He continued before she could answer. "See here? The next step down from this is going to be dog food." He shook his head sanctimoniously.

Theo couldn't help himself. He tried to control his laugher but it escaped. Jimmy stopped talking. He looked up at Theo as if he wanted to kill him.

"Just cause you about to be sixteen, a man I suppose," he grimaced. "Don't mean you going to disrespect me in my own house. Hear?"

Dora jumped in, hoping to change the subject and keep them from fussing at each other. "Theo has a job lined up. Don't you Theo?"

Jimmy clamped his mouth shut and tossed his fork onto his plate. He looked at Theo for an answer. Theo shucked his shoulders.

"I talked to Bell's uncle," he offered.

Dora explained. "He's going to help clean up one of them buildings on Washington Street in the evening," she smiled. "That will keep him busy over the summer."

"It's only for a couple of hours," Theo explained. "A couple of hours mean you got time to work in the daytime too." Jimmy picked his fork up. He pushed the food toward the middle of the plate before shoveling a forkful into his mouth. Dora clapped her hands together lightly before getting up from the table. She turned to smile slyly at Jimmy and Theo. They responded with queer looks in return until she pulled a cake out of the icebox. Jimmy pushed his plate out of the way and rubbed his hands together.

"What we celebrating?" He asked with a big grin.

Dora nodded at Theo, "Somebody has a birthday coming."

Theo immediately began to blush. Jimmy sat back and crossed his arms with a smirk. "I wish somebody baked me a cake for my birthday."

"I've baked you a cake many a time," Dora reminded him. She placed the cake on the table and stuck a handful of candles into the pink frosting. She lit them with a match from the stove.

"Go on, now. Make you a wish."

Theo closed his eyes for a second.

"Go on, boy," Jimmy growled.

Dora shook her head for him to hush. Theo tried to make a wish but he couldn't think of anything. He opened his eyes and blew the candles out. Dora kissed him on the forehead.

"What you going to do with that?" Jimmy asked him.

"What am I going to do with what?" Theo responded.

"The wish, fool! What you going to do with your wish?"

Jimmy wiped his fork off with his napkin and watched the piece of cake Dora cut travel the short distance across the table to be placed in front of Theo. He narrowed his eyes at her.

"Birthday boy gets the first slice," she reminded him.

She cut another wedge and placed it in front of Jimmy.

"I'm not saying," Theo answered Jimmy.

"It *is* bad luck," Dora agreed. "If you tell it, your wish won't come true."

"Bullshit," Jimmy answered. "Colored people's wishes don't come true no damn way."

He laughed out loud and kept laughing until tears came to his eyes.

Theo and Dora watched him in silence, both marveling at what a fool he was.

After dinner Theo went downstairs to meet Tony, Ray, and Bell. Bell was alone, sitting on the stoop. He reminded Theo of a boy in Tennessee who smiled all of the time. It was a good thing since Bell's teeth were so large they practically protruded out of his mouth. When he wasn't smiling his mouth still wouldn't close.

Theo climbed onto one of the pillars on either side of the steps. He shaded his eyes and searched the far end of the block.

"They're not coming," Bell told him.

"Why not," Theo asked.

The corners of Bell's mouth fell into a frown. "Police got Tony. They took him downtown. They're waiting on somebody to pick him up. And Ray's daddy found out he ain't been to school since November."

Bell hit his fist against his left hand, "His daddy beat him like he was a slave, man."

He shook his head mournfully. He grinned, even though a look of concern leaned more to his intention. "He's going to be busted up bad, man. He was looking like a rag doll. His daddy had him by the throat. I wanted to help him out but I can't mess with this face," he joked, running his finger lightly along his cheek.

Theo playfully tapped his shoulder. Bell responded with a straight face. "I'm serious man. This is all I got going for me."

"What did they pick Tony up for?"

"Listen," Bell adjusted the hat on his head. "Didn't today seem like a good day for a movie? I told that sucker not to go up in there! You know that store where you got your mama's tomatoes that time?"

Theo nodded his head.

"We was just in there last week." Bell held his hand up like a traffic cop stopping traffic. "Too soon. Too soon!"

He put his hands on his chest. "I have a gift, man. I can feel it when something ain't right. Tony doesn't know how to listen."

He shook his head. "They won't give him no time but they won't let him loose until his brother goes down there to take adult responsibility for him."

He looked at his watch. "If Artie don't get there before seven they will send Tony upstate for the weekend."

He shook his head again. "He won't have a bed." He counted on his fingers, "They'll beat him up real good on the first night and they won't feed him for two or three days."

He abruptly changed the subject. "Hey, man, you got a cigarette?"

Theo patted his pants pockets and shook his head, no.

"What time are we leaving tomorrow to meet your uncle," Theo asked.

"Round about four o'clock. He wants us down there by five."

Bell got up. "Alright, man, I got to see a man about a dog," he smiled.

Theo watched Bell walk away and then he pulled a cigarette out of his shirt pocket. He lit it with the lighter he'd stolen from a man getting off of the trolley the day before. He'd lifted it just seconds after the man lit a cigarette for himself and dropped it into his jacket pocket. It was still warm by the time Theo got hold of it.

He looked at it in the moonlight. It was silver in color with two eagles etched into the surface. The eagles appeared to be in battle above a mountain range. Theo spit on it and then buffed it against his shirtsleeve. He flicked it a few more times before closing it and dropping it back into his shirt pocket.

He practiced blowing smoke rings like Uncle Charlie did in Hitchcock's Shadow of a Doubt but his rings looked more like clouds. When he got to the end of the cigarette he flipped the butt into the street and then went inside to bed.

The next morning, Theo was lying on his pallet trying to ignore Jimmy who had perched himself on the corner of the chair to sermonize.

"Who got time to sleep? I don't got time to sleep. You don't got time to sleep," he called out to Dora. "If he got time, he can pull something over at the grocery store, bootblack down at the hotel or throw some newspapers or something."

Jimmy scowled at the boy. He ran the comb through his shining wavy hair, gently running his hand across the top to make sure the ripples were smooth and consistent. Theo rolled his eyes. Who could sleep with that nigger running his mouth, he thought. All he really wanted to do was get up and kick Jimmy's ass.

Dora was in the bedroom listening to Jimmy as she rolled one of her stockings on, twisting it tightly above her knee to stay in place. It was too early for Jimmy's bickering. One of the neighbors pounded the wall to shut him up.

It had been more than nine months since this unusual family dynamic had come together. She was trying desperately to keep it together but the threads were thin and barely holding. Jimmy banged the broom handle on the floor. His anger now aimed at poor Mr. Boykin who lived downstairs. Dora shook her head before reaching for the other stocking. She hoped that Mr. Boykin was already gone for the day since the neighbor who was banging the wall was from next door, and not down below.

Three more months would pass before the fragile arrangement would implode. It happened on a Tuesday night after the new school year started. When Theo walked in around seven,

Jimmy was sitting at the kitchen table in his uniform pants and undershirt. His jacket was hanging neatly on the back of the chair.

The creases in his pants were still sharp after working all day. Every few minutes he took the cuff and gave his pant leg a tug to keep it that way. Theo nodded a greeting and walked across to his bed.

"I don't want you bringing those hard heads in my house." Jimmy murmured. Theo sat on his bed and looked back at Dora Dear. She was folding clothes in the bedroom. She shook her head to indicate to Theo to ignore Jimmy.

"He's talking crazy," she mouthed the words.

She yelled out to Jimmy. "I'll have dinner for you all in about an hour. I got a good price on some turkey legs at the butcher."

Jimmy cut his eyes toward the bedroom before taking a sip of whiskey from a small jar that he was cradling in his lap. He tapped his finger on the rim and stared at Theo.

"How old you getting?" He asked Theo.

"You know he turned sixteen," Dora Dear answered.

She walked across the living room to the kitchen to check on her dinner.

Jimmy slammed his hand on the table. "If he sixteen, why you got to answer every time I ask him a question?"

"I'm sixteen," Theo announced.

His voice was deep and smooth, more confident Dora thought.

Theo had grown another two inches over the summer and that alone was enough to agitate Jimmy into a fight. A fight she was

141

certain Theo wouldn't back down from. She walked back to the living room to stand between the two.

"Look," Jimmy started. He turned his lips down and sucked his tongue against his teeth. "I don't believe in taking care of a grown man! This man is as grown as me. Look at you," he craned his neck to look around Dora Dear. "You *grown*, nigger!"

Theo pulled his sack from one of the crates under his bed. He stuffed his shirts and slacks inside but Dora immediately ran to his side to stop him. She turned frantically back toward Jimmy.

"What are you talking about, Jimmy. This boy is sixteen years old. He's not a man. He's not a man. He can't get out there on his own. Give him till he gets out of school at least."

She pulled a few of his shirts out of the bag and patted Theo's hand.

"You don't have to go nowhere. Don't worry, I'll talk to him."

Theo pulled his hand away and tossed the shirts she'd taken out of the bag back inside.

"Talk to him all you want. I never wanted to come here in the first place."

Dora stepped back. "Theo, you don't have to go."

He picked his bag up but when he saw his mother's face, he let it drop off of his shoulder.

Jimmy took another sip of whiskey. He watched Theo put his jacket on.

"Dora, honey," he whined. "Let the man grow up. You're going to ruin him pit patting on him like he's two years old."

Dora Dear turned back to Jimmy. "Where is he going to go?" She asked. "Where do you think he got to go? He lives here... right here. Where is he going to go?"

Jimmy chuckled. "I don't care where he goes."

He watched Theo walk past his mother with amusement. She reached for him but he pulled away.

Jimmy shook his head. "I couldn't care less."

He took another sip of his whiskey. "Not one bit."

Dora sat on Theo's bed. She unpacked the bag that he'd left there. She refolded some of the shirts then went back into the kitchen. She made Jimmy a plate piled high with turkey and potatoes. She poured enough gravy on top to turn the dinner into a soup just the way Jimmy liked it.

She carried the bowl across the room and placed it in front of him. He grudgingly turned in his chair to face the table and then he carefully placed a towel over his lap to protect his pants.

"I told you I wasn't taking care of nobody's kids," he reasoned. "I thought I told you that a hundred times. I don't take care of my own kids. What makes you think I'll spend money on yours?"

"I don't ask you for money," Dora reminded him.

She walked across the room and peered out of the window. It was already dark. She couldn't see if Theo was out front. Maybe he walked down to the store on the corner, she thought.

"Bullshit," Jimmy answered. "Lights cost money. Food cost money. Clothes cost money." He folded a piece of bread and dipped it into the gravy. "He's in my pocket regardless."

He wiped his mouth on the corner of the towel. Dora threw her hands up in defeat; there was no use. She went to the bedroom to fold the rest of the clothes. Jimmy went right on arguing and with no one to contradict him, in his mind, his argument grew stronger. She could see him from where she was standing. He waved his arm around in the air as if he was conducting the New York Philharmonic. A drink here a fork full there. Food flew from his mouth and off of his plate.

She turned her little transistor radio on to drown him out and finished folding the clothes. When she was done she opened the window to let some air in. The early autumn breezes were picking up off Boston's harbor. Winter would be coming soon. She leaned on the windowsill and stared into the distance. She wondered where Theo had gone.

## Chapter Sixteen

"Come on, man. Hand it here."

Bell reached for the cigarette the four of them were sharing on the rooftop. It was nearly eleven o'clock and it was getting chilly. Raymond, his face bruised from his father' latest beating shook his head when Bell offered it to him. He kept his arms folded around his thin jacket, too cold to want to move. Tony took a drag and then he returned to the money they'd stolen from the cash box at the bowling alley. It was only about twenty dollars. All of it was in coins since it was what the owner's wife used to make change in the kitchen. The larger haul that Raymond claimed they could have gotten was locked away in the office.

Tony shook his head, "You're trying to get yourself killed." He tapped his head with his finger and stopped counting the coins for a second. "Think about it. Trenton won't miss this chump change so fast. When he does he'll think Crystal took it. He already don't trust her."

He went back to the four piles of money, "Where was I?" He asked.

Theo pointed to the pile of change where Tony stopped counting. He'd been watching him divvy the money but knew that if he wanted to, Tony could slip half of it off the table without any of them even noticing. Instead of being a hustler, he could have been a magician. He was just that quick.

Bell looked down at the street. "Your daddy is in front of the building," he told Theo. "He's standing on the front steps. It looks like he's looking for somebody."

Theo knew Bell was talking about Jimmy. "If that little sucker was my daddy I'd jump off this roof and kill myself." He shook his head with a laugh.

Bell took a long drag from the cigarette. "I seen him around, man. I'm glad he ain't your daddy. He's about as big as a minute."

Theo playfully pushed Bell away from the wall. "He's with my mama but him and me is just a matter of time."

Tony looked up. "He looks like he got a little cash with all that gold in his mouth."

Theo thought about it before shaking his head. "I don't think so. He's one of them country boys who shine his pennies to make them look like dimes and still hold on tight enough to make you think he got a pocket full of silver dollars. He don't have shit."

Raymond got up and held his hand out for his share. "I gotta go or my old man will be out here looking for me."

"Do you want me to hold on to it?" Tony asked.

Ray shook his head. "No, I got myself a better hiding place. I don't think my daddy will find it."

"It's your mama you need to worry about," Bell teased him.

Tony laughed. "Man, you better watch your mouth talking about somebody's mama."

Ray shook his head. "I ain't worrying about Bell." He pushed Bell's shoulder. "He has problems of his own."

Bell stuck his chest out. He laced his thumbs under his armpits as if he was wearing suspenders. "My old lady don't drink but my young lady do!"

It was a joke but they all knew that Bell was known for fooling around with older women while his girlfriend Freda stood by to collect the money they gave him.

Tony handed each their share and they parted, promising to meet the next day at Tony's.

Theo stayed on the roof for a while and finished the last of the cigarette alone. He knew his mother was downstairs fretting over where he was but he didn't care. He pulled his jacket closer around his neck. He thought about Naomi.

"What you doing up here?" His mother was standing in the doorway. He dropped the cigarette to the ground out of her sight and mashed it with his shoe.

"I sent Jimmy down to look for you awhile back. I think he felt bad..." she trailed off.

Theo looked away, certain she was exaggerating.

"I heard your friends leaving down the stairs. I figured you'd be down directly."

When he didn't respond, she continued. "Did you eat?"

He nodded his head, yes.

She came closer to the wall and took a quick glance over before gingerly resting her arms on the ledge. The sky was black dark with only the brightest stars shining through the clouds. Someone was playing Double Crossin' Blues on the record player in one of the rooms down below.

"Somebody likes Little Esther," Dora remarked.

She sang along with a few of the words, laughing at herself before she finished the first verse. She hoped it would change Theo's mood, but he stayed quiet.

"We were worried about you."

Theo laughed out loud when she used the word, we. "What for?" he asked. "Is Jimmy missing more change?"

"He never said you took his money," Dora reasoned.

"I tell you every time it happens that I don't take his money." Theo responded indignantly.

"That's true," she answered quietly. "I believe you."

"Why do you give him money if you believe me?"

"Sometimes it's easier than fighting."

The record player whirred to the end of the song. They listened as the arm lifted and carried itself back to the beginning to start over.

"What are you going to do with yourself?"

"I already told you. I'm joining the army."

"Until then, I mean. What are you going to do with yourself until then, Theo?"

He shrugged his shoulders.   She waited for a long moment then told him. "The school sent a letter today."

Theo looked away. "I've been to school."

"The letter says you been missing.  It says your grades are low."

He wanted to throw up. "I don't care what it says.  I'm going to the army.  What do I need school for?"

She nodded her head. "You might be right but running the streets isn't such a good idea..."

"Who said I was running the streets?"

"What have you been doing with yourself all day?"

"Maybe I'm looking for work," he shot back.

She hesitated for a moment. "I'm your mama, Theo."

He shrugged his shoulder.

"Well, I do the best I can," she retorted. "I don't want to see you get into trouble, that's all."

"Don't worry about me. I've been fine all this time." He turned and walked past her.

She followed him down the stairs but when he passed the door to their apartment she called after him.

"Where are you going Theo?

"He didn't answer. She followed him down for a few more steps but when she heard the street door slam shut she realized there wasn't much she could do. She leaned against the cool railings and closed her eyes. She said a silent prayer and hoped the Lord was listening. Despite her desire to remain steadfast tears sprang to her eyes. She let them flow silently down her cheeks. Standing there in the hallway alone she wished she could just disappear. She looked up through the stairwell to the fifth floor ceiling. She wondered how far up God really was... too far to hear her she imagined.

She wiped her face with her shirtsleeve and went back inside. Jimmy was propped on the corner of her couch trimming his toenails.

"Niggers and flies," he curled his lip with a nasty laugh. "Niggers and flies. If you looking for shit, follow the niggers or follow the flies!"

Dora walked on by him. She stood at the window and hoped with every ounce that he would just be quiet for a change.

"I told you to leave it alone," Jimmy advised her. "You should have left him where he was. There's no telling what that boy is getting into. I'll tell you one thing, if you can't get a hold on him, I will."

She ignored him. Big talk, that's all he was. She looked out over the buildings across the street and into the black distance. She thought back to when her troubles began, all borne from one warm and lazy afternoon seventeen years ago. All coming from one slimy, snake-in-the-grass named Jesse Boy Minor. He was the cause of her having to give up her dream of becoming a nurse and the cause of her and Eliza pulling apart and never truly coming back together again. He was the reason she took up with Jimmy. She thought they were alike. And now, Theo was turning into a hoodlum because Jesse was too sorry to stick around to help raise him.   Over the years her heart had secured a safe and quiet place for Jesse Minor. Now the memory of him seemed more like a cancer that was lifting like bile from the pit of her stomach.

She ran to the kitchen, barely making it to the sink. Her stomach heaved every ounce of dinner into the basin.

"What the hell?" Jimmy jumped up to follow her.

He switched the light on. "God damn it, Dora! What in the hell is wrong with you?  Ever since you let that boy move up in here we have had nothing but trouble! I told you, didn't I? I let you know right from the get go, wouldn't be nothing but a pain in my ass."

He'd started with a roar but now seemed to be whining. "I won't have it. I can't stand it. What's wrong with you throwing up your food... all around here crying? What's wrong with you Dora Dear?"

She was bent over with her head against the sink. It hurt too much to look up but she could see him there with his hands on his hips, his tiny legs sticking from below his under shorts like burnt, brown, tree branches. His flat feet were pointed this-a-way and that-a-way like a fork in the road.

Her silence made him mad all over again. He pulled himself together, stomped his foot and pointing at Dora, he screamed.

"You bet NOT be pregnant!"

He hit the light switch with a bang. Then he tramped through the living room and into the bedroom. The door slammed with a loud clap.

Dora eased herself to the floor to sit against the wall in the darkened kitchen, where finally, everything was quiet.

## Chapter Seventeen

Theo walked the seven blocks or so to Tony's apartment. When he knocked, someone he didn't know answered the door. Before letting him in, the man turned to check with Tony's brother, Arthur, who nodded that it was ok.

There was a card game going on in the front room and Arthur's girlfriend was in the kitchen making bacon and eggs for everybody. Arthur spoke around the cigarette that was dangling at the corner of his mouth. He pointed the deck of cards towards the back room. "He back there," he gestured for Theo to go on back.

The bedroom had one bed set up along the far wall and a bare mattress was on the floor. There were boxes all around the room filled with enough candy and trinkets to open up a five and dime, which is about what the apartment was during the day. Everything in the boxes had been stolen from the store where Arthur ran deliveries.

One time he'd emptied the whole truck and then cut himself on the forehead to pretend he'd been robbed. He liked to tell the story, which broadened with every telling. Either the cut or the amount of merchandise got larger and larger.

"I'm out here, man." Tony waved Theo out to the fire escape.

He handed Theo what was left on his plate and then lit a cigarette.

Theo wrapped the bacon and egg inside the piece of bread. He ate it without a word.

"They're going down to the Bay later tonight." Tony blew a perfect smoke ring. "You want to go?"

Theo shrugged his shoulders. He didn't know what the Bay was but he didn't care.

"Will he let me go?" he asked about Arthur.

Tony nodded. "He don't care as long as you don't eat in his new car. Have you been upstate before?"

Theo shook his head, no.

"It's a couple of hours. We won't get back until late."

Theo shrugged his shoulders. "What time are we leaving?"

Tony stood up. He leaned around to the front window. "Hey Artie, what time are we leaving?"

Theo could hear Arthur in the front room talking trash to the others. He heard him slam his cards to the table with an apparent win. The other players groaned.

Arthur yelled back to Tony. "Right now, man. No better time than the present."

Theo walked across the fire escape and leaned on the windowsill next to Tony to peer inside. The cigarette smoke in the room made it look like a fog of blue, which along with the yellow light coming from the kitchen, snapped a permanent image in Theo's mind. He would remember it as the calm before the storm.

"Who's going?" Artie asked. He gathered his cash off of the table.

Dee Dee, one of his friends, shook his head. "I believe I'm going to pass on the liquor run."

Artie shot back. "What are you talking about?  This ain't no small time boost, Dee Dee."

He waved his arm around the room. "I'm upgrading this operation. Do you know how much money I can make selling shots of liquor?"

Dee Dee waved the opportunity away.

Artie dismissed him with a pivot. "Suit yourself my man. What about you, Tommy."

Tommy stood up.  He searched through the clothes on the couch for his jacket.

"No man, not me. They don't take to Negroes up Kings Highway. Why won't this cat bring the truck down here?"

"I told you, man.  He's not coming this way. We're going to get up there and be back before you know it."

He tossed his hands at Tommy. "You cats don't know when a good opportunity is knocking on your door."

Tommy looked at him skeptically.  His hand was already on the doorknob.

"What's going to happen when he shows up at his work place with half his load missing?" He asked.

Artie laughed. "We're going to knock him around a little bit to make it look authentic."

Tommy shook his head and laughed. "I wish I could, but I told my old lady I was going out to buy cigarettes and that was four hours ago."

"Oh, shit. You're in trouble." Artie reached into a box and pulled out a pack of cigarettes. He tossed it across the room to Tommy.

Dee Dee followed Tommy out the door.

Everybody piled into Artie's brand new Buick Roadmaster. Tony, Theo, and Artie's friend Bennie, climbed into the back seat. Anna May, his girlfriend, rode up front. Bennie quickly settled in for the ride. He fell asleep nearly as soon as they started out. Pattie Page was on the radio.

"Change that damn channel," Artie said. Then, he quickly shoved Anna May's hand away and turned the knob himself. He found Bukka White, who was whining through the tail piece of *Aberdeen Mississippi Blues.*

*Shout Baby Shout* came on next, and when Artie started singing along with L. C. Williams, Tony, Theo and Anna May chimed right in. When the station went out of range Artie fiddled with the knob to try to reclaim the station but all he got was static. He ran the knob up and down the dial trying to find anything that would come in clearly. He had to settle on a station where the DJ talked more than he played music. Artie argued at the radio as if he was having a one-on-one conversation with a real person.

"Don't nobody care what you talking about!" He admonished the DJ. "Play the damn song, man."

When he finally found a station playing *I Like My Baby's Pudding* they all started singing again. Anna May cracked a pint of whiskey open and passed it to the back seat.

Artie warned them, "Don't drink too much. That's just to keep your feets warm."

He laughed and reached for the pint almost as soon as it had been passed to the back. Both boys took a swallow before handing it back. Anna May grabbed it out of Artie's reach just as quickly.

"What you doing, Anna May?"

"My feets is cold too." She wiped the bottle top before taking a sip. The taste of it made her wince but she nevertheless nodded her head emphatically. "Oh, yeah," she said before taking another sip.

They finally arrived at the cutoff about a mile past a diner on Highway 6. Artie's friend was leaning at the back of his delivery truck. They all climbed out of the car and walked over the packed sand to the truck.

The roar of the ocean and the wind from the surf caught Theo by surprise. He hesitated for a second before searching the blackness until his eyes adjusted to what looked like the edge of the earth.

Artie laughed at him. "Look at this little pumpkin head. He's never been to the ocean before?"

Theo shook his head, no.

Artie pointed over the water. "You got your France. You got your China. You got your Africa." He waved his arm. "If you get in a boat you can sail around the world right from here."

Theo walked a few steps closer. He could make out the white foam and feel the mist from the water spray lightly across his face. He was in awe.

Artie shook his head in amusement before turning to the business at hand.

"Hey, Doc," he said. "What we got here?"

Doc opened the rear doors of the truck. It was stacked high with crates of whiskey, gin, vodka and rum.

He climbed up and started handing the crates to Artie who handed them down the line to Bennie, then Tony, then Theo. Anna May opened the trunk of the car and directed Theo as to where to place the crates. They were able to load six crates plus another twenty or so separate bottles in every empty nook in the trunk or under and around the seats up front.

When they finished, Doc jumped off of the truck, closed the doors and secured the latch. He tossed the padlock as far as he could into the distance and then he pulled the gold cover off of his front tooth and put it in his pocket.

"Alright, man. I'm ready."

He steadied himself by spreading his legs slightly. He tilted his head for the first punch.

He gave one final directive. "Try not to knock any of my teeth out."

"Come on, man!" Artie disagreed. "How can we guarantee that?"

"Just try, man, damn!" Doc steadied himself again.

Bennie stepped in. He socked Doc in the stomach with a clean right jab. Doc fell against the truck and after several more punches he fell to one knee. Bennie picked him up and holding him steady with one hand pressed against his shoulder he threw a punch to Doc's face.

"Sorry, man," he said before throwing Doc to the ground.

Bennie stepped back so Artie could help him back to his feet. He waved Tony and Theo over. He told them. "Come on, everybody got to throw a lick."

Theo stepped up, reared back and landed a punch to the side of Doc's head. Tony danced around for a second before throwing a one-two combination.

"There you go," Artie said as he counted the money.

He stepped forward to move the boys aside with his arm. He helped Doc up from the ground and handed the money over. Doc took it.

"I think one of you all broke my finger, man." He grinned, unable to contain himself despite the blood coming from his mouth and nose. He checked his teeth and was satisfied that they were all there.

Artie took Doc's hand and turned it over to inspect it.

"You want me to pull it back in place?"

"Naw, man. It hurts like shit but it'll be better like it is."

"Alright then, I guess we'll catch you on the flip side." Artie walked Doc back to the front of the truck and helped him climb inside.

"Let's get out of here," he told the others.

They all climbed back into the car with a sense of odd satisfaction. Tony was shadow boxing as if he'd been in the ring for an hour. Artie started the car and turned to back out of the opening. He nodded at Tony.

"I taught that boy everything I know." He turned back to the road. "I raised that boy from a piglet," he explained. "When he was born he was pink like a piggy, squealed like one and smelled like one too," he laughed.

"Shut up, man." Tony yelled. "You always tell this story." He turned to Theo. "It isn't true, man." He pushed the seat with his foot to get his brother to stop teasing him.

"How you know it ain't true? You was a pig! You didn't become human until you was about three... maybe three and a half."

"Go on, man. If you're going to tell it, go ahead and get it over with."

"He don't like to hear the truth but the truth will set you free. He was about this high." Artie held his hand over the seat.

He maneuvered the car back onto the road before continuing.

"Playing in the dirt, you know, like little piggies do. Daddy gone... been gone and your Mama acting a fool with big old Butch running in and out of the place like he the Daddy."

"We don't have the same mother," Tony explained to Theo.

Artie laughed. "Shit! We might not have the same daddy, neither! But like I say, I raised him from a piglet. Damn sure did."

"Pull over, man. I got to see a man about a horse." Bennie broke in.

"Come on, man, damn! I just did get back on the road good. Why didn't you take care of your business back there?"

"Hey, man. I can't tell my faucet when to run."

"Can't you wait until we get on the other side of the bridge?"

"For damn sake, man, I can't wait! We're far enough away. They're not going to pick up on that boy till the morning."

Artie checked his rear view mirror and after a slight hesitation he pulled the car onto the side of the road.

Bennie climbed out and walked off. After a few seconds, Artie opened his door.

"Shit," he said.

He climbed out and followed Bennie. "If you got to go, now is the time," he called back to the car.

Tony and Theo followed. The four of them stood there facing the beach.

"What time is it?" Artie wondered out loud.

Tony checked his watch. "It's almost six-thirty." And just as he said it, a tiny slither of sun peeked above the horizon across the ocean. It shot across the surface of the water with a blast. Theo's mouth dropped open. He looked at Tony. Tony smiled and then he ran down the hill to the beach. Theo ran after him.

"God damn it! Tony! Get your ass back here." Artie threw his hands up in dismay. "See what you did, Bennie?"

Bennie laughed. "What did I do? All I did was take a piss."

"Come on, Anna May," Artie called.

They all walked down to the beach where Theo and Tony were dodging the water and chasing tiny crabs, which were faster than they were. Artie took his shoes off. He tested the water with his toe. He turned back to Anna May and Bennie. "It's not too bad," he said.

He shook his head with a laugh. "I'm lying. This shit is colder than ice."

Nonetheless he rolled his pants up and stepped into the water with a scream.

"I'm a man's man!" He beat his chest like an ape.

He held his hand out for Anna May. She shook her head and stepped further away from the surf.

"Come on, Ben. You get used to it."

Bennie shook his head. He looked back up to the street where the car was parked.

"Come on, man. We ought to get on back."

"Alright man. Give me a minute."

He looked down the beach to where Tony and Theo had wandered. He yelled for them but the sound of the ocean was too loud for them to hear. He walked out of the water and fell onto the sand to put his shoes back on. When Benny uttered the word, "Fuck..." Artie knew something wasn't right.

Anna May breathed. "Oh, shit."

Artie turned to look in the direction of his car. The dark shadows of two policemen were standing at the ridge, both of them with their hands on their hips. When Artie, Anna May and Bennie got up the hill one of the officers was standing next to the opened back door of Artie's car. The liquor bottles shined brightly in the light of his flashlight.

The officers put handcuffs on all three and when a backup officer showed up a few minutes later, he drove over the dune and right onto the sand to pick Tony and Theo up.

When Theo and Tony saw the red police lights, they both ran. "We got to split up, man!"

Tony didn't give Theo a chance to disagree. He cut toward the dunes near the street. The police car veered to the right and followed him. Theo kept running across the wet sand. His heart was beating like a piston but he didn't look back and he didn't stop until he saw the bridge. He climbed the rocks near the wall and crouched low to the ground to catch his breath. He looked back.

The sun was rising over the water but it was still hard to see far off. He climbed further along the wall until he was under the bridge where he was hidden out of sight. Although the water was receding it was still high enough to lap against his sneakers. He tried to climb higher but the rocks were slippery. He clung to the bearings of the bridge and waited. He looked down at the dark water certain that he saw something moving around down there.

Something with eyes, with fangs... something that reminded him of when he was small and traveling alone on the train. He closed his eyes and held his breath until his lungs burned. He was hungry and scared but too afraid to move. He wished he could go back to earlier that night.

Why hadn't he ignored Jimmy? Why didn't he go in when his mother asked him to? He watched the sun brighten to a clear cool day and still he was paralyzed with fear. It felt like hours had gone by. He knew he couldn't stay there forever. He took a deep breath and with a pounding heart he shimmied back the way he had come. He peeked over the rocks just in time to catch one of the police cars swing around to the bridge road. Doc's truck was next and then two more police cars followed.

From where he was crouching, Theo could see Doc, Artie and Bennie in the back seat of the first car. Anna May and Tony were in the last one. Like strangers crossing in the night Tony and Theo caught each other's eye as the car passed. They simply stared at one another until the car moved on. A tow truck with Artie's car on the back followed about ten minutes later.

Theo didn't know where he was or how to get home. He had no other choice but to start walking. He climbed over the rocks and walked across the sand to the road. The ocean was still loud and the beach was undoubtedly still beautiful but all he could hear was the loud cry of the seagulls, mourning for him he was sure.

When he finally made it to the top of the bridge he controlled the strong urge to run. The other people walking across the bridge were white men on their way to work in the city and colored people walking in the opposite direction on their way to clean houses and watch babies.

He walked for hours and after awhile he realized he was the only one on the road, the others having made it to their destinations. He was thirsty and hungry and his legs felt like lead but he kept going. Finally, someone pulled over to offer him a ride. He accepted without a second thought.

"Where you headed," the elderly black man asked after Theo climbed inside.

"Roxbury," Theo responded.

"Me too," The man said.

Thankfully, that was all he said. Theo fell asleep almost as soon as the truck pulled back into traffic. The next thing he knew they were at the corner on Brookline Avenue. The man nodded his farewell.

Theo walked the few blocks to Dora's apartment and when he unlocked the door no one was home. He climbed onto his bed and tried to sleep. Every sound made him jump. He was sure the police would knock on the door at any moment but finally he slept.

When he opened his eyes it was the next morning. Dora was in the kitchen. Jimmy was sitting across the room hitting the side of his shoe with a shoe brush, flipping the shoe from one side to the other every minute or so. It was a practiced motion. So much so, that Jimmy didn't have to monitor the movement. Instead, his eyes were trained on Theo as if it was his job to make sure the boy didn't run.

Theo didn't move. He stared back until Jimmy rolled his eyes and put the shoe on. He slammed the door on his way out of the apartment. Dora came around the corner. She walked across the living room and looked out of the window to catch Jimmy walking out of the building. She stood there for a few minutes before taking a seat where Jimmy had been sitting.

She breathed in heavily before telling Theo that she'd bought him a bus ticket. She looked down at her lap. "Your aunt Eliza said it's a room come available in her building."

Theo didn't move. It wasn't a surprise. "When do I leave?"

"In the morning," she answered.

Her eyes were dry even though he could tell she'd been crying. She folded and refolded a ragged piece of tissue as if she may burst into tears at any second.

"I guess Jimmy got his wish," Theo said as he rolled over onto his back.

"You didn't help, son."

He wanted to respond but he suddenly felt the urge to cry himself. He turned toward the wall.

"All night you went missing. He was out looking for you. I was out looking for you." She took a long pause. "I know you've been through some things but I try my best. It isn't so easy as you think."

She walked over and sat on the cot beside him. She ran her hand over his hair, raking her fingers gently through it.

"I suppose I set the example," she said. "I should have stayed on track. It may have made it better."

She folded her hands in her lap. "The only chance you're going to have is your schooling... or else you'll only have what they give you. Jimmy don't think so but it's true. You don't want to end up like him or me, working too hard for too long. There's no dignity in it, son."

She stopped talking. Theo waited for her to continue but she didn't. She got up and went into the bedroom to get ready for work.

Later that afternoon, Bell called for him from downstairs. Theo ignored him. After a few more calls from the street Bell came up to knock on the door. Theo didn't move from his bed and after a while he heard Bell make his way back down the stairs.

That night after Jimmy and Dora Dear had fallen asleep Theo got dressed and slipped out of the apartment. He walked the few blocks to Tony's place. He was hoping to find them there but the apartment was dark. When he knocked, the door creaked away from the jamb. He pushed it and what he saw made his mouth drop open. The couch was cut across the top, its stuffing pulled out and strewn around the room. The chairs from the card table were thrown in every direction and the table had been tossed on its side. The curtains at the window were blowing through the opening as if Theo thought, they would run if they could and that he should do the same.

He ignored the warning and stepped inside. His foot crunched over the peanuts that Artie sold for five cents a bag. They were all over the floor. Most of them were crushed from the weight of whoever carried what they wanted out of the apartment. He picked the lamp up off of the floor and set it right side up before making his way as quietly as possible toward the

166

bedroom. He peeked around the corner but the bedroom was too dark to see anything.

"Tony," he whispered.

"Don't move." A voice came out of the darkened room and then a shadow as big as the door emerged through the opening.

It was Dee Dee, Artie's friend from the card game.

"If you're coming to take something you're late," he said.

He held a bottle of brandy up. "This is all they left."

He took a swig, nearly tottering off of his feet in the movement.

Theo followed him out to the hallway.

Dee Dee held a finger up before descending the stairs. He stepped back to pull the door to. The wood was splintered and the doorjamb was broken. The door squeaked away from the closed position as soon as he let it go. Dee Dee pulled it again with a loud bang.

"Come on, man." Theo whispered. "You're going to wake up the whole building."

He took Dee Dee's arm and helped him down the stairs and out to the street. Dee Dee handed the bottle of Brandy to Theo who took a tentative sip. He winced. It tasted like wood with a bitter bite. He tried to hand it back but Dee Dee pushed it away.

"Go on Man." He seemed to be sleepwalking. His eyes were half closed and he was speaking nearly without moving his lips.

"It'll get better to you."

He helped Theo lift the bottle to his mouth again. Theo tilted his head back. He held the alcohol in his mouth for a second before swallowing a bit at a time. Dee Dee took a moment to explain.

"Some folks like their brandy with a tiny bit," he held his fingers apart by about an inch, "of ginger ale on ice but if you know what you're doing you're going to drink it just like that, straight up."

He gestured for the bottle. He wrapped his big hand around it to balance it in the palm of his hand. He steadied himself with one hand on Theo's shoulder and moved the one holding the bottle in a circular motion.

"You warm it up in your hand. Give it a little sniff."

He put his nose close to the bottle top. He nodded his head with satisfaction before turning the bottle up for a drink. Dee Dee pointed his finger at Theo. "Don't ever forget it."

They stumbled along the empty street in no apparent direction. After more than an hour Dee Dee abruptly stopped in front of a stoop.

"This is where I live," he said it as if he was as surprised as Theo might be.

Theo looked around at the building. He pulled back. "Are you sure?"

Dee Dee stepped away. He checked his watch as if it may somehow support his theory. He nodded his head. "Yes. This is where I live."

He took a step up but lost his balance. Theo caught him before he fell to the ground.

"You got any money?" Dee Dee asked. Theo shook his head, no.

"Artie and them, they're going to need some cash to get out from up there." He shook his head mournfully. "I told them not to go up Kings Highway, didn't I?"

Theo didn't remember but he nodded anyway.

"The only folks they want up that way are the ones cleaning their toilets."

"And cooking their food," Theo added.

"And cooking their food," Dee Dee agreed.

He patted Theo on the shoulder. "And cooking their food." He repeated.

Dee Dee grabbed a hold of the banister and pulled his way up the three steps to the first landing. He turned back to hand Theo the bottle of brandy. He swirled it around in a circle. "Remember. Warm it in your hand and don't put no ice in it."

Theo took the bottle and watched Dee Dee climb the rest of the way to his front door. Once he got inside, Theo walked away cradling the bottle in the crook of his arm to keep it warm. He took a sip every couple of minutes. The taste was turning from tart and woody to a more pleasant and warm marmalade.

By the time he got to his mother's building it was nearly five o'clock, too late to go to sleep since he was due at the bus station in a few hours. He left the empty bottle down by the front door and climbed the stairs. He unlocked the door and slipped inside without a sound.

On the way to his bed he caught sight of Jimmy's prized uniform hanging on the back of one of Dora's kitchen chairs. Theo picked it up and carried it out the back door. He stuffed it into the basin that Dora used to wash the floor with and then he tiptoed back inside for the bottle of bleach. He poured until the bottle was empty.

A few hours later he smiled when he hugged his mother goodbye. She was relieved that he was taking the decision well and was not at all aware that he was actually imagining the mottled patterns that the bleach was forming over the gold braiding and dark wool uniform that Jimmy prized so dearly.

She fought the urge to pull him back as he climbed aboard but she straightened her back and remained steadfast. The doors closed and the bus roared and belched into a slow amble away from the curb.

The feeling of loneliness washed over her. Her heart slowly sank to the irreconcilable place where the hearts of all mothers one day fall as they realize their children remain so only in their dreams.

When the bus finally turned the corner onto Cambridge Avenue, she gathered herself together and headed back the way she had come.

## Chapter Eighteen

Six hours later the Greyhound bus pulled into Penn Station at 34th Street in New York City. Theo waited as the other passengers climbed down to the street, and watched as they were each greeted by their family and friends. He was in no rush. All he had was a slip of paper in his pocket with his aunt's address: 773 Seventh Avenue at 130th Street, 3rd floor, Apartment B.

The bus driver called back to him. "This is the end of the line." He lit a cigarette. "This bus will be headed on to Pittsburgh in about an hour and unless you want to go to Pennsylvania you're going to want to be on your way by then."

The driver hefted his weight around the steering wheel and gearshift before carefully stepping, one step at a time like a two year old, down to the ground.

Theo grabbed his bag and made his way off the bus. He wandered for a while around the station. The familiar rumble of the trains coming and going at the lower level gave him an odd feeling of ease. He watched them for a while from the main floor before following the arrows that led out to Broadway.

When he stepped outside and looked up he couldn't help but walk around in a circle. He was amazed at the size and beauty of the station. It took up the whole city block and rose a hundred feet in the air. Twenty massive pillars stood like soldiers along a waterfront battlefield. It looked like nothing *he'd* ever seen before but the people going in every direction stepped around him as if the station was just a minor distraction in their daily lives. He wanted to stay there all day.

After several hours of meandering about he set off for his aunt's house. He crossed over to Times Square then up to

Midtown and finally made it to Harlem.   Every ten blocks he saw something new; the architecture, the people, the smells or the languages.

Just before dark, he found the building.  It was a dingy six-floor walk up with a few raggedy cart boxes and an old kitchen chair sitting along the sidewalk out front.  The chair had cardboard aligning the seat and the mold of someone's rear end was creased into the corrugated paper.

Theo walked through the courtyard and went inside.  At the second landing, a little woman mopping the floor told him that if he was looking for Smithy, he wasn't in 5C no more.  When Theo didn't answer, she raised her voice several octaves.

"Smithy ain't in 5C no more. Are you looking for Smithy, boy?"

"No Ma'am. I'm going to 3B. My aunt lives there."

"Oh," she continued loudly. "You're looking for Eliza. She's not home."

She shook her head as if it was normal for Eliza to be gone.

"Her girl is there. Go on up and knock for yourself."

The woman waived Theo out of her space.  When he knocked at 3B the door swung open before he finished the third knock. His hand was still in mid air when his cousin CeCe greeted him.  Her hands rested on her narrow birdlike hips and a smile as wide as the cat rimmed eyeglasses that she wore spread across her face.   Theo didn't remember ever meeting her but he learned rather quickly that she was his favorite cousin and that they had in fact traveled many miles together as younger children.  He was apparently not the only one to be shuffled from one relative to another.  She wore tight pants, conked hair and the black-rimmed cat glasses with rhinestone studs in each corner.  If he'd ever imagined a Negro movie star, she'd fit the template.

172

"Talk to me, cousin," she grinned before cocking her head to one side. "Sit down here and tell me what you been doing?"

She patted the couch before flopping down herself.

"And please don't tell me they call you Othello. You might get beat up if you go around with that name for too long up this a way."

"They call me Theo. That's my name."

"Fancy prancy names may go over in Bean Town but here in the great state of Harlem you're going to have to follow a different rule, my man."

Theo smiled incredulously. He shook his head. "My name is Theo."

Cece got up and steered Theo onto the couch. It was the only place to sit in the living room.

She explained, "Who you telling? It might be what you think your name is but they named you Othello. "

When she saw his brow furrow, she waved the notion away.

"You go by Theo... that's fine with me. Better, even."

She hopped up and headed toward the kitchen but just before turning the corner she twirled around like a drunken ballerina.

"Are you hungry?" She asked. "We don't have no food but we got plenty of water!"

She laughed out loud at her own odd humor.

She leaned against the wall. "Your Aunt Liza..." she advised him, "she'll be home from church after awhile. She'll cook up something nice for you."

She always referred to her mother as everyone else's something or the other.

"Your Aunt Liza. Your sister Eliza. Your friend Eliza." But never "My mama."

It was peculiar but so was she. "Your Aunt Eliza goes to church more than the preacher. I don't go in for too much holy rolling. How do you like that cousin Othello... I mean, Theo? Do you go to church? I would imagine you do. You seem like a polite type of a young fellow. You're out of school by now aren't you? You look like you might be. I don't know."

She waved her hands out in front of her as if she wasn't trying to pry but continued, nonetheless. "You understand? I'm just saying, you look like you might be on this side," she gestured with her left hand, "of edge-u-ma- cation."

Theo tried to answer her questions but found it was easier to nod or shake his head. Eventually he didn't even bother to do that. He just stared at her until she was finished. She was no bigger than a ten-year-old but her mouth ran like a locomotive.

## Chapter Nineteen

*Frank Lee found him at the lake. He was sitting on the newly built dock. One leg was hanging below the pier just above the water. The other was pulled close to his body, his arm resting easily over it. He blew a plume of silver smoke into the moonlit sky. Its homemade bouquet seemed more like the aroma of a cigar than a cigarette. It tickled her nose as she came closer.*

*She walked silently to the edge, to lean at the far corner of the post. It reached just above her head. He noticed her hair escaping from the braids, as colored children's hair will do. It was fuzzy like a halo with a mix of curls and waves all exclusively set by God's intricate weave. With her bare feet she pushed a pebble from the dock into the black water. She watched as the moonlight caught the ripples as they ambled slowly across the inky pool.*

*She stole a glance at his silhouette, darkened by the light from the boathouse. Though her heart beat like a hammer in her chest, she mustered the nerve to whisper the one question she dared not ask her mother.*

*"Are you my father?" She kept her eyes on the water and could feel her hands begin to sweat. She hoped he hadn't heard and for a moment was convinced that he hadn't. She had often been accused of mumbling her words and was for the first time elated that her shy ways had come to some good.*

*She wanted to run but her legs wouldn't move. Her heart rattled in her chest. His voice was low, just barely audible above the crickets and bullfrogs singing in the woods around them.*

*"We live by the rules of our society," he said.*

*She could feel him peering at her through the short distance. Her face shone in the light of the boathouse and to some satisfaction he found his own mother's lips and high cheekbones clearly etched into the child's face.*

*Before looking off into the distance he added. "And we die regrettably deficient."*

*He flicked his cigarette into the water. Its singe melted into the air, replacing the sweet smell with a burnt one. Frank Lee was too young to understand the meaning. In fact, the moment seemed surreal as if it never really happened. For years later she imagined it to be a dream but she could always remember the odd smell of his homemade cigarette.*

# Chapter Twenty

*Down Home Prosperity*

I slept most of the way, dreaming of the sweet scent of green apples, which pretty much amounted to my 5-year-old recollection of South Carolina. Mr. Clovis drove the whole way with only one stop at a side street gas station. The people at the station let us fill the car with petrol but they wouldn't allow us to use their toilet. They eyed us suspiciously and when Sissy asked where the bathroom was they pointed to the field across the two-lane blacktop.

Their children, both with the same lopsided mushroom shaped haircuts, stared at us oddly. Their clothes were the color of slate and I couldn't tell whether they were boys or girls, or one of each.

We were somewhere south of Richmond and the whole bunch was proof enough to recognize that the south was far different from what I could recall. We climbed back into the car without another word.

We arrived in Prosperity early in the morning to find to Ludie's utter chagrin that Adele wasn't even at home. Juney said she'd left the night before, "heading off to the four corners for all I care to know."

While we waited, we ate corn fritters and orange syrup with our fingers. Ludie was angry beyond repair. Her dish sat beside her, being buzzed over by flies. I had never seen her in such a state. She sat straight as a board in the rocking chair on the porch. Its spindles set still by her rigid stance for nearly an hour.

The rest of us watched the crooked dirt road that ran out to the black top in silence. Waiting for Adele and I supposed for Ludie to get past her anger.

"She don't tell me nothing," Aunt Juney defended herself.

Not that she had to. Her promise to take care of Adele was supposed to have been for only a few months but had grown to more than ten years.

"I told her I don't know how many times to stay away from them boys. Ever since Jake pulled up from out of here she's been acting like a wild Indian with her hair on fire." Juney shook her head mournfully.

Her arms were stained a strange dark blue. Sissy said it was the mark of indigo set there when Juney was a young girl working on an indigo plantation. The stain had marked her arms with a permanent tattoo that looked like a pair of long gloves that reached to her elbow. Gloves like one would wear to a fancy place except that they were blue and not made from white silk or lace.

She said she was a lucky one even to survive as most folks in those days lasted for only a short while before dying.

"Daddy had us sprinkle a bit of sand over in it,"

Juney rubbed her fingers together to show us. "Kinda like sprinkling a bit of sugar in your tea." Her eyes closed and she paused for quite awhile.

She was young Sissy said but she was like an old woman. I watched her in awe. She wasn't sleeping. She spoke with her eyes closed.

"Premium is what they paid for but they got taken most of the time. It was the worst and foulest smelling concoction you would ever care to get a whiff of," she shook her head. "Twas't good on your lungs nor your eyes but you sure wasn't worried about the yellow fever. No critter nor even a mosquito would come near you for the stench."

Ludie wasn't paying her no mind.  Sissy and Mr. Clovis were sitting in the car looking out at the fields for as far as their eyes could see.

Juney started humming a tune. After awhile, the melody had her swaying gently back and forth. She was lost in thought to a time in her life long gone. I thought about Adele.  She was fifteen and clearly not keen on living out her life in Newberry County.  Her pleading notes and dramatics had done nothing to convince her mother to allow it until rumors floated north saying that she was hanging around with a man named Johnson Bowles.

Johnson was a nineteen-year old laborer.  He worked about as much as a cat swims in water.  His own family had nothing to do with him and his wife was known to cut anybody she thought was sharing his bed.

"I didn't raise you for all these years just so you could take up with a fool like that boy," were the first words out of Ludie's mouth when Adele finally sauntered home at nine-thirty in the morning.

It was the first time they had laid eyes on each other in nearly seven years.  Ludie glared at Adele until the smile on her daughter's face faded away.   I was sitting on the bottom step, grateful that Ludie's anger wasn't trained on me.  I looked at my cousin and was immediately confused.  She looked like a full-grown woman with breasts and hips, and long legs that I could see through the dress she was wearing.

I tried but couldn't capture even a glimpse of the girl who cleaned my fingernails up on the tall bed so long ago.

"What kind of mess is this?" Ludie was asking.  "You're staying out all night with God only knows who."

Juney opened her eyes and nodded her head. "Um huh." she said. "I have been telling her."

Then Adele, borrowing from the good sense Johnson Bowles had given her, crossed her arms pursed her lips together and offered the most minor degree of information needed at that particular moment.

"I been with Johnson," she said, and then to the astonishment of everyone there she looked down at me and winked.

The flash of her mother coming off of the porch was like a bolt of lightning. She pushed Adele across the yard with so much force it brought with it a gust of wind.

"You think I been working all these years so you could get laid up with some fool who don't got enough sense to pour water out of a boot even when the writing on the heel is telling him how?"

She held up her hand when Adele tried to respond. "You been wanting to come to New York well you're going to get your wish. Then you'll see what it's like working for them white folk up there. Then you'll see what it's like living in them rooms with heat melting you in summer and the cold freezing you in winter. You'll see. Uh huh. You'll see for yourself, for sure."

Adele let her head drop, with the hopes that her mother would believe her to be repentant. From my vantage point, I could see a smile spreading across her face. She was finally getting what she'd been wanting for her whole life. Her only problem was Johnson Bowles' baby growing in her belly.

No one knew she was pregnant, including Johnson. He was the last person who needed to know because he'd demand that she stay and marry him. Adele knew that would be a bigger mistake than letting herself get pregnant in the first place. She looked at her mother, who was still talking.

"Yes, Mother," Adele agreed, sounding as mournful as she could.

The next day Adele and I were in the back seat giggling like schoolgirls. Sissy sat beside us with a blanket over her head to keep out the sun. She and Ludie had gone out with their cousin Precious after supper the night before. Ludie got home around two o'clock in the morning but Sissy dragged in after breakfast. She hadn't even bothered to come in the house. She just climbed in Mr. Clovis's back seat and pulled the blanket over her head. She fell asleep, snoring loudly and stinking of root rot moonshine and stale cigarettes. She didn't wake up for the two hours it took to drive the distance to the dirt road that led back to Papa Jake and Jasper's property.

Their new house was set away back in the woods where a good number of Negroes lived on plots they thought they were buying. They were all, for the moment living in ignorant bliss with their chests stuck out proud to be landowners like the white folk. Years later, as the city proper grew and the land became more valuable, they would be told by a sorrowful enough looking representative of the bank that they had in fact only been leasing the land.

Like so many houses before this one, Papa Jake built it with his own hands. He started it off as one room but added on where Jasper supposed there should be a second room, a third and so on.

It was raining when we arrived. The ground around the front porch was muddy. An odd assortment of old tools and a rusted tractor rested around the edges near the trees. Papa Jake sat on the top step stuffing tobacco into his pipe. He smiled when he spotted the car. He waited there for us to climb out and up the stairs to greet him.

"What are you all doing this far down in the country?" He smiled while hugging each of us.

He held me at arm's length. "And look at you, growing like a flower."

Sissy pulled the blanket from her head.  Like a dead woman coming to life, her perfect hairdo from the night before screamed in all directions.

"She eats enough," she remarked while unceremoniously climbing out of the backseat of the car.

"Well," Papa Jake nodded his head. "I'm happy you all came so far out of your way to stop by."

He made his way to his feet. "Let's go see Jasperella. She won't believe her eyes."

Jasper was standing at the indoor spigot in the kitchen.  She was washing pole beans that she'd picked from the backyard garden a few minutes before.  Her face was the same as I'd remembered. She was heavier now and happier it seemed but certainly the same quiet woman I faintly remembered from years before.

She covered her mouth when she smiled and then she held her arms out to us.   We stayed overnight and the next day Papa Jake held on to me for a long time, asking more than once whether I'd like to stay there with him and Jasper. "I know how much you like Jasperella's pecan pies."

Sissy shook her head. "Is you crazy?  Where is she going to go to school down here?  She'll be starting at the sewing school as soon as she gets back.  How is she going to get a trade in backwards assed South Carolina?  Get in the car, child.  She won't be staying no matter how good Jasper's pies is."

With a laugh, she threw her hand at the lot of us.  She was feeling better.  She climbed into her spot in the front seat, ready to be the boss all the way back up the road.  Papa Jake laughed wryly.

"Don't listen to your mama. That city of yours has plenty more uneducated Negroes with high school diplomas than down here with no schooling at all.  If you want to, you can stay right here and be just fine.

"He hugged me one last time before letting me loose.  I settled in the back seat between Ludie and Adele, who were still not speaking to one another.  Jasper and Jacob waved from the top step as the car pulled away from the house.  I didn't look back. I could still feel his arms around me.  I fell asleep with the powerful feeling it gave me.

# Chapter Twenty-One

In New York, I was given the task to show Adele what was what and who was who. It wasn't long before she knew more people than I did. She tickled the fancy of everything she touched. She never met a stranger and she laughed at me when I suggested we stay in for a change. I thought I had died and gone to heaven.

We spent every moment together, either at Sissy's apartment or at Ludie's. At night we sat on the fire escape for hours, watching the comings and goings of everybody on the block. We saw husbands slip out and wives tip around the corner.

We watched Maxine on the first floor fight with her boyfriend, until one time she ended up knocking his front tooth out with what she called her nigger stick. Adele relayed the story to Sissy and Ludie the next morning.

"She swung that stick like it was a baseball bat. It popped that tooth right out of his mouth. It flew through the air like a baseball at Yankee Stadium." Adele twisted her body to simulate the boyfriend's near stagger to the ground.

"Before she hit him he was dancing around like Sugar Ray Robinson but when the stick cracked across his mouth," she deadpanned. "It sounded like a homerun to me!"

"Homerun," Ludie shook her head in disdain. "She better homerun out of there before he grabs that stick and whips her with it."

Sissy turned her lip up. "He should be happy all she broke was a tooth. Everybody knows that gun she totes in her purse can back up whatever her nigger stick won't."

Sissy was getting ready to go out, either to the Mandalay Bar in the basement of the building or to Small's Paradise down on a Hundred Thirty-Fifth Street.

We'd know which one depending on if she pulled her thirty-dollar mink stole out of the box that was stored on the top shelf of her closet. She saved the mink for fancy places. She wouldn't need it if all she was doing was going to the bar downstairs.

Adele gave me a silent smile when Sissy reached for the box. She pulled the furry creature out of its hiding place and wrapped it around her shoulders with a wide swing. The stole, along with the set of pearls she'd taken from one of her employers when they wouldn't pay her right were prized possessions. She wore them whenever she wanted to play it rich.

She dared anybody to touch either one. She smoothed her dress down along her hips and thighs and gave it a tug to lie just below her knees. She had on a shiny pair of high-heeled pumps that matched the dress perfectly. The little mole above her lip that she called her beauty mark was rounded out with an eyeliner pencil to a perfect circle. She winked at us as she gave herself a last look over in the mirror.

She was as pretty as a movie star. Pearl was out of town. She said they had an understanding and even though she mixed and matched her beaus around his schedule, she remained a steadfast believer in maintaining her independence.

"Never let anybody hold you back," she advised us. "And," she paused as she pressed a creased piece of toilet paper between her lips with a smack. "Don't wear red. It'll make folks think you're a street walker."

"Aunt Sissy," Adele laughed. "I've seen plenty of women at church wearing red."

Sissy turned away from the mirror. "That don't mean they're not street walkers, baby. That just means they're wearing to church what they wore out on Saturday night."

When she left, we climbed out onto the fire escape to watch her emerge from the front of the building. Everybody out there stopped to watch. The guys whistled and the women immediately fell silent as she breezed on by. Sissy held her head in the air, her nose tilted just high enough to let them know that she made her own rules and damn them if they couldn't understand.

We could hear her high heels clickety- clacking on the sidewalk. She raised her gloved hand in the air to hail a cab.

Pearlie wasn't the only man she had a crush on. Mr. Monroe, who lived across the street, was another one that Sissy couldn't get enough of. On Thursday nights we'd catch her sitting on the stoop late after midnight waiting for him to come home from his late shift at the hospital morgue.

"Hey stranger," she'd say, as he passed the building.

He always jumped back, pretending to be shocked at her being there. She would try to get him to stop to talk to her. "Come sit with me for a while?" she'd ask.

"We already tried that, Miss Sissy," he'd joke.

"You and me, we're sort of like oil and water ain't we?"

"She crazy about that boy," Adele would whisper.

I shrugged my shoulders and took another sip of my soda pop.

"I know she'd better hope Pearlie don't come around that corner."

"What Pearlie don't know, Pearlie don't need to know."

"Let's go down and sit with her," I whispered.

"Hell, no," Adele hissed. "I'm not going down there for her to cuss me out."

We watched Mr. Monroe reach inside his jacket pocket. He took a pack of cigarettes out and offered one to Sissy. She wagged the one she was smoking in the air.

"He isn't all that cute anyway," I remarked.

"How cute you think he got to be for an old man? Shoot, when I get as old as your mama and my mama, I guess I'll be happy with a bullfrog!"

From where we were the light from the street lamp floated in dimming layers to the street, casting Sissy and Mr. Monroe into what looked like one-dimensional cut out dolls. The smoke, mingling around them from their cigarettes reminded me of the plume of flour that danced around my grandfather when I was little.

When Mr. Monroe finished his cigarette he flipped it with his thumb into the street.

"I guess I'll be getting on," he said. "It's been a long day." He laced his thumbs under his suspenders and waited for Sissy to dismiss him. She watched him for a while before saying, "So long, then, Ronnie. So long..."

She dropped the cigarette she was smoking onto the step and twisted it out with her shoe. She pulled her sweater tighter around her shoulders and watched him walk away. She was lonely and she didn't care that Ronald Monroe thought he was too good for her. He strutted around like a Mister Big Stuff because he had a job working down at the hospital with dead folk but he wasn't so special with his smelly hands and bad haircut. Just because he had a penchant for ordering top shelf bourbon the two or three times that he'd taken her to the Lenox Lounge didn't mean shit.

She stood up. "Don't ya'll gals have school in the morning," she said up to the fire escape.

She didn't even say it that loudly. She could always tell when we were there, whispering above her head about grown folks business.

She stepped off of the stoop and followed Ronnie languidly across the street. My hand flew to my mouth. I looked at Adele and narrowed my eyes at her.

She laughed. "You talk too loud," she advised me. "Don't know a thing about a whisper."

"That was you talking, not me."

"Shit," Adele smirked. "Let her have her fun."

It wouldn't be long before Mr. Monroe moved away after the hospital hired some white fellow to do his job a few months later. After all, the war was over and a lot of colored people were being replaced at their jobs by returning soldiers.

Adele returned to school after more than two years running wild in the south. She would be starting in the senior class even though she could barely read. Her mother talked the Principal into letting her start in the top year so she'd have a high school diploma. She convinced him that it wasn't Adele's fault that she hadn't been to school. She blamed it on the South so the principal agreed to let Adele stay. By Christmas break she had stopped going, not because she couldn't learn or because she was more than four months pregnant, it was because she couldn't wake up in the morning.

Every night she snuck out with our cousin Deeda May to 125th Street where all the late-night clubs were. If she couldn't get Deeda May to go, she'd begged me to go along.

"Come on, Frank Lee," she'd whine, pulling on my arm and trying to drag me from the covers and out of bed.

I tried to be the voice of reason. "I have school in the morning and you do too!"

Sissy was out on a date with Mr. Porter a man she'd been dating lately and Ludie was working out on Long Island. Sissy had warned me more than once to stay put and I knew she had Mrs. Bailey, the neighbor down the hall, checking on me.

Adele threw her arms in the air. "You know your mama won't call that bitch this late at night. That lady won't come over here just to see if you're in your bed. Come on and go with me. I promise we'll be back before your mama gets home."

When she saw that I wasn't about to budge she changed her tactic.

"Didn't I go with you to see that crazy movie with the lady stuck in the bed getting ready to get herself killed?"

I knew she could and would go on like this for hours. It was only a matter of time. It was easier to give her what she wanted than to listen to her whine or pout about it for days afterwards.

I climbed out of the bed and grabbed what I'd worn earlier that day.

"Oh, no you're not." Adele grabbed the skirt and blouse from my hands.

"I got something for you to wear. You never know you might get lucky if you dress up a little bit."

I blushed. "I don't know why you act so silly over them boys like you do. Number one," I counted on my fingers, "All you know is what they tell you. They could be lying from the minute they open their mouths. They probably got the law, wives, children, all sorts of mess following behind them."

Adele twisted me around to button the back of the dress that she had pulled over my head while I was trying to make my point. I looked down and smiled.

"Wow!" I breathed.

I ran my hands across the front of it.

"Your new dress. I didn't know Deeda May finished it. Does your mama know you're wearing it before Sunday?"

"Deeda May fixed it too tight around the middle," Adele grumbled before grabbing my hand and pulling me to the living room.

She pointed at the floor to where her new blue patent leather pumps were.

"You're going to let me wear the shoes too?" I gushed.

"They go together, Frank Lee. And you better not get them dirty, neither."

I slipped into the shoes and before I could get the buckles fastened Adele was pulling on my hair, pushing the stray strands back around my ear. I stopped her when she started to take the braids out. She pushed my hands away and pulled the comb from somewhere like magic.

"I won't do nothing fancy." She looked around to check on my silent opinion. I rolled my eyes and crossed my arms. She shook her head.

"You don't have to worry about being pretty."

Before we left, she dabbed lipstick on my lips and pinched my cheeks.

"Ouch!" I protested.

"Look here," she lowered her eyes at me. "I'm sick of people asking me if you're a white girl.  At least now, you got a little color."

I double checked the door to be sure it was locked and hid the key under an old pair of boots that had been propped there since before we moved in.  I followed Adele down the stairs on tiptoe, making sure to hold my breath when we passed Mrs. Bailey's door.

It was after eight o'clock but kids were running around outside as if it was the middle of the day.  Miss Hicks was at her window.  Her fingers were laced around a coffee cup that everyone knew was filled with Schlitz malt liquor. She kept the bottle on the floor and when her cup got low, she'd lean down out of sight to refill it.

We walked around the corner from the courtyard and ran into Cece.  She lived in the building next door.  A toothpick was sticking out of the corner of her mouth and her short hair was conked to the side. She looked more like a twelve-year-old boy than a seventeen-year-old girl.  She eyed Adele and me up and down as if she was the boss of Tammany Hall and we needed her permission to pass.

"Well..." She said slowly. "Where do you think you're going this late in the evening?"

Adele stepped back and put her hands on her hips. "I'm trying to figure out why where we're going is any of your business."

Cece hopped down from the step. "Don't you know it's too late for good girls to be out in the streets?"

Everybody in the building and all along 163rd Street gave her a hard time for wearing dungarees with button down shirts and ties. They called her a bull dagger behind her back and if you let her, she could talk till Sunday. When I asked Sissy what a bull dagger was she told me it wasn't nothing I needed to know nothing about.

Adele took another step back to get a better look. Cece straightened her tie for the inspection. She leaned to the left, stuck her left foot out in front of her right and transferred the toothpick from one side of her mouth to the other.

Adele studied Cece's outfit. It didn't matter that she had just recently come up from the south where it was widely regarded as a land of poor Negroes with bad taste. She still considered herself to be a fashion icon. You couldn't put it past her to remind you that the swing skirt was in style but the bobby sock was not.

"How you like me now?" Cece asked with a grin as wide as her face.

Adele fanned her away. There was obviously not enough time to help.

"Listen here," she said. "We're grown just like you and your little boyfriend there."

She jutted her head toward a boy who was leaning against the basement railing a few steps away. Cece chuckled. It wasn't often that anyone responded to her annoying prattle. She was more than willing to take a few insults in order to keep the conversation going.

"These mean streets don't care how grown you is. They'll eat you up one side and down the other."   She tilted her head to one side to indicate that she was about to reveal something clever.

"I know you read about that gal up in Hollywood getting cut up?" She raised an eyebrow. "She was grown... she was colored too. Just like you.  Me and my cousin, we'll walk with you."

She waved the boy forward. "We don't mind. Do we, Theo, my man?"

Adele didn't believe her.  She shook her head.  "I read about that gal," she said. "She wasn't colored. They called her black Delilah... or something like that because she wore black clothes and her hair was black."

She laced her arm with mine and we started to walk away. "I don't think you need to worry about us. We can take care of ourselves but," she stopped and turned back to Cece. "The streets... they're free. You can walk wherever you want.  I'm not the boss of nobody."

Adele and I sashayed toward the corner.  Cece's cousin silently watched us as we headed up the block.  I could tell he was young but his eyes looked old, like they weren't afraid of anything.

My preoccupation with him took me off balance.  I stumbled behind Adele for a second, nearly scuffing her new blue shoes. By then Cece had grabbed her leather jacket off of the post and jerked her head forward for her cousin to follow.

They trailed behind us all the way up Eighth Avenue and then across to 125th Street.  Cece jabbered the whole way.  Every now and then Adele stopped to give her an earful but my own voice was lost in thought over the equally silent boy.

According to Cece's non-stop chatter, Theo had just arrived from Boston by way of Tennessee. He would be living with her and her mother until Mr. Mooney's rooms were cleared of his belongings. She told us that Mr. Mooney died in his sleep but not in his own bed. She raised her eyes dramatically. She added, with a wink, that everybody should have known that Mr. Mooney and Miss Alberta had been sneaking around, "ever since Miss Alberta's husband left to go back to Charlotte."

Adele stopped. She turned to say, with a look of utter disbelief, "I have never heard of nobody leaving here to go back down south."

"She was right. It wasn't often that folks left Harlem to go back down south, although there were plenty arriving every day. Sissy always said folks were searching for their pie in the sky and streets paved in gold when they came to Harlem.

She said they never would find what they were looking for. We all run up here, she'd say and after awhile we all wish we stayed where we came from.

At the corner of Broadway and 125th Street, Adele and Cece got into a long debate over why they should or shouldn't walk with us the whole way and then back again.

Adele waved her hands and shook her head. "No, no, now. You don't even know where we're going! This is far enough. We don't need a bodyguard."

The two of them went back and forth with each other for more than ten minutes.

I peeked at her cousin. He was standing a few feet away with his hands held loosely in his pockets as if he was bored.

"How long have you been here?" he asked me.

I stepped closer to him, almost losing Adele's shoe off of my left foot for the second time. It was one size too big and the toilet paper she'd stuffed in the toe had worked its way out and into the arch of my foot.

"I've been here ever since I was five." I answered. "I moved here on my birthday."

I wanted to bite my tongue out for saying something so stupid.

"When is your birthday?" He asked.

"Oh, um, September. It's already passed."

I could feel the blush rise to my cheeks as soon as I said it.

He smiled. His teeth were perfect like Pearl's. The lights on the street made his dark eyes dance with glitter.

Before I knew it, Adele pulled me across the street. Cece and Theo stayed on the other side. Adele had apparently won the debate.

"What were you talking to that boy for? You know your mama would skin you alive if she caught you talking to some boy. You're not but fifteen." Adele reminded me.

I blushed and shook my head in mock distaste. "I wasn't talking to him. He was talking to me."

She thought about it. "He might make a nice little first boyfriend for you."

I stopped, shocked at the idea. "I don't like that boy! We weren't talking about anything."

I had to turn away from Adele because I couldn't control the smile that was spreading across my face.

"Uh huh, see there? You better be careful before you end up like me."

As soon as she said it, she realized her mistake. She quickly changed the subject. No one knew she was pregnant and even though I'd covered for her as a guard at the washroom door when she threw up a time or two it hadn't dawned on me until now that she was going to have a baby. I stared at her quizzically but she refused to answer. She quickened her step ahead of me.

When we got to the Savoy, Plaxico let us in without paying. He was from Prosperity and had known Sissy and Ludie since they were all children. He liked Ludie and we knew she liked him even if she would never admit to it.

"Plaxico is a married man!" she'd exclaim with a wink just so we'd know that some things were better left unsaid. They were always making eyes at each other and whenever they got close they'd touch hands or smile quietly, as if their secret was safe.

We found a table and waited for Teeny to make her way over with two soda pops. "What you all up to tonight?" she asked.

"We're alright," we answered in unison.

"Have you seen Stanley?" Adele asked.

She squirmed in her seat to check every corner of the small club. Teeny smiled and nodded her head towards the bar. Adele craned her neck to see around the crowd. I sipped my pop. So long as Sissy wasn't there it didn't matter to me who was. Within seconds Adele was on her way across to the bar. She promised not to be gone for long.

The next time I saw her she was jitterbugging across the floor. Her legs were high in the air in one second and then her under drawers flashing in the next. Her new swing skirt was

197

apparently doing what she paid for it to do. They called her a tart in our building but to let her tell it, she didn't give a damn.

I smoothed my hair down across my shoulder. Quickly, so no one would notice. Having straight hair was a goal worth achieving if you got it that way with a straightening comb. If you were actually born with it you had to be careful not to look like you were bragging about it. You could get into a fight real fast if you flaunted around or swung it like a white girl.

When I asked Sissy why my hair was straight or why I was light skinned she told me her grandmother was an Indian. She said she didn't know what tribe. I knew my father was probably white but my Aunt Ludie only admitted to knowing that he *looked* white.

I was lost in thought when I glanced up. Plaxico was standing there smiling at me. He held a short glass of bourbon in his left hand, his pinkie finger with its bouncing diamond ring sticking out to the side.

"Hey there," he smiled. "What you all up to tonight?" He asked, leaning forward to hear my reply.

I knew he was being polite. He could barely care what we were up to. Aunt Ludie was the topic of all of his conversations even if her name never came up. His gold tooth glittered when he smiled.

"Oh, we're just having a little fun." I smiled.

"You look really cute with your hair down like that." He nodded.

I felt my face blush red but I struggled to accept the compliment like a lady.

"Thank you, Mr. Plaxico."

I stared at my soda and waited for him to leave.

"How's your auntie?" he asked, leaning closer across the table.

"She's ok. She'll be home this weekend," I offered.

He stood up and nodded as if he couldn't wait. Then he waved like a window washer before side stepping away through the crowd.

By the time I was on my third pop, Adele fell into the seat beside me. She was drenched with sweat. Her hair no longer resembled the pageboy she'd carefully crafted before leaving home. She pulled my drink over and took a long gulp.

"I could dance with that boy all night!"

I looked across the floor where she nodded towards a tall fellow who was smiling in our direction.

"Oh, he's so cute! Don't you think?" She asked.

"He has nice teeth," I nodded my head in agreement.

I let her ooh and ah for another five minutes before pointing to the watch on her arm. It was nearly ten thirty and I had to go to school in the morning.

"All right," she reluctantly agreed.

We inched through the crowd until we made it to the front door and out to the cool night air. We headed back the way we'd come, skipping and stopping along the way so she could fill me in on yet another notion about Stanley. She couldn't stop talking about him.

We made it more than halfway home when Adele suddenly pulled me with her to lean at the corner of a building. She groaned that she had a cramp in her stomach. She laughed about it at first but within a few seconds she was in too much pain to move. Her forehead was suddenly awash in sweat.

"What's wrong with you?" I grimaced.

She eased herself down to sit on the sidewalk.

"What's wrong?" I asked again.

"My stomach... I got cramps! I think I'm about to be sick."

Her face grew ashy and tears sprang to her eyes.

"What do you want me to do?" I squealed.

I'd do anything. I looked around, desperately wishing to take back my agreement to go out with her in the first place. I could be at home, warm in my bed but instead I was out here in the street surely inching closer to Sissy and her belt.

"I told you we should have stayed in tonight. I told you I have to go to school in the morning. I told you!"

"Won't you shut up? Damn!"

She clenched her teeth together and then stumbled to her feet. Tears were running down my face by now and my heart was beating like a drum. It seemed like it took forever to get back to the neighborhood because she could only take a few steps at a time.

When we got within a block she tried to walk on her own. I wiped my face and tried to look normal. If we didn't, by morning the whole building would be buzzing about the probable cause of the little gal in 4C needing help to walk.

When we got into the stairwell, she took one step at a time each one seemed more painful than the last. We made it to the first landing and then the second.

I was scared to death that Sissy would come home and find me gone but I couldn't leave Adele alone. When we passed our door on the third floor, I listened to see if I could hear anyone inside.

I shook my head and whispered, "I don't think she's back yet."

We made it to the fourth floor but within a few steps inside the door, Adele vomited all over the small hallway. She crawling into the kitchen and pulled a basin from under the sink. She squatted over the basin and within a minute or two the secret she had been hiding aborted from her body.

Her eyes were as wide as saucers and mine probably were too. I helped her onto the couch in the living room. I went back and grabbed the basin and scrambled into the stairwell with it. I dumped it along with everything in it down the incinerator. I did it without thinking. Anything to get whatever it was out of sight.

I ran back to the apartment and cleaned the floor. I tossed the rags I used into the incinerator too. Adele watched me from where she was lying. I covered her with a blanket and sat beside her until her eyes finally fluttered closed.

I quietly closed the door and then tiptoed down to our apartment. When I got there the door was now open, just ajar enough as if someone opened it for me. My heart beat like thunder as I silently pushed it open and stepped inside. The lamps were off but I could see light from the street through the doors of Sissy's bedroom. Mr. Porter was telling her to shut up or he'd slap the black off of her.

I leaned into the shadows of the kitchen. Sissy wouldn't shut up for nobody and Mr. Porter answered her rebuttals with hollow punches. I involuntarily stepped further into the kitchen and ended up under the counter where we kept the hotplate. There was usually a curtain covering the hollow but I'd taken it down earlier that day to wash it.

I closed my eyes tightly. What should I do? I covered my ears.

My mind raced, searching for someone to run to for help. Ludie was gone and Adele was sick. Would Sissy want me to find help from somebody in the building? I suppose if he killed her she wouldn't mind but if not she'd be damned mad if I put her business in the street.

It seemed like hours but in fact within minutes, Mr. Porter pounded past the kitchen and out to the hallway. I squeezed further into the recess hoping he couldn't see in the dark as well as I could.

I don't know how long I sat there but the next thing I knew Sissy was dialing the telephone, calling Plaxico's. I heard her ask for his brother Dominick but before he came to the phone, she put the receiver down and rushed to the door to lock it.

I climbed from under the counter and stood there. She didn't even turn around when she heard me.

"Bring me some ice," she said before returning to her bedroom and closing the door.

I scampered for the pick, opened the icebox and chipped a few chunks from the block. I wrapped them in a dishtowel and carried it to her bedroom. She was lying on the mattress in her nightdress. The blankets and sheets were on the floor near the window. Her back was to me. When she heard the door open, she lifted her hand to accept the ice.

I rushed to my bed and pulled the covers off. I carefully laid them over her and then I climbed into the bed with her. I wrapped my arm around her waist and waited for her to pull away but she didn't.

The next morning I quietly slipped out of her bedroom. I got dressed for school. Her doors stayed closed for two days and when she came out I could see traces of the bruises Mr. Porter had left on her face and arms. I pretended she was normal. Mr.

Porter never came back around but whenever his name came up Sissy would curl her lip and laugh as if he'd gotten what he had coming.

Don't ever let nobody kick you down, she told me once. "If one of them hits you one time, they keep on 'til they kill you."

Ludie came home for good that weekend. Her Long Island family let her go after she requested extra money for watching some neighbor's kids.

She told us, "Money is money but one of them kids is like the devil! He'll stare you in the face and turn his food over onto the floor if he's not in the mood to eat it. I watched him scream like a monkey for thirty minutes just because he didn't want to wear a particular pair of shoes one morning... and they want to drop their asses off like I have the patience for two more bad assed children. The two already there are bad enough. Shit," she laughed.

"I bet you these twelve dollars right here." She pulled a small wad of bills out of her bra and unfolded it for us to see. "That heifer will be calling me to come back before the week is out."

She was right. The mother changed her mind and started calling Ludie to please come back the next day. She blamed the whole thing on her husband and promised to pay Ludie whatever she asked.

Ludie held the telephone away from her face. With a smirk, she shook her head. She transferred her weight from one leg to the other before putting the telephone back to her ear.

"I would love to come back, Miss." She rolled her eyes and checked her fingernails. "It's that..." she lied. "I already found a situation."

When the woman told her what she would be willing to pay, Ludie brought her hand to her chest in mock surprise. "Why that's nearly double what you was paying me, Miss." She gushed. "No, Miss." Ludie said about her fake new job. "The hours are day time and they only have the one and he's no trouble, just the sweetest little fellow. I come home every evening to be with my Adele. Adele, Miss? She's my daughter, Miss... yes. I have a child. Yes, I do." Ludie paused again.

"That's alright, Miss. I don't expect you to remember that I have a child of my own." When she put the handle back onto the receiver she did a little dance in the middle of the floor. We celebrated with a piece of her pineapple cake.

Everything changed after that. Adele calmed down considerably and just before Thanksgiving she and Stanley announced their engagement. She announced it just like that, hadn't bothered to tell me first. I left the apartment too excited to be mad and too mad to be part of the celebration.

I found a spot on the steps outside their apartment to pout. When I heard footsteps, I pretended to be finding the chipping paint on the wall engrossing enough not to have to greet whoever it was. When I looked up, it was CeCe's cousin Theo.

He asked me if I wanted to go to the roof to share a soda pop.

I looked at him oddly.

"The roof?" I asked.

He shrugged his shoulders. "I go up there all the time. The roof in my building is always locked.

"Okay," I answered.

He held his hand out and helped me to my feet.

I'd never been on the roof. Stepping out onto the black top made my stomach feel funny. He pointed across to where a bit of the streetlight shined.

We walked over.

"I read or sometimes I just sit up here to think. One time I fell asleep." He smiled and handed me the soda.

He shoved his hands into his pants pockets and watched me take a sip. I motioned to hand it back but he said he'd bought it for me. He stooped and picked a small stone off of the black tar. He tossed it above his head a few yards before catching it easily in his cupped hands. He told me about the room he had next door.

"It's the one that Mr. Mooney lived in before he died. It's not so bad since they left some of his stuff up there."

He counted the things he inherited from the old man. "An icebox, but I can't afford to buy ice," he smiled. "A chair and a chest of drawers. An old trunk full of old magazines, his daughter or somebody came and took his bed I think. It was gone when I moved in. But I like the magazines," he smiled. "Maybe you can come up sometime, before I go?"

"Before you go?" I asked.

"I'll be leaving soon," he said. "My friends from Boston and I, we're joining the Army."

I looked away at the sky across and beyond the buildings on the other side of the street. It was early evening. The sky was an odd mingling of pink and yellow. The pale and almost fading full moon floated just above the dancing horizon waiting it seemed for its chance to brighten the darkening sky.

I pointed at it. "My grandfather calls that a sugar moon."

Theo smiled. "Sugar water moon," he smiled. "My Aunt Sula says it's supposed to light up the sky."

I studied him. "I didn't know you were old enough to go to the Army."

He shook his head. "I'll be seventeen but they don't care how old you are if you look old enough."

"You don't look old enough to me."

He touched the faint line of hair on his upper lip and deepened his voice. "Well," he smiled. "I'm glad you're not the one I have to convince."

"Why do you want to go to the army?"

He shrugged his shoulders. "They pay for college and I'll get to travel. I'll end up messing up if I stay here."

I was impressed that he wanted to go to college. I didn't know anyone who did.

"The Army has a thing that lets you sign up with friends. We'll all go to boot camp together and get stationed in the same place."

"Overseas," I whispered.

He leaned on the pillar and spit through his teeth over the side.

"Probably," he answered.

I leaned against the pillar beside him. He smelled like lemons. When I smiled at him he reached out and held my hand. After awhile he turned and kissed my cheek.

"I have to go back down." I wasn't lying, "My mother will be looking for me."

We held hands down the stairs until we got to Ludie's landing. He turned and kissed me again before saying good night. When I told Adele the next morning, she lowered her forehead in my direction.

"That boy better go to the army before your mama finds out he been kissing on you. Lord, have mercy!"

"He'll be leaving next month."

"I thought you had to be out of high school before they let you join the army? He sure don't go to school no more."

"He goes to school," I defended him.

Adele sucked her tongue against the roof of her mouth. "Not unless they teach school to Negro boys on the corner! Please, now. I know I don't go myself and all and don't have too much room to talk about it but he sure hasn't been to school since I been here."

I shrugged my shoulders. A lot of boys were dropping out of school to go to the army. Adele went on and on. I pretended to listen but I was daydreaming about my new boyfriend and nothing she was saying could change my mind.

## Chapter Twenty-Two

On Saturday Adele and I were out front, standing in the sunny part of the courtyard. Stanley was balancing on the rails that led down to one of the basement units.  He was teasing Adele about her new hairdo.

"It makes your head look like a poodle," he said apologetically.

She crossed her arms and frowned at him.  He jumped down and grabbed her around the waist to twirl her around.

"Stop it before you mess it up!" she laughed. "Then you'll be going in your pocket to pay for it to get done all over again."

"Hell," he threw his head back with a laugh. "Just stick your finger in the socket up to your bedroom. You'll get the same thing for free."

They could go on for hours back and forth like that. I pretended to laugh along with them but I could barely contain myself because Theo had captured my eye.

He was across the street, sitting on a car that was parked at the curb tossing a baseball from one hand to the other.  Cece kept tapping him on the shoulder, trying to get him to pay attention to what she was saying but he was finding me more interesting.

"There you go again," Adele grumbled when she saw me smiling at Theo.

She pushed Stanley away and turned around to yell across to Theo.

"Will you go on out from here, boy?"

He shook his head, no.

That made her mad enough to curse. "That damn nigger." She furrowed her brow.

"Come on, baby." Stanley pulled her back to him. "Leave the little love birds alone."

She snatched her arm away. "Didn't I tell you to stop hugging all over me out here?" She huffed.

"Baby," he whined. "What's wrong?"

I took the opportunity to walk out to the sidewalk.

"Frank Lee..." she called my name sternly as if she was somebody's daddy.

I walked a few feet further away. Theo hopped off the car. He began to match my steps on his side of the street. Cece was still talking, not yet realizing that her audience was no longer there.

"Frank Lee..." Adele called me again, this time much louder and even more demanding. "Keep it up..." she sang. "Keep it up."

I ignored her. My eyes were on Theo. By the time Cece realized he was gone. He was halfway down the block. She called after him. Her hands were out in wonder.

"What the hell is going on," she queried.

I quickened my step further down the block and when Theo stepped off the curb to start across the street to where I was, I took one last look back at Adele before holding my hand out to him.

I could hear Cece yelling for her cousin.

"These are them gals you want to stay away from," she bellowed.

"Don't nobody want that raggedy mangy cousin of yours." Adele rebuffed.

Then she hollered out to me one last time. "I'm telling your mama!"

Theo and I laughed as we ran towards the subway station. By then Adele and Cece were long behind us. My heart felt like a huge vibrating walnut aflutter at the idea of defying everyone and everything.

A train was waiting at the platform when we got there. Only a few people sat here and there. Each with their assortment of bags clutched close to their bodies; their faces with far away looks hoped that we wouldn't disrupt their quiet survival on this chilly afternoon.

I sat on an empty row of seats and Theo sat across from me. His dark eyes were as clear as glass and his chin was almost square but it had the smallest cleft etched into it. His hands were large and crossed peacefully in front of him.

I thought they looked like piano playing hands, which was a strange thought because I didn't know what piano playing hands looked like. He winked at me and after a moment I winked back. When the train started moving, he got up and sat beside me.

"Where are we going?" I asked.

"Around the world," he answered.

I smiled wryly. He hopped up to look at the map. He traced his finger from where we started to the Central Park station. Then he tapped his finger on the map.

"Right here," he said.

He sat back down beside me and I rested my head on his shoulder. Our fingers laced together between us.

"I'm in big trouble," I told him.

"Do you want to go back?"

I shook my head, no.

The train rumbled along the track. The flickering lights and squealing rails propelled the car into complete darkness in one second and then into sky blue sunshine the next. The train shook and rattled as if at any moment it would jump free and into the air like a spaceship.

At the Central Park Station, he pulled me to my feet. We walked up to the street to find it had been raining. Umbrellas were being deflated and rain hats were being removed and shaken out by the ladies who were trying to preserve their fancy hairdos. The smell of a newly washed city greeted us but only for just a moment. As soon as the wet sidewalks dried, the trash bins that were lined along the alleyways slowly sifted the air with the unpleasant pall that everyone was used to.

Across the street at the park we sat on a bench near the pond and ate hot dogs and drank soda pops. At one point, a man walking by suddenly slowed to a stop to stare at us oddly. He moved on after a few seconds but glanced back a time or two, a look of confusion on his face. Theo looked at me incredulously before laughing out loud.

"What's funny?" I asked.

"He thinks you're white. Can't you see?"

I shrugged my shoulders. People always stared at me.

"I don't care what they think."

"You could easily pass for white," he suggested. "Then you could do whatever you want. You could marry some white cat and live in a big house on Park Avenue."

"Sure... good idea," I joked. "And when my mother comes to visit, what am I supposed to say?"

Theo shook his head. "That's just it. She wouldn't be your mother anymore."

"And you wouldn't be my boyfriend."

He smiled at the distinction. Then he shrugged his shoulders as if it would be worth the sacrifice. "Park Avenue, baby. It could be yours."

"For the small price of giving it all up," I waved my hands around to indicate everything that I knew.

I hit him on the shoulder. "Why don't you cross over before me and then tell me how it all works out."

He held his arm out. "Cross over with this black skin?"

I lifted my nose in the air. "Tell them it's a suntan."

"What about my hair?"

"Tell them you paid a lot of money to get it that way."

He laughed. "Your father must be white." He shook his head as if there could be no other explanation. Then he thought of one. "Maybe you are white and maybe your mother stole you out of your crib one day."

He took one of my braids in his hand to study it. Then he ran his finger along my arm. He nodded his head. "You have to admit. It's a possibility." I pulled my arm away.

"Are you crazy?"

I ate the last bite of my hot dog before I lied. "I know who my father is. He's not white. My aunt told me that he was just really light skinned."

"At least you know who he is. Mine could have sold me that hotdog and I wouldn't have known any better."

"Do you know anything about him?"

He shook his head. "My aunt says he was just another nigger."

I stopped. "What?"

I couldn't believe it. "She didn't say that."

"Where do you think Cece gets it from?" He asked. "The apple didn't fall far from that tree."

"I don't believe it."

"It doesn't matter," he assured me. "That's all I got. I don't know his name. I don't know what he looked like. Nothing, not a thing."

I took his hand. "You have me."

"I have you today. What about tomorrow?"

"You have me tomorrow, too."

He smiled. "Do you want to see a movie?"

I wanted too but I shook my head because I couldn't. "I work at the factory on Mondays and Thursdays."

"What kind of factory?"

"They make lamp shades and draperies." I blushed. "One of the shades I made got bought by somebody famous."

"Who was it? Bette Davis? Steppin Fetchit?"

I shrugged my shoulders. I didn't know. The owners had appeared at my worktable, both bobbing their heads in unison with identical smiles of pride on their faces. They told me that my work was exceptional.

They had already offered me a full time job after I graduated.

"They wouldn't tell me but they said whoever it was they were from Hollywood."

Theo shook his head in awe.

"Sissy doesn't want me to work there, though."

"What does she want you to do?"

"She wants me to find a job in an office."

"What do you want to do?"

I shrugged my shoulders.

The next evening, I sat on the windowsill trying my best to ignore Adele. She was still giving me grief about running off with Theo.

"It just wasn't right," she said.

"Alright, I heard you the first fifty times. Sissy won't shut up about it and now you won't leave it alone."

She was sitting on the bed with our cousin Deeda May. Her wedding dress was spread between them like a huge puffy cloud. Thankfully, Sissy had finally left to go upstairs to Ludie's. She had spent nearly the whole night reminding me of what a fool I was to think that I was grown enough to run off like I did.

"This isn't Prosperity!" She kept yelling. "It isn't like it is back home. You can't run off like some silly little fool with little niggers from nowhere. This is Harlem, damn fool! This is a great big old city with all kinds of foolishness out here."

"She's right," Adele was saying. "You running all over with that boy that nobody knows nothing about. You mess around and get yourself pregnant and that's going to be it! You know your mama's going to hurt somebody."

She pointed a sewing needle at me. "She may just send you back south to live down there. How are you going to like that?"

I blew my breath on the window and traced Theo's name on the glass.

"Look at her!" Adele stood up and screamed. "She's going to drive herself crazy over that boy. I'm the one getting married. You don't see me falling all over Stanley do you?"

Deeda May stopped. Her needle raised in midair.

"The closer you get to your wedding, the more crazier you get. Why are you worrying about that child and her little boyfriend? You need to be worrying about your husband and this dress, here."

"He's not my husband yet," Adele rolled her eyes.

216

Deeda May asked me. "She got the right one, don't she? She tell him to shut up and all he's going to do is bring her cake and pie from the bakery.  And all that's going to do is make her mama mad for bringing food in here everybody knows she can make better."

Adele and I were supposed to be helping Deeda May sew little cloth petals onto the wedding dress but so far Deeda May was doing all the sewing.  I pressed my face sideways on the windowpane to see further down the block, trying to catch a glimpse of Theo on his way in or out of his building.

Adele whined, "That boy is about to get up and out of here and she's over there about to break her neck."

"What's wrong with Donald?" She asked me.

Deeda May looked confused. "Stanley's friend," I filled her in. "She wants me to like somebody I don't. She wants me not to like somebody I do."

Adele sat up with her arms outstretched in wonder.  She tried to get Deeda May to hear her argument.  "He's alright, Deeda May. He really is. What's wrong with him? He has a job over there with Stanley and he looks better than that somebody-nobody-knows-nothing-about out there." She nodded her head, agreeing with herself if nobody else would.

I rolled my eyes. "Not again," I pleaded. "I already told you. I'm not interested in Donald."

I turned away from the window to face her. "He came over here the other night and never stopped talking." I held my finger up. "Not a one single time."

I turned back to the street. She threw her hands in the air again. "I suppose you like the quiet type like that one you got. The cat caught his tongue. He doesn't ever have nothing to say.

He just sits there and looks like he's afraid to say a word. Who wants a boyfriend like that?"

I pointed at myself, "I do."

Deeda May picked up another petal from the pile on the bed,

"Listen, here," she announced. "If you want to show up at your wedding with half this dress looking plain as a sheet, keep on talking."

Adele rolled over onto the dress but after Deeda May threatened to stick her with the needle, she rolled back and sat up. She found a petal in the pile to sew into place. She held it up for me to see.

"You're the one who said to sew them on in the first place, and you're not even helping."

I retorted. "I said they would be pretty. That's all I said. I didn't say nothing about helping to sew them on."

Deeda May reminded Adele, "You'll be glad once we're finished."

"Shit," Adele rolled her eyes. "You're used to all this sewing."

Deeda May shifted her weight on the bed. "I like to sew when I'm getting paid, actually."

"You didn't say that when you made Annie's dress."

"How can I make my own sister pay?"

"I'm your cousin," Adele answered. "That's just like sisters, isn't it?"

Deeda May changed the subject. "Watch what you're doing before you stick yourself with that needle and get blood all over everything. You won't have to worry about wearing a white dress no more," she chuckled.

I had to admit, the dress was finally looking more like the wedding gown that Adele had found in a magazine and less like the simple and plain one that Ludie bought for fourteen dollars from a store on Fifty-Ninth Street.

I sat on the wide sill and I pulled my legs up close to my body. I rested my head on the window.

"Don't you know not to lean on a window pane?" Adele tested me with one of her mother's favorite warnings. "If it breaks, you'll be on the ground faster than a sack of dirt off the back of the dirt truck."

I gave up. I hopped off of the windowsill and pulled a straight-backed chair up to the bed. I found the needle I'd threaded earlier and picked a petal out of the pile to sew on. Deeda May turned the radio up when Nat King Cole came on. We all sang along with him,

"Mona Lisa... Mona Lisa. Men have adored you..."

Adele teased Deeda May who was smiling widely as she sang, "I believe you love Nat King Cole more than you love that man of yours."

Deeda May responded in between the lyrics. "Don't you be worrying about who I love."

It took another hour to sew the rest of the petals on. Adele tried the dress on after it was finished. She twirled around like a princess. Deeda May and I clapped because Adele looked like the perfect bride and for the moment she was happy.

It was nearly eleven o'clock when Deeda May left. Adele carefully wrapped her dress in a plastic liner to carry upstairs. She stopped before stepping clear of the door.

"You know," she whispered. "Your mother is going to be upstairs at least until midnight."

She nodded her head toward Theo's apartment.

"Is you crazy?"

I involuntarily began to search the hallway and stairwell for anyone who may be listening. I shook my head vigorously but at the same time my heart started pounding at the idea of sneaking out to the building next door.

"Have not, want not." Adele atoned.

She raised her eyebrows and fluttered her eyes to let me know that she wouldn't let the opportunity pass *her by* but that if I was too chicken... oh, well.

"I thought you didn't like him," I said.

"I don't but what does that have to do with it?"

She wrapped the wedding dress around her shoulders like a mink stole and left to go upstairs. I closed the door and leaned against it, debating in my head whether or not to take a chance and go to Theo's apartment. I traced the steps in my head.

First, I'd have to pass the nosy neighbors sitting outside in front of the building. They looked like a row of beetles sitting on a windowsill. Old Mrs. Palmer and her daughter-in-law, new Mrs. Palmer, would be there. Mrs. Connelly, the one with the blue hair and one short arm that she tried to hide behind her purse, would be there too. Old lady Simmons, the meanest one of the bunch, would surely be sitting on her box with her legs splayed out like a third base-coach sitting on the side of an inning long lost. She'd be slouching with one arm resting on new Mrs. Palmer's chair and a cigarette hanging from the corner of her mouth.

None of them would say a word loud enough for me to hear. They would silently shift their eyes back and forth at each other. They'd wait until I was out of earshot to rake me up one side and down the other, all bobbing their heads like toads.

I'd have to pass Cece and her friend Andrew who would undoubtedly be hanging out in their favorite spot near the basement stairs. Cece, looking like a boy and Andrew looking like an ugly flat-chested girl would watch me until I was far enough away to have to ask as loudly as possible why I was out so late.

"Why you out so late little gal," Andrew would bellow in his mouth-full-of-honey way, switching his narrow behind back and forth about to break his back from the effort. They would cackle at each other like hens but ultimately they would find *themselves* more interesting, and leave me alone.

Once I made it inside his building, I'd have to pass Miss Tiny somewhere in the stairwell, sweeping or mopping. She'd stop the broom or mop and set it to the side to let me pass. She'd ignore any greeting from me before going back over my footsteps, silently fuming at the intrusion so late after hours.

I decided to go the back way through the alley instead. I prayed as I walked that no one would throw their trash out of the windows as I passed below them.

It was a new practice that had folks cutting out the necessity of walking down to place their trash in the cans that lined the back of the building. They simply tossed what they didn't want, letting it land where it would. Sissy, Ludie and many of the longer standing residents argued with the landlord to find out who was doing it. He refused, staring back at them as if they were speaking another language.

I held my nose and scampered around the trash towards the one dim light that sat above Theo's building's back door. I made my way up the stairs to the first level and then across the small foyer to the first flight of stairs.

I looked up the stairwell to see if Miss Tiny was around. It looked as if she had already finished her self-imposed chore and had gone inside for the night. I ran up the steps two by two, making it to the third landing before stopping to catch my breath.

Inside his apartment, Theo adjusted the blankets on the floor. He turned his back away from the window. The light from the street lamp lit the room in a powerful yellow haze, strong enough to make the sheet hanging over the window useless and any chance of getting any sleep doubtful.

He wasn't sleepy but he knew the next day would be long. Raymond and Bell, his friends from Boston, were sprawled out on opposite sides of the room. They seemed to be oblivious to the light and were both sleeping like babies. They had arrived in New York earlier in the day. The three of them spent the afternoon hanging around downtown near the Bowery and on Delancy Street.

They didn't have much money but Bell bought a comb and Raymond bought razorblades to trim the back of his hair. He was hoping the army barber would accept it and let him pass without getting sheered. Theo was just about to doze off when he heard a slight tapping on the door. When he opened it, I was standing there.

"I had to see you before you left," I smiled.

He looked at me oddly. I reminded him, "I didn't get a chance to see your room."

"Bell and Ray...my friends from Boston," he nodded his head sideways into the room. "They're asleep."

"I won't wake them up," I smiled.

Theo stepped out of the way and opened the door wider.

I stepped forward and tentatively peered inside. The room was small, probably no bigger than the bed Mr. Mooney's daughter had taken when her father passed away.

I wrinkled my nose at Theo and backed out of the room. He followed me to sit on the steps in the hall. Thanks to Miss Tiny the stairwell was spotless, unlike my building which Mr. Peterson barely swept.

I smoothed my skirt over my knees and waited. I knew my heart should have been pounding like a drum at the thought of deceiving Sissy twice in two days, but it wasn't. I supposed I was getting good at it.

"We'll be leaving out tomorrow." Theo's echoed whisper broke the silence in the quiet stairwell.

He set his hand loosely on the iron railing and I took his other hand in mine. He'd been working down at a grocery store on 37th Street, washing vegetables and fruit in the cold back alley behind the store. His hands were ashy and his cuticles were cracked from the cold water and winter air. I measured my palm with his.

"Your hand is too big," I teased him.

He smiled. "How can my hand be too big? I'm over six feet tall. How would I look with little hands?"

I shrugged my shoulders and laced my fingers into his. I popped a bubble with the mint chewing gum in my mouth and then brushed kisses across his fingers.

"Do you want a stick of gum?" I asked.

"Sure," Theo answered. I took the wrapper off and when he opened his mouth I touched it to his lips before pulling away.

223

He grabbed me around the waist and lifted me into the air.

"Alright, alright..." I laughed.

He put his hand over my mouth, "You'll wake up the whole building."

He leaned against the wall and wrapped his arms around me. I closed my eyes and rested my head against his chest. I don't know how it happened but I started to cry. I was immediately embarrassed.

"Why are you crying?" He asked.

I shook my head. I didn't know why.

"I'm not going to be gone that long," he assured me.

He wiped my tears away.

"You'll be fine. You'll have a new boyfriend in no time."

"And you'll have a new girlfriend."

He shook his head. We looked at each other for a long time and then he asked me if I would marry him. He blurted it out so fast that I had to take a second to compute it in my brain. A smile spread across my face. He immediately waved his hands.

"I don't know what I'm talking about. I mean, I don't even know you that well. Don't say it." He pulled away. "It's the army talking. They told us about this."

He pulled his pockets inside out. "Look, I don't have shit! I don't even have a high school diploma."

I answered, "I don't care. I will marry you."

I patted my skirt. "I don't have pants on but if I did they would be empty too."

He took my hands and pulled me to him. When I started to talk he held his finger to his lips and pointed up the stairs. We ran to the top floor where we found the roof latch broken and the door swinging open in the midnight air. The wind picked my skirts up with a whoosh when we stepped outside. We ran across to the far end where Theo picked me up and swung me around and around. We screamed into the night. When he finally put me down, I kissed him on the cheek before pointing back and forth between us.

"We're engaged!"

"You're my girl," Theo nodded down to me.

"What are we going to do? I mean, when are you going to tell your mother?"

Theo shrugged, "I'll write her a letter. I'll tell her tonight. I'll tell your mother tomorrow."

"Oh..." I pulled away with a frown. "I don't know. She might not let me get married until I finish school. I think we should wait before we tell her. Just until you get back from training. That's only a little while, right?"

"I think its eight weeks but I'll be right over at Fort Dix," he pointed toward New Jersey. "I can leave for a few days halfway through or you can come and visit me," he trailed off.

Eight weeks was forever. I'd be a nervous wreck by the time he got back.

I smiled at Theo. "Let's be happy," I reminded him. "We can worry about everything else later."

We sat together until the breeze picked up off of the Hudson and swam across the rooftops suddenly making it too cold. We climbed over to my building and walked hand in hand down the steps to the fourth floor. He kissed me gently on the lips.

"You smell like Ivory soap," I teased him.

"I should," he smiled. "I use it for everything... my clothes, my hair."

I laughed gently, "Soap is soap."

He nodded and then waited for me to go down to my apartment. I peeked up through the stairwell and whispered. "Have a safe trip."

He nodded and then I heard him heading back up to the roof.

## Chapter Twenty-Three

I kept my secret for nearly a week. I could have held it longer but Adele guessed something was odd when I was too busy daydreaming to keep up with what she was telling me about her wedding.

"You're looking as silly as a moon pie," she accused me.

She playfully knocked one of my braids off of my shoulder and when I smiled she evidently knew there was a secret hiding behind it. We were sitting on the steps in the courtyard. After checking to make sure Mrs. Hicks wasn't eavesdropping at her window, she scooted closer to me.

"Theo and me... we're getting married," I whispered.

My eyes closed at the thought.

"What!" Adele hissed.

She grabbed me by the arm and pulled me away from the building.

She checked back to see which old busy bodies might be close enough to hear. Old Mrs. Ritter, the only white resident still left in the building was alone. She was sitting with one foot propped on the chair while she clipped her thick gray toenails.

Adele held tight to my arm and leaned in as close to my ear as possible. "If that boy made you pregnant, Sissy is going to kill him, you and probably me too!"

I screwed my face into a grimace and shook my head. She turned me to the side and studied my stomach as if she had x-ray vision and then she stared into my eyes as if she could read my mind.

"I'll show you how to get rid of it. I know what to do."

I suppose she was referring back to her own experience because she assured me, "Mine was worse than it was supposed to be. I've seen girls do it, you know... without any pain at all."

She shook her head in awe. "He must be out of his mind! Who does he think he is?"

I pulled away. "I'm not!" I whispered. "We haven't been... even... I mean I'm not having a baby, fool!"

Adele put her hands on her hips. For a moment she was at a loss for words. Her head finally wrapped around the idea that it was possible for a girl to get a proposal of marriage without a baby being part of the equation.

She fell against the building and wiped her arm theatrically across her brow.

"Boy. That was close. Jesus! I thought I was about to have a heart attack! Anyway," she put her hand out. "Let me see the ring. Where you got it hid?"

"He ain't got no money for no ring," I snorted.

"If he ain't got no money for a ring then he ain't got no money for a wife!" Adele replied. "Come on, here."

She took my hand. We walked arm in arm down the block while she broke down the semantics of boys trying anything to have their way with girls, even if it meant asking them to get married.

"He seemed like he was innocent," she pondered. "Hmm, but them the ones you got to watch. Listen here," she got closer to my ear. "One time I heard they buy a fake license. You know, a wedding license, and get one of their friends to pretend to be a preacher. They go through with 'I do this' and 'I do that', then after they sex you on the wedding night," she stopped for a second to peer at me, to be certain that I understood *wedding night* to be part of the ruse.

When she was satisfied that I understood, she continued. "The next day they tells you to get lost. They say they're not married to you no more than the man in the moon."

I shook my head, "Theo isn't like that. He just isn't."

Adele patiently yet knowingly let me defend Theo but she knew well enough that even cute shy acting boys would lie to get into your drawers.

"Oh, yes, ma'am!" She shook her head like a fat black preacher.

"Listen to me and listen to me good," she sermonized. "I wouldn't put it past him. Don't you let that boy turn you around, hear? Give Donald a chance. If he talks too much maybe he's just nervous," she reasoned.

By the time we walked the block four times, I was dizzy with a headache trying without much success to convince Adele that there was no way Theo would lie to me just to do the you know what. She stopped me in front of the building with one last piece of advice, which she rendered with all sincerity.

"He's a boy, Frank Lee." She put her hand to her chest. "I've been there, done that. If you're going to get married... if you want to get married, just don't marry him. Find you a man to marry. Somebody who's twenty or twenty-one, somebody with money in his pocket."

She thought about it for a minute. "There's something about that boy that ain't right."

She paused, shaking her head again. "He shouldn't have asked you to marry him. He just shouldn't have."

When she finished I got the strangest feeling, so much so that the hairs on the back of my neck tingled. I looked up and there in the window was Sissy. My eyes nearly popped out of my head and my breath involuntarily drizzled out of my lungs with a tiny squeak.

Adele looked up to see what was the matter.

"Jesus," she uttered.

I narrowed my eyes at Adele and clamped my mouth shut. I was angry enough to twist her head off. I wanted to run but I was too scared to move. I followed Adele up the stairs to the apartment like a prisoner on my way to the gallows. We both fell onto the couch to wait for Sissy to speak.

Ludie and Mr. Harris were there too. He was Sissy's new friend. He was as skinny as a beanpole and if she wanted to she could blow him over with a hand fan.

He once worked as a cook on a Pullman train out of Pennsylvania, so had many a tale to tell about his travels along the railroad tracks. He had a tendency to say *listen here* as a precursor to every other sentence.

We called him Mr. Harry, usually in unison and usually with disdain because another of his annoying habits was to tell jokes back to back. He told silly riddles, made obnoxious sounds and funny faces. His stories were far too long and drawn out and with a kick at the end, which was usually not worth waiting for. He could make us laugh over a wilted carrot but so much so that after awhile it got on your nerves.

Sissy folded her arms and stared at us until even he was wise enough not to find it funny. Finally after more than five minutes of silence, she asked,

"Who is this boy?"

Everybody in the room looked at me. I scratched the back of my neck and tried to speak but my throat was too dry.

Adele answered for me, "He's that nephew for Miss Eliza."

Sissy swiveled her head in Adele's direction. Adele's mouth immediately turned to a grimace as if she could already feel the smack across the head that might be coming.

Her mother breathed in deeply and then looked at the ceiling as if to wonder why her daughter always had something to say when any fool could see it was best just to keep quiet.

"Who is talking to you, Miss Adele?" Sissy asked. "I believe that somebody who is getting married ought to be able to say what they have to say on their own."

She rotated her attention back in my direction and waited for me to answer.

"His name is... um... Theo... um... Miner."

"Theo um Miner?"

"Yes, ma'am," I stammered  "Who is he? Where did he come from? What does he do?"

I glanced at Adele and then repeated what she'd said. "He's Miss Eliza's nephew."

Sissy shook her head. "He's not the one that lives up in Mooney's room?  The black one that's always with that gal from across there?"

I nodded my head.  She mimicked the movement until I said it out loud. "Yes."

"What does he have?" She asked around the room. "He's a boy, Frank Lee! He can't give you anything. He ain't got a pot to piss in or a window to throw it out of. Nothing!"

She searched around the room again, trying to see if they knew something she didn't. Finally she turned back to me.

"How old is he? He couldn't be older than fifteen years old... talking about marrying somebody. I thought you had a little bit of sense. Hell, if you wanted to get married I could set you up with Mr. Raskin. At least he can take care of you."

My breath caught in my throat. "Mr. Raskin doesn't have any teeth," I reminded her.

Harry pulled the top set of his dentures down from the roof of his mouth with his tongue. "He can borrow mine," he mumbled around them.

He pushed them back into place with his finger. We all looked at him somberly.

"Harry," Ludie whispered.

He smiled and settled back into his seat.

"He's seventeen and he's a nice boy," I offered. "He joined the army and..."

"And that boy better not be thinking about taking you off from here. Make sure you let him know that. He's going to get you away from here and the next thing you know we'll probably never see you again. You got school to finish. Don't think you're grown little gal. Don't think you're grown enough to go off with little niggers from nowhere."

"Come on, now," Ludie interjected. "Frank Lee's not thinking about going nowhere. She's not but a baby herself."

Sissy gave me one last look and then went to the kitchen to tend to her fried chicken. Ludie stuck her lips out and shook her head letting me know not to worry, she would talk to Sissy.

A few seconds later, we heard Sissy open the icebox. She poured the melted water into the basin at the sink and then walked through the living room carrying the brown chunk of ice in a dishcloth. She opened the side window, peered out and below and then threw it out to the alley.

She turned, stopped and then thinking better of it, changed her mind and stomped back into the kitchen.

Harry watched her leave before turning to me. "Listen here," he said. "Fellows are a dime a dozen. You have but your one mama." He nodded his head as if he'd just imparted the wisdom of Job upon the masses.

Adele and I glared at him until he chuckled and clattered his false teeth at us.

The next morning I woke up to Sissy banging pots and pans in the kitchen. I got up and quietly got dressed for school. I could hear her mumbling over the idea of me getting too grown for my own good. I sat down on the bed after tying my shoes. I needed to leave before I'd be late but I was afraid to take a chance of crossing her path.

She finally stepped into the living room and put her hands on her hips.

"I need to ask you a question," she started.

"I'm not pregnant." I answered before she could get the words out.

Her hands came together as if she was about to pray. She brought them to her mouth and closed her eyes. I don't know whether she was happier that I wasn't pregnant or that her second senses hadn't failed her.

She sat on the couch.

"Is that all you want, to get married?  Can't you wait until you graduate?  Can't you at least find a job first?  You're going to meet all kinds of folk outside of here." She waved her hands to indicate the block or Harlem or the state of New York in general.

"What does he want from somebody like you, Frank Lee? You're a good girl," she reasoned.

She shook her head before I could answer and in the blink of an eye her mood changed from what had seemed to be a heartfelt plea to that of sharp-knifed condemnation.

Her voice got louder with every next word. "There's no telling what he has on his mind.  I heard his own mama kicked him out. What kind of foolishness is that when you're not welcome in your own mama's house? Tell me that, Frank Lee. Tell me that?"

I didn't know and wasn't sure to which question she expected a response.  I kept my eyes on the floor.  She gave up. "Go on and get to school before you be late."

From then on, Sissy found her way in our little apartment as far away from me as possible.  If I was in the kitchen, she waited in her bedroom until I was somewhere else.  When I asked if I could go to the Savoy with Adele and our cousins Vela Mae or Deeda May one night, she remarked that I was grown and that I never asked permission to get engaged so why was I asking permission to go dancing.   She mostly responded to the ceiling and usually left the room before I had the chance to ask a second question.

When I wrote to Theo, I didn't mention anything about my mother. I only told him that I couldn't wait to see him. Yet on the same token I had no idea how I would manage to since Sissy said that if she caught sight of him, she would kill him on the spot.

"Your mama is in love with you!" Adele teased me.

"She don't want to let her baby brown eyes out of her sight."

"You don't know what you're talking about," I told her.

"She may love that leopard skin jacket Harry bought her but she doesn't love me. That's for sure."

Adele gave me a funny smile. "What are you talking about? She came and got you didn't she? She didn't leave you down there in the country like Ludie did me."

"She may love her mink stole." I responded stubbornly.

"You're the only gal out here with a nickel in your pocket every time you ask for one. You call for it and she throws it down to you, don't she?"

I shook my head no but it was true. When the candy man stopped at our building, I was the only one who could call up to the third floor for Sissy to throw a nickel. Five cents was enough to buy sweets for three whole days.

I shrugged my shoulders. "It wasn't for me," I said. "She just didn't want anybody to think we were poor."

Adele stopped applying polish to her fingernails. She looked up. "Everybody out here is poor. That don't matter one way or the other."

I looked away. "Her pride made her throw the money."

Adele went back to her nails. "Your mama is proud, I will give you that." She nodded her head towards the new black sling-back Mary Jane's that Sissy had left on my bed a few days before.

"Did pride make her buy them shoes?"

Tears came to my eyes. "You're just jealous," I told Adele. Even though I knew she was right. Sissy may not have been the perfect mother but she loved me in her own way.

Adele smirked and nodded her head. "I am! I do wish Ludie did for me like Aunt Sissy does for you. Call me jealous if that's all you got. I'll be jealous. I surely will be."

She screwed the top back onto the polish and held her hands out to admire her nails.

But," she said after a moment of thought. "I don't know what you're going to do about your little boyfriend. She's not having her baby brown eyes getting away with the likes of that boy."

I wiped my tears away and shook my head. No, I agreed. She wouldn't.

## Chapter Twenty-Four

When I graduated from high school Sissy, Ludie, Adele and I crowded into Harry's car for the ride down to 24th Street.

"Why are you looking like the sky is falling?" Adele asked me. "You should be happy."

Ludie corrected Adele. "She should be proud. She's the first one of all of us to get to high school let alone graduate."

"Wait a minute, now! I got to high school." Adele pouted. "I may not have finished all the way through but I got far enough."

"I am happy," I lied. "I am proud."

Harry pulled up to a stoplight. He turned around and made a sad face by pulling the corners of his mouth down with his fingers. We ignored him until he turned back to the front.

Sissy pulled the rearview mirror her way so she could see herself. She readjusted the bobby pins that were holding her hat in place.

"You don't have a spoonful of sense, Harry. Not a spoonful. There's nothing wrong with Frank Lee," she said. "She's just wasting time worrying about that boy across the river over there."

I turned away and looked out of the window. I knew I should have been happy but it felt like something was missing. Maybe it was Theo, who I hadn't heard from since he left. Maybe it was Donald, who was hanging around more and more. Maybe it was just that it was raining outside and the city looked dirty and gray.

When we arrived at the school's auditorium, Ludie kissed me on the cheek and told me to keep my chin up. I followed the other girls to the dressing area. I watched them squealing in delight at new hairdos in one second and then screeching in anguish when one of them discovered a run in her stocking. A few had plans to go to college, some had jobs lined up and others had beaus waiting in the wings to marry them. A few I knew were leaving for the courthouse as soon as they received their diplomas. None would admit why but everyone knew what they were hiding under their extra large graduation gowns.

At the principal's sharp clap we lined up in our pre-assigned positions and followed him to the stage. Chairs were lined up in rows facing the audience. The Gants, who owned the lampshade factory, were sitting on the front row.

Sissy shook her head with a laugh when I told her they offered me a ten percent raise on top of the full pay if I agreed to work for them.

"You wasn't raised to work in no factory. I don't care how much they want to pay you."

She had forbidden me to accept their offer for a job and I didn't know how I would tell them. I pretended not to see Mrs. Gant when she fanned her paper thin hand at me. I didn't think I was too good to work there. I enjoyed sewing and making drapes and shades from scratch but it wasn't the first time Sissy had reminded me that she had greater expectations for me.

Adele teased me about it. "You're damn near white, Frank Lee! You'll be a fool if you don't take advantage of it. Shit. There are people in them offices downtown that will pay you good money. They'll stare at you and ask if you're Italian or some other such nonsense but you'll be able to get up and out of here."

"I like where we live," I'd told her.

She put her hands on her hips and cocked her head to the side.

"You like sleeping in that little bed against the wall?" She shook her head as if there was no talking to me.

Sissy had warned me that if I couldn't tell the Gant's what she said, she would. Thankfully, she didn't know what they looked like and I had no intention of introducing them to one another.

Afterwards, we headed over to Plaxico's to celebrate. He opened the club early and had it decorated with balloons and ribbons. Adele winked at me from across the table when Stanley walked in with Donald. I wanted to strangle her. She ignored my glare and waved them over.

"Shush, honey. He brought you a present. Act like you're surprised."

"Hello, Donald," I responded, trying not to appear perturbed that he was there at all.

He placed a long slender box on the table. It had only been a second ago that Adele told me to act surprised, but I didn't have to act. I was surprised. It was wrapped in a golden colored wrapping paper and had a large red bow on top. It was wrapped so nicely that I didn't want to tear the paper away.

"Open it," he said.

I turned the box over in my hands a few times. I could feel a blush rise to my cheeks since I knew everyone in the room was watching. I untied the bow and carefully pulled the wrapping paper away. Just before I pulled the lid off, I thought of Theo.

It didn't feel right. I paused for a second before handing the gift back to Donald. Everyone who was watching groaned with regret. It was like listening to a deflating balloon.

Stanley and Adele discretely glided away from the table and everyone else immediately went back to finding each other more interesting than us. Donald's face was flushed red with embarrassment.

"I'm sorry, Donald. I just don't think I should take it."

He tried to laugh it off as if his feelings weren't hurt. He pulled a chair out and sat down.

"It's alright."

He pulled the lid away and took the bracelet out of the box. He showed it to me. "It's just a stupid bracelet."

I immediately felt sorry for him. "It's pretty," I said.

He shrugged his shoulders.

I took it out of his hand to get a better look. It reminded me of something an old lady would wear.

"Here," I held my arm out. "Put it on for me."

"I can take it back to the store. The man said that I could."

"No. I like it," I lied.

After he clipped it on, I turned my arm this way and that to allow him to admire it.

"It's pretty just like you," he smiled.

"Come on," I took his hand. "It's too smoky in here. Let's go outside."

240

Plaxico's club wasn't very large but it took a couple of minutes to make our way through to the door. The rain had stopped so we walked down the block and away from the folks who were standing around outside.

"You have a lot of family," he sounded impressed.

I shook my head. "Not really. Most of them are from where we're from, back home."

"Back home?" He asked.

"We're from a place called Prosperity. It's in South Carolina." He nodded his head as if he knew it, which I was certain was impossible.

He told me that he was born in Mississippi but had moved to upstate New York when he was two or three.

"My mother works at the school up there for people who are deaf."

I looked at him quizzically. I'd never heard of such a thing. He nodded his head.

"It's true," he said. Then he tilted his head sideways as if he was telling me a secret. "It's for rich white people."

I raised my eyebrows. "I guess so," I agreed.

He had been quietly cared for on the grounds there and I supposed he must have started talking as soon as he left and never stopped. He showed me how they spoke with their hands and tried to show me how to hold my fingers to make the signs for hungry and sleepy.

The more he talked, the less I heard. I had to make myself look interested even though all I wanted to know was the sign that meant to shut up.

Adele and Stanley finally came outside. "Come on," she waved us on. "They're going to be in there all night. I'm ready to go home."

Stanley, who was trailing behind her threw his hands up in frustration. "I'm not walking all the way up to a Hundred Thirtieth Street!"

He headed out to the curb to flag a cab. Adele kept walking and after he realized she was going to have her own way, he ran to catch up.

Donald laced my arm around his and we followed them.  He told me about how his father left them and was likely passing for a white man wherever he was. He pulled his wallet out of his back pocket and showed me a picture of when he was a boy.  It showed him standing stoically on a chair.  His parents were positioned on either side of him. They all looked like they could pass for a white family but the father especially so.

I looked up at the dark sky and wished Theo could have come instead of Donald. When he saw me look away, he immediately clamped his mouth shut. I pretended I hadn't noticed. I watched in amusement while he fidgeted for something to say without speaking.

He actually seemed more handsome when he wasn't talking. His skin was pale, even lighter than mine and his hair was cropped close with a patch of dark curls at the top. His eyelashes were long like a girl's and his eyebrows were thick like an old man's. There was a small mole just above his upper lip that I suddenly couldn't take my eyes off of.

When we got to my building Adele was telling Stanley that he was a pain in her ass and he better watch out or he might end up getting married all by himself.  She pushed past us and up to the fourth floor.

Stanley stood out on the street and yelled up to her window.

"It might be you standing up there by yourself!"

He stood there waiting for an answer that he should have known by now he would never get. He walked back and forth with his hands on his hips, staring up at her window.

The streetlight shone down on him like a spotlight on a stage for which he was unfortunately at the end of his scene but didn't quite know how to exit. He finally shook his head in dismay and walked out of the spotlight and up the block.

"Thanks for walking me home," I told Donald.

He shucked his shoulders and smiled. "I better catch up with him," he said.

He kissed me on the cheek and ran off after Stan. When I got upstairs and closed the door I leaned against it until my heart stopped pounding. I twirled around in a circle and danced through the living room to my bed.

The smile on my face dropped like an apple from a tree when I saw the letter on my pillow. It was from Theo. Sissy had apparently left it there before leaving for the graduation. I wondered when it had come. I sat down and opened it. I pulled the single sheet of paper out and read it by the light coming through the window.

Dear Frank Lee,

I will be in New York the first week of July. I hope we can talk. I miss you and I love you. Othello Miner

I love you, he'd said. No one had ever told me they loved me. I couldn't believe it. I read the letter over and over again. I finally fell asleep with it in my hand. The next morning Sissy watched me from her chair at the kitchen table. She took a sip of her coffee.

"What did your little boyfriend have to say?" She asked sarcastically. "Will he be riding through here on his white horse to take you away any time soon?"

Before I could answer she got up and walked to the sink where she poured what was left in the cup down the drain. She rinsed the cup out and dried it with a dishtowel.

"You got your diploma," she acknowledged matter-of-factly. "You're eighteen years old. I can't tell you what to do. If you go, you go," she trailed off.

"I like Theo," I told her. "I do! I don't like anybody else the way I like him."

I looked away.

"His own mama don't want to have nothing to do with him, Frank Lee."

I wanted to tell her that those were just rumors. They were lies that people in the street didn't know a thing about. Instead, I kept my mouth shut.

"What do you think is going to happen?" She asked. "You think he's going to ride up to carry you off and away to the happy ever after land? He don't have nothing and you can do bad all by yourself."

She tossed the dishtowel onto the counter and put the cup away. "You're grown," she told me. "Live your life."

She raised her arms in the air, a gesture meant to give it up to God. She walked out of the kitchen.

I tried to talk to Adele about it later but she wouldn't listen. She stopped me by holding her hand up and placing it across her chest.

"I'm getting married in three weeks," she explained. "I'm not talking about nothing but me up until then. If you have to talk about you," she pointed away in the distance, "you'll have to talk to somebody else."

She wrinkled her nose and smiled at me impishly. "I'm just so tickled to be the center of attention for a change."

"...for a change?" I asked sardonically.

"Don't worry," she laughed. "Your time's coming soon enough."

I sat back and listened for the thousandth time about how her wedding day would transpire from start to finish.

"First thing, I'm going to tell that lazy fool down in the basement to sweep the courtyard which he's supposed to do without nobody asking.  Then I'm going to tell Miss Ritter to stay out from in front of the building until after everybody is gone."

"How are you going to do that?" I asked. "She lives here."  "

I live here too. Nobody wants to see her cleaning her toe jamb all out in the open where any and everybody can see!"

I grimaced, "That's nasty."

"Who are you telling?" Adele agreed.

She got up and looked out of the window. "Look, there she goes again. I ought to toss some cold water out the window on the old heifer."

She shimmied up on the sill. "Fifty degrees out there and she has the nerve to be propped up like it's the Fourth of July."

Adele leaned back against the windowpane. She let her eyes flutter closed, "This feels so good," she said about the cool glass.

She fanned herself with her pad of paper. It was decorated all over with the scribbled plans for her wedding day.

"Don't you know not to lean on a window pane?" I teased her. "If it breaks, you'll be on the ground faster than a sack of dirt off the back of the dirt truck."

"Very funny," she rolled her eyes. "Why are you so hot all of a sudden?" I asked.

She fanned the tablet at me. "Shush, with your little nosy self."

She hopped off of the windowsill and fell across the bed. She rolled over onto her back. She ran her pen across the items on her list. "I'm going to make sure Pastor Thurmond is on time and out of the kitchen eating on any and everything. Don't nobody want to be smelling his breath when they're trying to say *I do*."

I shook my head in regret. "You need to stop talking about people like that. Especially Pastor Thurmond."

"You weren't there when Stanley and I met him at the church!" She shook her head and lowered her voice. "His breath smelled like fish ass."

I laughed, "Fish butt."

"Fish Butt Thurmond," she pointed the pen at me. "Jesus knows it sure can't be no secret."

She flipped the page on her pad of paper. "Then I'll get Stanley to move the couch and chairs against the wall so there'll be room for everybody. Ludie..." she laid the pad on her chest and looked at me. "Do you know after all this time she asked me why I don't call her mama?"

"She is your mama. Why don't you call her mama?" I asked.

"Why don't you call Aunt Sissy, Mama?"

"I thought we weren't supposed to be talking about me, remember? Besides, if she asked I think you should try. It can't hurt anything."

Adele thought about it for a moment. She shrugged her shoulders.

"My baby sure won't be calling me by my first name... when I have one. Anyway," she got back to her list. "Ludie is already shopping for food. She's going to make my cake too even though I wish she would let me buy one."

I shook my head. "Her cake will be better than one from some old bakery." Adele corrected me. "I'm not complaining about how they taste. I'm talking about how they look. Don't forget Stanley's old uppity people are going to be there." She pointed her finger this way and that. "They be putting their finger on everything they see."

She sat up and put check marks on the rest of the items on the list. "You only get one wedding cake in your lifetime; it ought to be like you want it to be. Check, check, check." She atoned before hopping off of the bed. "I believe I'm ready. All Stanley has to do is get his people in line. Tell his mama and sister's that if they can't pretend to be happy for real they're going to need to take an eyeliner pencil and draw smiling faces from here to here." She traced an invisible line from one cheek to the other.

Adele knew Stanley's mother and two sisters held a quiet contempt over his choice for a bride but she didn't care.

"They can kiss my butt. They should be happy I'm marrying his ass at all. That's why nary one of them got nobody. When folks are too picky they end up by themselves with nothing better to do than worry about what everybody else is doing."

She turned and pointed the pen at me. "And you," she warned me. "Be nice to Donald. You know he can't help himself."

When I smiled she lowered her head and narrowed her eyes in my direction.

I shook my finger at her. "No, no... we're not talking about me, remember."

"Okay, okay. I take it back. He is a nice fellow. Much better than that one you got. He's older. He got a job. He likes you."

I shook my head, no. She pleaded with me. "Tell me everything. Please!"

I pressed my lips together and shook my head again. I kept my secret. She pestered me for the next two weeks up until her wedding day when she walked down the hall of her mother's apartment with her wedding dress on. She was still trying to read my mind and Donald's lips when he finally found his way to me during the reception. I smiled at her and then I blocked her view.

"I know I talk too much," were the first words out of his mouth.

I returned a look of shock. I wasn't surprised that Adele had probably told Stanley and Stanley had undoubtedly passed the opinion on to Donald, even though that wasn't the real reason I hadn't seen him. I knew he'd been coming over to hang around in the courtyard and ask where I was and if I was mad at him.

I'd been peeking at him from behind the curtains, afraid to take the chance of seeing him...afraid that if I did, I'd end up with a mess on my hands.   I shook my head and lied. "You're alright. You can talk if you have to."

I crossed my legs and got comfortable on the couch, sure that I'd be stuck there for the next three hours saying "uh huh" and "oh my" while at the same time trying to ignore the most adorable things about him.

As he spoke my eyes wandered around the room, hoping someone would save me before I went crazy.  Ludie was busy cleaning out ashtrays and fretting over the wedding cake, which was yet to be cut. It was leaning just slightly to the left. She tried to readjust the tiny little painted faced bride and groom on top to lend the cake the illusion of being straight but it didn't work.

She shook her head with a frown.  "This old cake just isn't going to do right," she said out loud.

Sissy was busy going through Harry's L.P.'s, while he was trying to stack them on the record player in the order she was dictating. I was surprised he was there since I knew she had been trying to get Pearl to come to the wedding.

"What's the matter?" Donald asked.

I shook my head, "Nothing."

"Come on, let's dance," He said.

I shook my head and shifted a few inches away from him. The last thing I wanted to do was to be in his arms, to smell the orange spice cologne he wore or to imagine running my fingers through his curly hair.

He misunderstood my hesitation and dragged me to my feet. His arm went around my waist and before I knew it, I was having my very first dance with a boy. And it wasn't even with my boyfriend.

Ludie started clapping and she and Sissie shared a secret nod at one another. "Go on, now," she yelled over the music. "Have your fun. We'll get to that poor little lopsided cake after a while."

After a while turned out to be the next day since everybody including Adele forgot about the cake. A little after midnight Adele and Stanley finally gathered their things together to leave for his new apartment up in the Bronx. We opened the windows and climbed out onto the fire escape to catch them leaving the building.

We threw handfuls of rice into the air from a bag that Ludie brought out from the kitchen. The rice drifted like snowflakes until the street lamps caught it and then, like glitter, it fell over them like rain.

Adele screamed in delight as they ran to the car that was waiting. Her wedding had turned out exactly as she had planned it. Everyone was happy because she was happy but as soon as the car pulled away from the curb, Ludie started crying like a baby.

I put my arms around her. "Lord, Jesus!" Sissy put her hands on her hips. "What are you crying for?"

Ludie shook her head fretfully but she kept right on crying.

"Listen here, honey." Sissy gave her some advice. "This is not the end of the world. She'll be back tomorrow like she never even left."

Ludie threw her hands toward Sissy. "Oh, we'll see what you do when this one gets up and goes her way."

Sissy shook her head. "Oh, she's not going nowhere. You're not leaving your old mama behind is you?"

She put her arm around me and kissed me on the cheek. I couldn't believe it. I thought she may have been drunk.

Ludie took my hand in hers. "Why do you want to put that on her? Of course she's going to get herself a husband. We raised them right, didn't we? Neither one of them can cook a meal to save their lives," she lambasted. "But they'll be leaving here, sure enough. It's a fact. Just because you never found nobody to marry and the one I did find turned out to be piss poor, don't mean they won't."

Harry did a little dance before falling to one knee beside Sissy. We could tell he wasn't serious because he kept winking his eye in every direction. Sissy hit him on the arm. She tried to pull him up.

He wobbled his head from side to side. "If I wasn't already married to my Betty, I can tell you straight I would beg you to be my wife."

She hit him again. "Shut your mouth, old fool." She pushed him away and headed back inside.

If what Ludie said was going to be true, I suppose Sissy was going to do her part to pick the husband she wanted me to have. She pointed at Donald and volunteered him to wash dishes with me. He jumped at the chance.

It took more than an hour to clean the whole kitchen and when we got through, Harry was the only person left in the little living room. He was sitting up, asleep on the couch. His mouth was wide open in a snore. Pearlie showed up some time after midnight so Harry was unceremoniously left alone to wonder where Sissy had run off to.

I walked Donald to the door and when he tried to kiss me, I turned my cheek. He planted it there and smiled. He waved goodbye before leaving down the stairs. I covered Harry with a blanket before slipping into the bedroom to sleep with Ludie.

## Chapter Twenty-Five

The next morning just as Sissy had predicted Adele was back. She woke me up with a shake. She was draped down in the brand new suit Deeda May put together for her as a surprise wedding present.

"Look at you," I nodded my head with a smile.

She turned around, sashaying this way and that as if she was posing for a glamour magazine.

"Where did Ludie go?" She asked as she walked to the kitchen ahead of me.

I didn't know. I shrugged my shoulders. Harry was gone too.

"I didn't hear her when she left," I offered.

She took the tin foil off the cake. After a night in the warm kitchen, it looked like a lopsided mountain slope with the bride and groom on their sides adrift in the snowy frosting. She looked at the cake with a frown, "Didn't I tell you?"

She put her hands on her hips and turned to me for validation. I nodded in agreement. She was right the cake wouldn't win any prizes for appearance. I took a butter knife and cut two fat pieces for each of us. We sat down at the small kitchen table and when Adele took a bite, her eyes fluttered closed.

"This tastes so good," she grinned.

"Better than last night," I teased her.

She shook her head. "Honey, by the time we got all the way uptown that boy fell on the bed and was sleep before his head hit the pillow. The better part of being married so far is not having to live here."

She pushed the cake away and stood up. She twirled around in a circle. "I can do what I want, when I want to. If I don't want to wash the dishes, I don't have to. Stan don't care," she shook her head with laugh and plopped back down in her seat. "I sure don't care."

She twirled the fork around in a circle. "It isn't like we needed to do it last night." She stared at me mysteriously. "The bun is already baking in the oven."

She crossed her arms and waited for me to catch the hint.

I looked at her oddly. "I'm pregnant, crazy gal," she confided. "Don't you get it? We're going to have a damn baby! I can say it now. I'm good and married."

She raised her eyebrows for emphasis. I dropped the fork. "I knew it," I pointed at her. "I knew it!"

She grabbed my hand and ordered me not to tell anybody.

I laughed, "Why not? You're good and married."

"Just don't."

"I won't, but how do you think you're going to hide it?"

I pulled her plate across the table to finish her piece of cake.

"Let me worry about that, Miss Thing. Come on," she pulled me up. "Let's go out and see what's going on out front."

We went down to Sissy's apartment where I washed up and changed. Then we went downstairs and found a spot in the sun to talk. I was getting ready to tell her about my conversation with Donald when I spied a familiar face turning onto the block.

"Theo?" I squinted.

Adele craned her neck to see. "Look at that boy with his little uniform on," she teased.

Theo stopped to talk to Mr. George, the number's runner.

"Oh, my goodness..." I stammered.

Adele pulled me back into the courtyard. "Pull yourself together before you pee in your damn pants. All you need is for them old busy bodies to start cackling out there," she said, referring to Old Mrs. Palmer and Mrs. Connelly who were sitting in front of the building.

I winced, "Why are they out so early in the morning?"

Adele pushed me toward the building. "If you run fast enough you can get to him before he gets too close."

I nodded my head. "Don't worry," she said before I left. "I'll go out there and give their old asses something to talk about."

She turned and strutted back out to the sidewalk. "You all want to see my wedding ring?" She asked loudly.

I scooted through the lobby, down the back stairs and out the back door. I ran as fast as I could to the building next door and flew up the stairs and through to the front so fast that I almost slipped on the wet floor.

Lettie, the Super's wife, stared at me as if I must have been crazy.

"Morning, Miss Lettie." I stopped for a split second, catching a hold of the banister to keep from falling before hitting the

255

heavy front door with both hands. I caught Theo just as he and Mr. George parted.

I tapped him on his shoulder and when he turned to look, I laced my arm with his and walked him in the other direction away from my building.

"Frank Lee!" He looked around. "Where did you come from?"

I shrugged my shoulders casually, fighting the temptation to stop and catch my breath. "I saw you from down the street."

He shook his head and laughed at me. "Why are you out of breath?"

I faked a look of awe. I shook my head. "I'm not out of breath. I'm just happy to see you."

I could hear Adele laughing way too loudly, showing off her ring and acting the fool just so no one would see me leave with Theo.

"You look nice in your uniform," I smiled at him.

"I wanted to surprise you," he said.

He pulled a small envelope out of his pocket and handed it to me. By then we were on Broadway near the little store where Ludie bought her ginger root and sassafras leaves from. The old man who ran the shop was from Jamaica. He smelled like pickled mackerel and always wrapped his medicines, as he called them, in torn pieces of newspaper.

I hated to go inside because he kept a pot of callaloo cooking in the alley behind the shop that smelled like burning collard greens. He sold small containers of the stuff to the old ladies who believed it would keep them from catching the apoplexy. The smell of it was enough to turn your stomach. Sissy said it may keep you from having a stroke but it sure wouldn't keep you from falling down dead from the stench.

We stepped into the shade of the blue and white awning that ran across the front of his store.

I turned the envelope over in my hands. "I'm surprised." I tried to read his face for a clue but I couldn't get past his dreamy eyes and oh so perfect lips. "What is it?" I asked.

Theo let his sack slip off of his shoulder to the ground. "Open it," he winked his eye and waited patiently.

I pulled the flap up and unfolded the tissue paper to find a ring inside. It had a tiny yellow stone with four small diamonds around it. My heart started pounding and blood immediately rushed to my face. I kept my head down to hide the tears that sprang to my eyes.

"Don't you like it?" he asked.

I nodded my head. When I looked up he asked me why I was crying. He wrapped his arms around me. I shook my head. "It's nice. I love it," I answered.

He took it out of my hand and slipped it onto my finger. I couldn't believe it. I wanted to smile but my lips trembled and my eyes flowed with tears. He kissed me on the forehead and picked his bag up to toss it over his shoulder.

I wiped my tears away and took a big breath to compose myself. I smiled at him before stepping back to admire his uniform. He stood at attention and saluted me.

"You look so handsome," I told him.

He kissed me on the lips.

"Come on," he said. "Let's get something to eat."

I followed him. At this point, I would have followed him anywhere even though I was sure Sissy wouldn't have appreciated me disappearing in the middle of the day. We rode the train down to 59th Street where he bought me a hot dog and a bag of greasy French fries. He told me about his training and how he would soon be going to a place called Korea.

He explained, "South Korea is different from North Korea. It looks like one country but they're fighting one side to the other.

"Why?" I asked.

He shook his head slowly back and forth as if it didn't matter. "In the army you do what they tell you." He took a bite out of his hot dog. "They put me on a medical detail, whatever that means. I'm going to learn how to take blood and stitch up bullet holes," he smiled.

It sounded important but my eyes widened at the thought of bullets and blood. "I thought the war was over?" I asked.

"There's always somebody fighting. It just depends on whether the States decides to jump in or not."

"Aren't you afraid?" I asked.

He shook his head. "When I come back, I can go to college for free and I can buy a house too."

He raised his eyebrows for emphasis.

"You can buy a house?" I asked incredulously. "What do you mean?"

He smiled wider and almost with disbelief himself, he explained. "It's some kind of a guarantee."

I couldn't believe it. "Do you think it's true?"

"It's true, for sure." He popped the last of the hot dog into his mouth and got up.

"Come on. I want to show you something."

We walked a few more blocks to a small hotel on Second Avenue. As soon as I realized what it was, I stopped.

Theo stepped back and gently put his arm around me. "What's wrong?"

I couldn't believe it. What did he think I was? Adele was right. Boys will do anything to get into your pants. He must have read my mind.

"Frank Lee, you must be kidding?"

He let his hand drop and took a step back. "This isn't what you think," he said with a laugh.

He looked around for some sympathy but no one along the sidewalk seemed to care what the two of us were talking about.

"Listen," he reasoned. "I'm your boyfriend... your fiancé for Christ's sakes. I'm just showing you where I'll be staying for the next few days."

I shook my head uneasily. I peered around him to see if I believed what he was saying. The outside of the hotel was filthy. The only reason I knew it was one was because of the tiny piece of tin hanging off near the entrance. It was faded so badly that I could barely decipher the word *hotel* along the bottom.

An old white man was leaning against the wall and after a second I realized he was actually sleeping standing up! Theo started laughing so hard that his duffle bag fell off of his shoulder and onto the ground. He held himself up by placing his hands on his knees. He looked up at me.

"I've never laughed so hard in my life," he said.

I pushed his shoulder.

"I don't see what's funny."

"Come on." He stood up. "I just want to put my stuff away."

He picked his duffle bag up off of the ground to show me how heavy it was.

"That's it!" he added with wide eyes. "Where else am I going to stay? I lost my room when I left and I don't have enough money to stay at the Waldorf."

He smiled in a puppy dog kind of way. "I promise. Nothing is going to happen."

He stood and waited for me to agree. We stepped into the dark lobby where a man was sitting behind a small table near the elevator. He was the cleanest thing about the building. His suit was black like an undertaker's and his shoes were shiny like a car salesman's.

He joggled the cigar in his mouth to the side so he could speak around it.

"What'll you have this fine day?" He sounded like a salesman, too. "I have the penthouse available for the taking."

He pulled the cigar out of his mouth and carefully set it on the edge of the table. He flashed his shiny white teeth at us and reclined back in the chair, lacing his fingers together across his chest to wait for Theo to speak.

"I'll... we'll take one room."

The man continued to grin, "For how long, young man? For how long," he sang.

"Three days," Theo answered stoically, almost as if he was surprised that he had gotten that far.

The man still seemed not to be impressed enough to take Theo seriously. He picked the cigar up. He carefully tapped it with his finger away from his body so that the ashes would fall on the floor away from his clothing. He paused for a second before asking.

"Are you paying for one night or all three?" He said three like the people in Brooklyn, "You paying for one night or all tree?"

"All three," Theo pulled a small fold of money out of his pocket. He turned away from the man to count out six dollars and then turned back to hand it over.

The man nodded as if he was impressed.

"Just leave it right there," he pointed.

He sat up and slid the clipboard across the table to Theo. When he pulled his hand back across the money was in his hand. He flicked his thumb across his tongue before counting the six dollars. He dropped each bill onto the tabletop and then picked them back up to count again. He counted them three times. He finally looked up.

"Six dollars," he said.

He held his hand out toward the elevator, which was standing open.

"Upstairs to the tird floor; get off and go to your right. The room is at the end of the hall."

"What about the key?" Theo asked.

"What about it?" The man grinned. "It's in the room under the pillow just like a present from the toot fairy."

Theo took my hand and we stepped into the lift. The man, without turning called out the instructions.

"Pull the door until you hear the latch. Take the pulley from the right to the left. Press the number tree and hold on tight."

Theo looked at me and I nodded for him to go ahead. I held onto his arm while he followed the directions. When the elevator jerked into action, I yelped. The man's chuckles faded as the elevator squealed with what seemed to be its last breath of life to the third floor.

It wheezed and moaned until it jolted to a stop with a loud clang. The sound of a tiny bell demure in its otherwise unpleasant setting signaled that the lever could be pulled back along with the cracked and faded caged door.

Theo hefted his bag onto his shoulder and led the way. I followed him to the end of the narrow and dingy hallway. He opened the door and peeked around the room before satisfying himself with the belief that it was worth the money he paid.

"It's safe," he smiled.

He swung the door wide to reveal a room that was the color of dingy underwear. Even the cover on the bed and the single curtain panel covering the window were the color gray that could only appear that way after having been white at one time, a long time ago.

I wrinkled my nose.

Theo laughed. "Come on," he pulled me inside. "Don't be timid. It's not going to bite you."

I stepped far enough into the room for him to be able to close the door.

"I'm not afraid." I looked around. "This room," I brought my hand to my nose. "It stinks."

Theo sniffed the air around him. He shook his head. "I don't smell anything."

I fanned the air around my face with my hand. "You've got to be kidding me if you can't smell anything."

He bent low to smell the bed. He shook his head again. "Maybe we need some air." He went over and pulled the curtain to the side. He opened the single window. He turned to me.

"It's in the airshaft."

I crossed my arms and looked at him skeptically.

"It is," he held his hand out for me to see.

I walked around the bed and peered out of the window. If our arms were a foot longer we would have been able to touch the building next door. The ground below was littered with odds and ends that folks on this side of the building had tossed out.

"Out of sight, out of mind," I murmured.

"Dried fish and curry," Theo nodded his head.

I agreed. He turned to close the window but I told him to leave it open. It helped a little bit. I perched myself on the narrow sill. He leaned over and kissed me on the lips. My heart began to beat faster because I knew I should have waited for him downstairs. My mother would wring my neck if she knew I had even left the block with him. He kissed me again. I maneuvered around him and stood up.

"What's wrong?" he asked.

"I should go," I reasoned.

"Ok," he answered and then waited for me to respond.

I closed my eyes for a second to think about it. "I'll stay for a few minutes."

I ended up staying all night. The next day, Sissy miraculously believed Adele when she told her that I'd been helping to paint their little apartment with Stan and Donald.

"Donald's a nice boy," Sissy suggested with all sincerity as if he were her son and I wasn't her daughter.

"I know he's nice," I answered sharply.

Sissy looked up from her magazine and stared at me until I gathered the good sense to look away. I didn't dare to add that Theo was nicer but I thought it just the same.

The ring that he had given to me was laced around a ribbon hidden under my blouse. The weight of it gave me enough confidence to disagree with Sissy but not enough to stand up to her. I sneaked back to the hotel every day until he had to go back to the base. Three months later after missing my period three times too many, I confessed to Adele that I was pregnant.

## Chapter Twenty-Six

We were on a Hundred Thirtieth Street coming back from Adele's seventh month check-up. She sprinkled hot sauce on the oyster she was about to swallow.

I looked away. "I don't know how you eat them things."

The man who sold them looked up from his steaming pot. "Don't knock it if you never tried it," he teased.

"You got that right, Mister." Adele turned the shell up over her mouth and let the grey clump slide down her throat.

"See there," I responded. "What's the point if you're not even going to chew it?"

"You never chew," the man advised shaking his hand like a fan. "You never chew. Swallow it whole, like a man."

I watched Adele prepare another one and swallow it with a smile. I shook my head. "That couldn't be good for your baby."

"This baby will be fine, won't you little fellow?" She asked her belly.

"Little fellow?"

"Your mama says it's a girl but I don't think she's going to be right this time."

"She's been right every time so far," I answered skeptically.

"She's not the only one who can tell just by looking whether or not it's a boy or a girl. Cousin Minnie says it's a boy."

Cousin Minnie wasn't our cousin but I suppose she was somebody's cousin because everybody called her Cousin Minnie. She was always invited over whenever Ludie had folks stop by but she and Sissy were often at odds over whose premonitions would come true. Mostly, they competed with each other by contradicting the other. I wasn't sure about Cousin Minnie but Sissy spoke to her long lost kinfolk all of the time. If anyone was too loud in her house, she would ask them to lower their voices because her grandmother or some other dead relative was sitting close by and was bothered by their tone.

"My money is on Sissy," I said.

Adele and I walked up to Broadway to catch the bus back home. When we climbed on board and found a seat, I leaned over and told her.

"I missed my cycle," I said plainly put.

She was speechless. She shook her head silently and then absentmindedly rubbed her hand across her own belly, which was by now as round as a kickball.

Sissy is going to kill you." She said it mournfully as if there could be no other reaction.

After awhile she turned to me and asked, "How did you let this happen?"

I didn't understand the question. "I don't know," I answered.

I shrugged my shoulders. "It just happened."

"Didn't you learn nothing from me? It's bad enough to get tied down when you don't have nothing going on for yourself, it's worse when you have a chance to get someplace and you throw it all away."

I stared at her.

"Listen," she said. "Do you think I love Stanley?" She shook her head before I could answer. "I don't."

"He's nice," I protested.

"Do you think that's all it takes... to be nice, to be good to you? That's not even half of what it takes, Frank Lee. That's not even a little bit. I don't want somebody who's nice to me. I want somebody who can take me out of here. I want somebody who can teach me something, show me something. Somebody who has money in the bank."

I shook my head in disbelief. She looked away.

"It's no secret," she said. "He knows."

"I think Theo will make a good husband."

"You think so," she asked with a smirk.

She shook her head back and forth as if explaining would be useless.

"You have your high school diploma," she reasoned. "You can live your life easy and *damn it*, you can take me with you!"

"What about your husband?"

She shook her head, "Don't even talk to me right now," she hissed but just as quickly she kept talking.

"If you get a job in one of them offices, they're paying thirty dollars a week to them gals that work down there!"

"Thirty dollars isn't much."

"After about a year it's a whole lot more than what you got, and if that won't make a difference to you, you can give it to me. I'll trade places with you. Anyway," she changed the subject. "When are you going to tell your mama?"

"I'm afraid," I said.

"If you're not going to get rid of it you might as well get it over with because you know she's going to know.  She probably already does."

We rode the rest of the way in silence.  Stanley was waiting for her when we got to my building.  She took his hand and walked off with a single forlorn look back at me.  I didn't know if the look was for me, and my troubles or because she was walking away with a husband she would never be satisfied with.

I climbed the stairs to the third floor barely able to breathe. Later that night, I waited until Sissy was in bed and was about to turn her light off.  I stopped at her doorway and told her I was pregnant.

She fluffed her pillows and remarked, "I know."

I was too shocked to respond.  I couldn't believe Adele would betray me.

"Nobody had to tell me," she read my mind. "I can tell when it's going to rain and I can tell when bad luck is coming, I can sure as hell tell when my own child is pregnant."

She turned over and away from me. "Cut the light off in the kitchen before you go to bed," she said.

I wrote to Theo and waited for his letters but by now they were far and few between.  I took the ring from around my neck after a month went by without a letter from him. The whole engagement seemed contrived. When I told Donald that I couldn't see him anymore, I could hear Sissy in the kitchen clucking her tongue in dismay.

He looked dumbfounded but nevertheless gathered himself off of the couch and left. Sissy walked through the living room shaking her head. "You don't have a spoonful of sense," she told me.

When Adele had her baby, a girl as Sissy predicted, I couldn't stop crying. Tears poured out of my eyes like a dripping faucet. Ludie explained it away by rubbing my stomach knowingly. "That's because this here is a boy, that's all."

"How do you know," I asked.

Adele lifted her baby toward me but when I reached my arms out, the baby screamed and squirmed away. Everyone laughed except for me.

"It's a boy alright," they all said in unison.

Ludie shook her head at me, "Look at that face. Just look at it."

I diverted my eyes away. They were having a great time teasing me. I wasn't in the mood.

This ought to cheer her up," Sissy said with a frown.

She pulled an envelope from her pocket and handed it across to me.

"Super's wife give it to me this morning."

I got up and walked out to the hallway. I sat on the bottom step to open the envelope but before I could read it Sissy came out and closed the door. I folded it in my hand and looked up at her. She crossed her arms and stared at me.

"What does he have to say?" she asked.

I shrugged my shoulders.

"I told you Frank Lee" she started. "That boy over there is no good."

"You just don't like him."

"I don't like him for you, Frank Lee. I don't like him for you."

"What's so special about me?"

"If you can't see it..."

I looked away. Sissy shifted from one foot to the other. She searched around the hallway to measure whether or not anyone was behind the other doors listening to her private business.

"I wasn't raised up on a whole lot of talking but right is right and wrong is wrong. That boy should have been here by now. He should have put a ring on your finger if only to make you honest."

I bit my bottom lip but what was on my mind slipped out, "You ran him away."

It felt like I'd bitten into a bitter lemon. I was afraid to move, afraid to look up, afraid to take it back.

"What you say," she said. It wasn't a question. It was an acknowledgement that I had an opinion, a voice even. To my astonishment, she smiled. I knew she was biding her time. I knew she would say what she came to say before we were through.

She shook her head. "You can blame it on me if you want to but if he wanted to be here, this is where he would be."

I shook my head, "No."

"No? What's going to happen to you Frank Lee? You let the other one get away from you. Who do you think is going to take care of you once you have this baby? Who do you think is going to want you and a baby too? What are you going to do then?"

"He'll be back to get me."

"Is that what the letter says?"

I didn't answer.

She shook her head, "I don't believe that boy no more than the man in the moon. After what he did," she shook her head, "you may never see him again."

"He loves me," I told her.

"What do you know about love," she shot back.

I clamped my mouth shut. I didn't want to say.

"Go ahead," she warned me. "Say what you got to say."

I thought about Adele. She was certain that Sissy loved me but only because she measured her life with mine. I looked up at Sissy.

"Maybe *I* don't know. You never said it."

I let the words fall from my lips one word at a time as if at any moment I could pull them back if I needed to.

"What does that mean," she looked at me in awe.

"You never said it," I almost cried because with every word another weight seemed to lift from my shoulders. I took a deep breath. "You never did."

A single tear rolled from my mother's eye and slowly ambled down her cheek. She tried to speak but her lips pursed tightly together until I thought she might disappear like the wicked witch did when Dorothy threw water on her.

She closed her eyes for a second and then gathered herself together.

"Listen child," she started. "My daddy raised me for some of the way. He was a fellow of few words and long between them, if he said anything at all. I've been told since I was small that he and I are alike in that way."

She suddenly looked uncertain, as if she wanted to say more but wasn't sure how to go on. She took another look around the stairwell before turning back toward our door. "Don't you to be bothered by me loving you or not loving you," she said. "I love you alright. I do. "

As soon as I made a motion to go to her she opened the door and went back inside. I watched the door after she closed it. I knew she wouldn't come back out. My head was spinning but instead of following her I ran up the stairs to the roof so no one would see me crying.

I sat at the corner where the rooftops meet. It was just getting dark and was a little cool. I buttoned my sweater and crossed my arms to keep warm. I knew I'd have to go back down but I hoped she would be in her room pretending to be asleep by then. When Adele stepped through the door and walked across to where I was sitting, I wiped my face with the sleeves of my sweater and pretended nothing was wrong.

"What the hell happened to you two," she asked with a laugh.

When she saw that I'd been crying she sat beside me and put her arm around my shoulder.

"She told me she loved me," I told Adele.

"As much as anybody could love their child. No less, that's for sure." Adele assured me.

"Why can't I feel it?"

"Why did Ludie leave me?" Adele countered. "Everybody's not the same I suppose," she suggested.

I rested my head on Adele's shoulder. We watched the moon lift up above the buildings across the street. I t bathed the roof in a bright white light.

"What did your letter say?"

I'd forgotten about it. I pulled the single sheet out of the envelope and read it.

"Theo will be here in the morning," I smiled.

"Amen," Adele brought her hands together.

## Chapter Twenty-Seven

The next day Sissy answered the door and led Theo down the hallway to the living room.

"Hello," he said when he saw me.

I smiled my greeting but quickly diverted my attention when Sissy pulled a chair up for Theo to sit on. She sat on the couch beside me and waited for what seemed like a solid minute before speaking.

"I'm not going to play around with you, hear?" she asked. "I know what you've been up to. I know what you done. It isn't right. You know it and I know it."

She stared at him. Her eyes were narrowed to slits, daring him to defy a word of what she was saying.

He looked at me. "I'm here to marry you."

It sounded like a song. I'm here to marry you, he'd said. I looked at Sissy.

"Tomorrow," she told him matter-of-factly.

"Tomorrow," Theo agreed.

The next day Sissy stood as a reluctant witness. She seemed to be getting what she wanted but nevertheless kept accusing him of every evil thing she could think of. The judge finally asked her to keep quiet or step outside.

For the rest of the short ceremony she glared from me to Theo to the judge and back again all the while maintaining her vexations within the tapping of her foot. When we walked out of the courthouse, Sissy folded the piece of paper declaring that

Theo and I were married and put it in her purse. She told Theo to get gone.

We walked away from him and out to the bus stop. Theo stood on the other side of the street and watched us board the Number 58 uptown. I couldn't take my eyes off of him and when he started to run my heart started to race. He caught up to the bus at the next stop and boarded. Theo stayed at the front of the bus but he never took his eyes off of mine. I didn't know what to do. I dared to think what she might do if I went to him. When it was time to transfer, Sissy pulled me with her to the street.

Theo stayed where he was. I stared at him through the windows of the bus until Sissy warned me not to make her miss the next connection.

Theo shipped off without a word. By August I was six months pregnant and the heat in the city was unbearable. It hung around us like a heavy cloak. My perch on the windowsill didn't help. Sissy and I had meandered into a quiet dance, existing mainly by pretending that she wasn't bothered by my growing belly, and I wasn't bothered by her hatred for Theo.

I fanned the air with an old magazine, trying to stay cool with as little movement as possible. I watched a man work a large wrench around the fire hydrant in front of our building. The children were in a frenzy jockeying around him to be the first to feel the cool spray of water.

Sissy came to the window and balanced across my shoulder to see. She'd never touched me much. As hot as it was, I leaned into her. She wore Lily of the Valley talc and even though it was the first thing that hit you when you came into our apartment, up close it smelled sweeter.

"Look at them fools down there. He goes through the same thing every other day," she remarked. "And every other night they send somebody over here to turn it back off again."

When the cap fell away, the water shot nearly twenty feet into the air. The kids squealed and ran in every direction.

Sissy walked across the room. She pulled her uniform off of its hook and then searched for a matching set of stockings in the drawer. I turned back to the window. I wished I had taken the job at the factory. At least I would have had something to do all this time. I rubbed my hand across my stomach. I had only gained ten pounds and as long as I could hide it I would have been able to keep working.

"I hope these folks don't give me no mess," Sissy remarked about her newest situation.

She was up to four apartments now and if this one worked out she would have the five she deemed to be enough to make a good living. "One day for each one of them. One day to clean my own and one day to rest."

She pulled the dress over her head. "I like it better than working with one family day in and day out," she said. "When I get there, they're gone. I can do my work in peace without somebody telling me what to do and how to do it. They leave the money on the kitchen table and when they get home their house is nice like in a magazine."

She stopped to pin her hair up. "Do you need some help?" I asked. "Can I come with you?"

She laughed. "Honey, no. You're married. You don't have to work no more!"

She kept laughing until she closed the door on her way out of the apartment.

"How am I supposed to be married if you ran my husband off?"

I scowled and stuck my tongue out at the back of the door. I looked down at my stomach. I ran my hand over the small hump.

"We'll probably never see him again," I said before turning my attention back downstairs. I watched her walk across the street to the bus stop. As much as I wanted to be angry with her, I couldn't be. I smiled and shook my head at the way she walked with her head held high, as if she was the richest and finest woman on the block. She looked as smooth as Bette Davis in All About Eve.

I stood up and walked across the room in the same fashion, tipping my nose in the air and walking on my tiptoes. I fell onto the bed and stared at the ceiling. It was too hot to pretend. I wanted to scream. What was going to happen to my life, I thought. The walls of the apartment were moving in on me. I thought I might lose my mind.

## Chapter Twenty-Eight

The Indian summer waned into a cloudy and cool autumn. Snow came early and by December the steaming hot ground of summer was no more than a distant memory.   The day the baby was born it was so cold I didn't want to get out of bed.  All night, my stomach had been cramping and by six-thirty in the morning I couldn't ignore it any longer.

Sissy followed me to the bathroom and made Harry guard the door. Anyone who needed to use it would have to go to another bathroom in the building or wait.

"Take your time," she kept advising me. "It's too early for you to have this baby. You're not but seven months."

I was actually nine months.  When she heard my water break she jerked the door open and told Harry to go and get his car. The baby was born later that morning.  I named him after his father but just like Theo the name morphed into a shorter version soon after. We called him Teddy and every time a nurse brought him into the room, Sissy swept him out of my arms as if she was the mama and I was there just for the ride.

By the time Theo came home, Teddy was almost three months old. I started scouring the streets for a glimpse of him as soon as I heard.  Finally there he was, standing on the corner with Cece and her friend Andrew staring up at my window.

When he saw me, he waved.  Cece hit him on the arm and then turned to stare at me with her hands on her hips.  I picked the baby up out of his crib and carried him to the window.  I held him up for Theo to see.  He placed his hand over his heart and then he pointed to let me know he was coming up.  A few minutes later I heard a tap on the door.  I opened it wide for him to come inside.  He shook his head, no.

"But, she's not home." I told him. "You can come in."

"I don't care if she's not here. She doesn't want me in there. I'll talk to you from here."

I stepped out into the cold hallway and put the baby into his arms.

"He's so light skinned," Theo remarked at Teddy's fair complexion.

He laughed when he saw his eyes. "I got a blue eyed baby. It's just something that's not right about that," he teased.

When I pulled my sweater around my shoulders he put his arm around me to pull me close. He kissed me on the lips.

"He's handsome like his daddy and pretty like his mother," Theo whispered.

I blushed. "Handsome is better."

"Handsome," Theo agreed.

He didn't stay for long but he promised to be back the next day to take us out.

When I woke up the next morning, I checked to see if he was there yet but the street was so scarce of people that it looked like it was the end of the world. The snow that had fallen during the night was already pushed into dirty piles around the car tires and curbs. The middle of the street was black with what I knew was a thin layer of ice and the sidewalk was drawn with a narrow path.

The few people who were out were the number's runner or their customers chasing after them. I heard Sissy moving around the apartment so I got back into my bed and pretended to be asleep.

She turned the radio on in the kitchen. "Baby need a bottle?" She asked.

When I didn't answer, she came to the side of the bed and picked him up. I suppose she could tell I wasn't asleep.

"I can't tell you what to do," she said. "I know he's over there. These streets don't hold no secrets, Frank Lee."

The way she said it sounded more like a warning.

After a few seconds, she turned and took the baby back to the kitchen with her. While she fed him, I could hear her telling him what she wanted to tell me. She told him to put on his heavy coat and two pairs of socks. She told him to put his hat on and she told him to drink a warm bottle of milk to chase the chill away once he came back home.

After Sissy left for work, I got dressed and pulled a chair up to the window to wait. Theo didn't come around until later in the afternoon. He walked across the street and waved for me to come down.

I put the baby in as many layers of clothing as he owned and when I opened the front door, Theo was standing there waiting. He took the baby and kissed him on the cheek. He held my hand and we went downstairs and out to the street. We walked up to Broadway to find a place to eat.

We ordered our food and then he told me, "They're sending us to Texas."

I laughed involuntarily since I didn't understand what he meant.

"We're married, Frank Lee. I know your mother doesn't like me but you're my wife and we're supposed to be together. She can't stop you."

"I know she can't stop me. That's not the problem. She's my mother is all."

"Listen," he said softly. "Do what you think is best. You're a woman. You're a wife. You're a mother."

"I'm a daughter too."

"You're not a little girl and I'm not going to beg you."   He fished into his pocket and pulled out some money.

"Here," he said. "Get what you need for the trip. If you decide not to go, well... spend it on the baby."

"I want to go," I assured him.

"Then come on and go." He held my hands across the table. "I have to be there by the first of April or I'll be in trouble. I want you to be with me." He paused for a minute. "We'll be leaving on Monday."

My heart dropped. Monday was in five days. My eyes filled with tears. Theo stared at me. I suppose he was wondering who the tears were for... him or Sissy.

He walked me back to my building and when I got upstairs Sissy was there. She watched me undo the baby's layers of clothing in silence. I put him down in my bed and came back to the kitchen.

She was sitting at the table. She looked up when I came in.

"I'm going to talk to the folks I work for. Maybe one of them can help you with a job."

She said it hesitantly, almost as if it would be a long shot if it happened at all. She shook her head as if she meant to convey it in another way.

"I suppose you'll be running off with him?"

I shook my head. "I won't be running off."

"Leaving, then if that's the way you want to say it. Leaving off and away from here."

I nodded my head and sat down on the edge of the other chair.

"Where is he taking you?"

"Texas."

She reared back. "Texas! You won't like it down there Frank Lee! They got nothing but wild Indians and gun toting cowboys down there."

How could she know? Theo wouldn't take me to a place like that.

"Theo told me it was pretty there. That it was warm and the sky was filled with stars."

She looked at me skeptically and seemed to be about to argue the point but she thought better of it. "When are you supposed to be going to this pretty place with a lot of stars? I suppose he won't be wasting any time?"

"We're going to catch a bus on Monday."

"Monday!" she screamed. "Today is Wednesday! What in the hell is he trying to do, Frank Lee? I don't like it. I don't like it one bit."

She shook her head and walked out of the room. She went to her bedroom and closed the door.

Later that afternoon Ludie, Adele, and her baby dropped by. Adele and I sat on my bed with the babies and listened to Sissy and Ludie whisper in the kitchen. Every now and then Sissy would get loud but we could hear Ludie trying to reason with her.

Adele looked at me somberly, "You're going to have to run away from home like she did."

I'd never heard that before. Adele shook her head back and forth.

"All I know is she up and left. She run off and left you behind. I don't know why and I don't know how. That's all I know." She refused to tell me more.

I waited until they left but before I could go to Sissy she came into the living room and sat down on the couch. She folded her hands together in her lap. Ludie had evidently convinced her to speak to me.

"I'm going to tell you everything you need to know. I'm going to tell you all about your old mama so that when you leave here and maybe we won't see each other no more, you'll know firsthand who I was and who I is."

I sat down beside her and listened. It grew darker in the little living room but the full moon outside the window lent enough light to see. She started from the beginning, to the very first thing that she could remember. She reached over to hold my hand while she spoke.

"My daddy bought me a pretty white dress, you see... with a pretty green lace from the colored seamstress in town," she started. "She only made dresses for white people but he paid her to make a dress for me. I was to wear my new dress to the river to see my mama but my mama wasn't there. She was gone to heaven but nobody told me. Nobody told me," she wiped the tears away from her eyes with her free hand.

She continued through the night. She told me everything she could remember and when she had nothing more to say, I hugged her and for the very first time I didn't want to let go and neither did she.

*The End*